DEATH OF A SCHOLAR

FIORELLA DE MARIA

Death of a Scholar

A Father Gabriel Mystery

IGNATIUS PRESS   SAN FRANCISCO

Cover photo illustration and
cover design by John Herreid

Photographic elements from
istockphoto.com and unsplash.com

© 2022 by Ignatius Press, San Francisco
All rights reserved
ISBN 978-1-62164-517-7 (PB)
ISBN 978-1-64229-200-8 (eBook)
Library of Congress Control Number 2021940727
Printed in the United States of America ∞

I

Stands the Church clock at ten to three?
And is there honey still for tea?

Gabriel had been warned many times against the sin of dissipation. Those idle moments of daydreaming had the power to tempt the soul down all manner of blind turns, and Gabriel knew the dangers of journeying too far into the past—even the happy past, and Gabriel did have a happy past hiding away somewhere, waiting to be found. His destination today was to be the town where he had lived and studied, in which he had spent his most joyful and carefree years.

Gabriel sat alone, in the carriage of a train chugging its way slowly towards the hallowed spires of Cambridge. A priest could always be sure that he would not be disturbed on public transport; there was something about the clerical collar and soup-plate hat that made fellow travellers pause at the door before moving farther along the corridor to seek a seat elsewhere. It was preferable to spending hours being subjected to the regrettable company of unchurched agnostics, who were always desperate to share their potted philosophy of pointlessness with him, all the way from Salisbury to London Paddington and beyond.

Gabriel had some sense that he ought to welcome such interactions as an opportunity to evangelise, but he never found that his own views were particularly welcome during these lengthy lectures, and he told himself that his time was better spent in prayer for the conversion of England. He had left the Wiltshire village he now called home a little after dawn, said his breviary, prayed the rosary and drifted off to sleep several times before the dining car had opened and he was able to enjoy a modest lunch.

It had been the sight of a group of students in the dining car that had set Gabriel on edge and sent him hurrying back to his seat as quickly as possible. There had been nothing wrong with them, a smartly dressed group of young men returning to halls, after what had no doubt been an enjoyable jaunt in the Big Smoke. There were five of them, a little garrulous but no more than Gabriel would have expected of youths who still retained the fresh, untroubled faces of boys who—not so very long ago—had been playing cricket and rugby all afternoon within the secure parameters of school. That was all that marked them out as different to Gabriel. They were young, and they had had the privilege of coming of age as the world was celebrating peace.

He had no business resenting them their innocence, Gabriel rebuked himself, settling himself back into his seat with what was almost sulkiness. No one chooses the moment of history into which he is born, and there had undoubtedly been happier times in which to be a young man on the threshold of life. And how on earth did he know if those boys were as carefree as they looked? They had been children of the war. Had they lost their fathers? Older brothers? How many of them had been Londoners, tucked away in their country boarding schools, living with the constant anxiety of knowing that their mothers and grandparents were stranded in the city, directly in the path of the Luftwaffe's reign of terror? The war had done nothing to shake the English resolution to conceal wounds from the world, and Gabriel knew better than to assume anything about the people he met.

The scene outside the train window was bleak and unchanging. Gabriel had forgotten how inhospitable the Fens were, flat and featureless, a barren wasteland compared with the gentle rolling hills and green valleys of Wiltshire. But then, Gabriel was not sure he had wasted much time looking out the window when he had come up to Cambridge as a freshman at the start of the Michaelmas Term of 1919. After a brutal six months in the trenches in the path of the ill-fated but ferocious Ludendorff campaign, all Gabriel had wanted to do was to throw himself into the glorious madness of student life. He had sat in a carriage very like this one, except that it had been full to bursting point, and he had been crammed into the corner next to the rather-more-substantial bulk of his school friend Alan Ellsmore, who was coming up to Cambridge to read archaeology and anthropology.

Alan had had a rather worse (or better) war than Gabriel, depending upon the way one looked at it. Always the dreamy academic, Alan had been even less suited to armed combat than Gabriel and had managed to get himself shot in two places on his first mission in no-man's-land, ending his time of active service after a whole three days. One of the bullets had caused so much damage to his femur that he had been encased in plaster for months and gone on to make a full recovery just two weeks before the armistice.

Dear Alan. Gabriel had received a letter from his old friend shortly before embarking upon his journey, informing him that he had finally plucked up the courage to pop the question to his Polish ladylove and that they planned to marry later that year. Gabriel chuckled just thinking about the letter, written in Alan's characteristically self-deprecating manner. He wondered if he would ever be naughty enough to tell the lovely Beata that her infinitely sensible fiancé had been the brains behind the student Popish Plot Society during his second year at Cambridge. Alan had come up with the idea as a way of making fun of the unchecked anti-Catholic prejudice still rampant in the university of those days. It had involved pranks—usually concocted after a little too much wine had been imbibed—such as placing a mantilla on the head of a statue of Vile Queen Bess or bursting in on parties dressed in the white of the Dominicans, brandishing egg whisks.

Gabriel felt an intoxicating muddle of pain and pleasure at the memory of the Popish Plot Society's last foray into madness. He could not remember now whose idea it had been to drape the statue of Henry VIII in a Vatican flag, but it had very nearly ended in disaster. The statue in question was positioned above the Great Gate of Trinity College, and Gabriel had had to shinny up a wall at least one storey high to reach the graven image of the Old Tyrant. Had he really been capable of such a feat?

"You'll break your neck, you crazy man!" called Giovanna from the cobbled pavement below. Gabriel looked down at her from his vantage point, one arm hooked around Henry VIII's ample neck, and felt momentarily dizzy, but not from fear of heights. They had met just a few hours before, at a concert at which Giovanna had been singing. Alan had introduced them during the interval drinks, inviting Giovanna to join them for dinner and revelry afterwards. She stood now on the cobblestones in a pool of lamplight, dressed in a demure blue gown, her black curls arranged like a Pre-Raphaelite lady.

Looking back, Gabriel had no idea why Giovanna had agreed to meet him again after that. Trinity Street was far too public a thoroughfare for such antics, even late at night, and Gabriel had been summoned before the dean of college the following morning. The dean, an old scholar aged about a hundred and fifty, had smirked at Gabriel as he stood cowering in his college gown, asking the question he asked all miscreants who came before him: "I wonder, young man, if you might give me a reason not to have you sent down?"

The question had not demanded an answer, but Gabriel had never understood the concept of a veiled threat and had proceeded to give the hapless dean a long list of reasons why it would be inopportune to send him packing. In the end, the dean had been so wrongfooted by Gabriel that he had thrown him out of the room—but thankfully not out of the university. And Giovanna had answered his nervous invitation to dinner that night.

It was raining heavily by the time the train pulled into Cambridge station, and Gabriel fumbled with his umbrella as he descended onto the platform, joining the other passengers like a cloud of bats making for the arched entrance. Further down the platform, he could still hear the group of students he had met in the dining car, talking noisily, their spirits undampened by the terrible weather. They probably had not stopped talking for the entire journey, thought Gabriel, handing his ticket to the stationmaster.

Gabriel felt irrationally offended by the rain, though standing under a dripping umbrella was hardly an unusual occurrence for any Englishman who was fond of stepping out of doors. It was just that, in his memory, it never rained in Cambridge. It was either bitterly cold, the immaculate college lawns sparkling with frost, or he was punting down the Cam to Grantchester under impossibly blue skies, the sunlight kissing his face as though he were the romantic subject of a Rupert Brooke poem. The station was some distance from the rest of the town, built out of earshot of the colleges on the insistence of dons who had refused to allow a nasty newfangled railway to wreck their lovely university. Nevertheless, Gabriel had intended to walk to his old college and enjoy the experience of being back in an old haunt. For a country dweller as Gabriel had become, the space of a mile or two was nothing, but the rain made him hesitate.

He pondered hailing a cab, but this was not London, and he suspected he would have to compete with a large number of damp passengers for the privilege. In any case, he had very rarely climbed into a car when he had been a student. He had travelled everywhere on a very smart Raleigh bicycle, bought for him by his proud and relieved parents, the summer he was preparing to come up to Cambridge. Gabriel marched determinedly down Station Road in defiance of the downpour. Cambridge was still Cambridge, even in the rain.

Cambridge may have still been Cambridge, but what with the relentless drizzle all around him and his black umbrella obscuring much of the view, Gabriel might have been walking anywhere. On either side of him, shop fronts and college entrances—Downing, Emmanuel—all melted away in a hazy blur of grey, punctuated by a flash of green as he passed the vast open space of Parker's Piece. *Leaving not a rack behind* . . .

Raindrops were starting to soak through Gabriel's worn coat, sliding their way under his collar and down his neck. It was no use pretending, thought Gabriel, trying unsuccessfully to stifle a bout of shivering; he had often been freezing cold at Cambridge in those austere days after the Great War. He remembered with a chuckle how his mother had sent hand-knitted socks and vests to him when he had served at the Front, only to receive a plea for a continuing supply of woollen socks and underwear when he was a student. During his first Lent Term at Cambridge, Gabriel had felt relieved that he no longer lived in fear of bombs and bullets, but he retained a morbid fear that he might freeze to death in his spartan room, with a coal ration that never lasted beyond the first hours of the morning.

There it was. Saint Stephen's College. The alma mater itself. Gabriel stood outside the unimposing façade and took in the fact of his return. He knew it would not have changed, and he took in the battered wooden doors he knew led to the porter's lodge, and the Tudor decor encrusted around the wide stone arch—engraved lions and unicorns, heraldic badges Gabriel thought he ought to recognise—the fingerprints of past ages Gabriel had never noticed as he had dashed in and out on his way to lectures. As one of the smallest colleges, Saint Stephen's did not have the grandiose atmosphere of Trinity or Saint John's, tucked neatly, almost apologetically, away from the narrow street. Saint Stephen's had few famous alumni—a couple of minor poets whose names escaped Gabriel, a pioneering surgeon from the 1870s—but its modest status in a world-famous university had always suited Gabriel. He took a deep breath and pushed open the door, aware of no other emotion than relief to be escaping the inclement weather.

In the porter's lodge, an elderly porter sat like a time-travelling anchorite behind the counter, dressed in a thick winter coat and fingerless gloves. At the sound of the door opening, he looked up from the *Times* crossword and regarded Gabriel closely from beneath a pair of thick white eyebrows. A moment later, the porter's heavily lined face broke into a boyish smile. "Good afternoon, Mr Milson," he said, rising to his feet.

Gabriel extended a hand to the porter, who shook it with the warmth he would have reserved for a family member. "It's good to see you again, Mr Derrick."

"Dr Kingsley told me you were coming," said Derrick, taking a key down from a rack, "and here you are, as though you never left."

Gabriel realised he had forgotten to remove his hat when he stepped inside and snatched it off his head a little too quickly, spraying water around him like a dog giving himself a shake. Derrick laughed. "I'm awfully sorry," said Gabriel, unbuttoning the top of his coat. The wet, rough collar was beginning to prickle against his neck. Derrick noticed Gabriel's clerical collar for the first time.

"I'm that sorry, I'd forgotten you were a man of the cloth now. *Father* Milson." Derrick hesitated, as though wondering whether it might be cheeky to continue, but he added, "That sounds a bit grown-up for you, young man. The missus would have been so proud. She were a Roman like you."

"Were?" Gabriel floundered. "I'm so sorry, Mr Derrick, has she . . . ?"

"It were during the war, lad," Derrick confirmed, his voice taking on a more halting tone. "Though it don't seem so long ago. She were visiting her sister in Croydon. It were a doodlebug."

Gabriel shook his head in disbelief. He had rarely conversed with Mrs Derrick, but she had worked in the college kitchens, and he had often passed her as he had entered or left the great neo-Gothic church of Our Lady and the English Martyrs. She had always smiled in his direction and given him a little wave but had seemed reluctant to chat with him in case it appeared presumptuous. Madness, of course, to be so horribly aware of one's place immediately after celebrating a redemptive sacrifice made for all, but Gabriel had assumed at the time that Mrs Derrick would rather talk to her lady friends than have a polite conversation with a gawky student. Mr Derrick had a more ambiguous role in the life of the college, crossing freely between students and servants. The rowdiest students were a little fearful of him as they might have feared a school prefect, whilst the quieter ones like Gabriel had looked up to him as a substitute father figure in moments of panic.

"I'm so sorry, Mr Derrick," said Gabriel warmly. "She was such a good woman." He made a desperate attempt at a smile, not sure if he ought to lighten the subject. "And such a good cook."

To Gabriel's relief, Derrick returned the smile. "Ay, that she was. She were always giving me cakes and buns to give you. Remember?" Gabriel nodded, thinking of the hamper Mr Derrick had used to carry his wife's baking about, that

13

little shiver of childish excitement Gabriel had felt when Derrick had heaved it onto the counter with the words, "Wait there one moment, if you please. I've a little something from the missus for you. She says you were looking a bit peaky." And out would come a round of lardy cake or half a dozen sticky buns wrapped in greaseproof paper. Gabriel was never sure why Mrs Derrick had taken to feeding him during his time at Cambridge, whether it was that he was one of the only Catholics in college and she sensed that he might feel a bit of an outsider (though he seldom did), or whether he just looked a little more battle-fatigued than the others. Whatever the motive, Gabriel had always been grateful for her kindness to him.

"I heard about your own loss," said Derrick, intruding upon Gabriel's happier thoughts. "What a dreadful shame, and such a beautiful girl too. You know, I remember watching the two of you walking arm in arm along Trinity Street, thinking what a lovely, lovely lady she was. Like one of them angels you see in frescoes. What was her name now? I've never been very good with foreign names . . ."

Gabriel heard the scrape of the door opening and let out an audible sigh of relief when Arthur Kingsley stepped inside. "Good heavens, man!" he exclaimed, looking Gabriel up and down with a broad smile. "Did you swim here? The Cam is frightfully dirty these days, you know."

Gabriel returned the smile and shook hands with his old friend. He would have liked to have been able to say that Arthur Kingsley had not changed a bit, but the white-haired man before him was unrecognisable when compared with the skinny, eager boy Gabriel remembered from years ago. Not that Arthur had been a boy in Gabriel's opinion at the time. When Gabriel had come up to Cambridge as a first-year undergraduate, Arthur was already a junior research fellow who talked obsessively about his area of research and dined at high table with learned old profs who remembered the Great Exhibition and the building of Big Ben. The ravages of time had not evaded Arthur; his girth had thickened at the same rate at which his hair had thinned and whitened, and his winter coat was frayed at the cuffs and collar, the striped college scarf doing little to hide the missing buttons and threadbare patches. But Arthur had greeted Gabriel with a daft joke and a mischievous smile he remembered all too well, placing him completely at ease. "Arthur, old chap. Splendid to see you again."

They walked across the quad, Arthur nodding and touching his hat to various young men who passed them. Gabriel could not get over how much like a monastery Cambridge college looked, built around a central quad so very like a cloister, with a prominent chapel and even gowns that made the inhabitants look a little like monks at a first glance. It was hardly surprising since the first colleges had been built as places for clerics to study long before the Reformation, but it amused him that even the newest colleges aped the style of the contemplative life, perhaps unintentionally. He did not recall much in the way of monastic behaviour occurring during his time in college, and that was an understatement.

"Does it all come flooding back?" asked Arthur, only semiseriously.

"In a way. Part of me feels as though I never left." *Part of me*—a small part, barely palpable beneath the morass of time and memories, the many unexpected twists and turns his life had taken. It was a little like that giddy, disorienting sense he had felt on the train. Gabriel was doing something he had done hundreds of times before, walking across the quad of his college, down one of two intersecting stone paths that cut through beautifully kept squares of lawn, going about his business as other students and fellows went about theirs. But somehow, between one stroll through the quad and another, time had rushed past him in a blur of weddings and births and jobs and disasters and flames and novitiates and ordinations . . . and a war that should by rights have left them feeling as though they had been hurled into the depths of hell. And yet he was walking down this path, quite naturally, as though he had never been away.

"I daresay it feels very familiar and very alien at the same time," said Arthur. He paused as the college clock struck the hour, a low, rumbling timbre more reminiscent of a passing bell than a college timepiece. "It felt quite like that for me when I returned. Before you know it, you'll feel quite at home again."

"I'd forgotten you'd left," commented Gabriel, following Arthur through an archway onto a staircase, which looked a good deal steeper than he remembered. Student accommodation was built around staircases, and he had never entered this one, but they were all much of a muchness in this college: the creaking wooden steps, the oak-panelled interior, the leaded windows so hopeless at keeping out draughts, the rooms with their inner and outer doors, the outer doors always kept open when the room was occupied. The wooden, hand-painted sign with the student's name on it.

"Well, they couldn't keep me away for long," said Arthur, halting by a closed door. He reached into his pocket for the key Derrick had given him. "A few years in industry were quite enough for a dull old chemist like me. I missed college life a little too much.''

''We always used to joke that one became a don when the outside world was a little too threatening,'' mused Gabriel, stepping into the guest room ahead of Arthur. He felt himself reddening with embarrassment, wondering whether he had just been appallingly rude. It was like returning to one's old school to find that the head boy was now the headmaster. He felt the need to make some kind of readjustment in his relationship with Arthur but was not sure what he was supposed to do.

Arthur gave a hearty laugh. ''My, my, I do believe I was the one who said that! And here I am, happily hiding away from the world.''

''I'm hardly in a position to throw any stones in that direction,'' Gabriel replied, surveying the guest room contentedly. It was perfect for him, not very different from the monastic cell he had so recently left. The room was spacious if spartan in character, containing a bed, a desk and a tattered green armchair. The only difference between this room and his own cell back at the abbey was the greater space and the fireplace, though it did not appear that anything had burned in the grate for quite some time.

''Sorry it's a bit cold, old man,'' said Arthur, also noting the empty grate. ''Let me see if I can't get that fire going for you.''

''It's quite all right,'' Gabriel demurred, but Arthur was already on his knees, picking bits of coal out of the scuttle and depositing them into the grate with a huge pair of grimy tongs. That was something else he remembered about Arthur: he defied the stereotype of the daffy academic by being quite practical. It had been Arthur who had mended Gabriel's bicycle on that terrible occasion when he had collided with a motorcar, destroying the front wheel, twisting the handlebars and making an ignominious dent in the passenger door of the mayor's splendid Humber.

"You don't want to be dressing for dinner in the cold," said Arthur, "and you're frightfully wet. We had terrible trouble with students going down with flu last year. Dropping like flies, they were."

Gabriel removed his coat and hat with some reluctance, as they offered a modicum of protection from the cold room in spite of being soaking wet, but he knew the risks of staying in wet clothes for too long. Arthur was using his silver cigarette lighter and a copy of yesterday's *Times* to light the coal and encourage the smoke up the chimney, as it seemed intent upon whispering into the room. It was strange, but the sight of a fire did not trouble Gabriel; it was the sensation of smoke stinging the back of his throat that made his heart race. He sat gingerly on the edge of the bed, afraid of making the counterpane wet. "Really, Arthur, you'll get ever so dirty down there."

"You sound like my mother," protested Arthur, but he looked up and noticed his ashen face. "I'm frightfully sorry, old chap," he said, rising to his feet immediately and fanning more vigorously at the fireplace as if to remove the evidence. "You just sit tight a moment. There, the smoke's clearing. I'm afraid the chimneys . . . the chimneys probably haven't been cleaned for a while. I . . . I should have thought."

"I haven't seen them since the funeral," Gabriel blurted out, but Arthur did not appear surprised at his friend's apparent non sequitur. He continued, "I used to write to Gio-

18

vanna's parents quite regularly, but not at all after I joined the Benedictines. To be honest, I'd rather run out of things to say."

"You are going to visit them, aren't you?" asked Arthur gently, but Gabriel lowered his head. "Come now, you can't travel all this way and not pay your in-laws a visit. They'd be hurt if they knew you'd been in Cambridge and not taken the trouble."

Gabriel could not look up. "I'm not ignoring them, Arthur," he said, so quietly that Arthur had to step closer to him to hear what he was saying. "I just don't want to hurt them. I cannot think of anything worse for them than opening the door and seeing me standing there."

Arthur patted Gabriel on the shoulder. "You know that's not true. They never blamed you for what happened. Might you take a bit of advice from an old friend? Tomorrow morning, you pay them a visit."

Gabriel nodded noncommittally. The thought of walking down that street and knocking on that particular door was already making Gabriel's stomach churn. "Perhaps I should," he said, standing up to indicate that the conversation was over.

"Good man." Arthur stepped towards the door. "Let me leave you to settle in. I'll come for you in an hour."

Gabriel waited until Arthur had seen himself out. As soon as the door closed, he slumped into the old armchair, grateful for the feeble warmth of Arthur's fire.

2

One of the many advantages of his clerical state was not having to dress for dinner, but Gabriel was not a philistine. He took the time to splash cold water on his face and run a comb through his hair to make himself as presentable as possible. Arthur had promised to introduce Gabriel to a number of his colleagues who would be dining at high table, and Gabriel had no desire to let the side down. He was not a man who had a great appreciation of silver forks and cut-glass decanters, but he had loved the traditions of Cambridge when he was a student—those in which he had been permitted to participate. A nasty thought struck him at the sound of Arthur knocking at the door.

"I'm frightfully sorry," Gabriel began, before Arthur was properly through the door. "I'm afraid I've just realised something."

Arthur glanced at Gabriel's Roman collar and burst out laughing. "It's I who should apologise, old chap! No evensong for you, I suppose?"

"Not to worry," said Gabriel hurriedly. "You go along to evensong, and I shall take a little stroll around the college. I'll be waiting for you on your way out."

"Poor Roman candle," chuckled Arthur as they walked towards the chapel together. "It's a funny old world we live in, where a crusty old atheist is more at home in the college chapel than a man of the cloth."

You are at home in an Anglican chapel that means nothing to you, thought Gabriel, but he kept the notion to himself. *When you step into that chapel, all you see is a beautiful oak-panelled room with statues and flickering candles. You see boys in period costume, intoning antiquated words you barely understand. What reason would you have to quarrel with any of that?*

"Well, I would have been welcome once, before they pinched it from us," quipped Gabriel. "If the college wishes to hold on to its traditions, it should really celebrate Mass in that chapel, just as they did for the first two hundred years of the college's history."

"If we had been at Cambridge in those days, you would have been celebrating Holy Mass while I was being burnt at the stake in the marketplace, on account of my godlessness."

Gabriel did not flicker. "Ah, but would you have been so very godless hundreds of years ago? I daresay we should have attended Mass together."

To Gabriel's mortification, Arthur's good humour vanished for a moment. "Not so godless, I suspect, nor many other things. One cannot be tempted when the temptations do not yet exist."

They were standing at the entrance to the college chapel, and Gabriel could see the chaplain and the choir processing across the quad towards them. "You'd better go in search of God, my friend, and I shall keep myself out of mischief."

Arthur smiled. "If God had a mischief maker, Gabriel, it would certainly be you." With that, Arthur stepped inside the chapel, to worship a God he did not believe in and to pray for the protection of a king towards whom he was at best indifferent.

Gabriel stood alone in the quad and glanced up at the row of stone angels guarding the outer flank of the chapel. From within, he could hear the magnificent organ roaring to life and the soft tones of the congregation singing:

> The day thou gavest, Lord, is ended,
> The darkness falls at thy behest.

Gabriel had always admired the Anglican choral tradition, but that particular hymn, with its monotonous melody and seemingly endless verses, had a tendency to destroy his will to live. He walked out of earshot. Strange to think that once, not so long ago in a nation with such an ancient history, monks like Gabriel had filed into that very chapel to pray. Gabriel snapped himself out of his own wistful thinking. Yes, and not so long after, his co-religionists had been fined, arrested, imprisoned, tortured and judicially murdered for doing what he was doing—refusing to enter the establishment place of worship. He buried the murmur of self-pity he had felt at being an outsider, in the knowledge that the worst he was about to suffer was a perfectly pleasant half hour strolling around his old college.

Gabriel's college, built in the shadow of one of the largest of the Cambridge colleges, consisted of just two quads, one on either side of a quiet road. Gabriel made his way across the road to the newer of the two quads, an early eighteenth-century set of buildings built around the same familiar square, though the lawns were not quite so well kept on this side and the buildings were less uniform architecturally, having been built in stages over a period of some forty years. It was a cold, clear evening, and the full moon looked huge and eerily close with no swathes of cloud to obscure it.

There was a passageway between two buildings which led directly out to the riverbank, and Gabriel was minded to walk that way. He knew that the river would be very quiet at that time of the evening, with no boats or punts making their garrulous way downstream, and there was something liberating about water, even a river as murky as the Cam. He wondered whether the remains of his old bicycle were still rusting down there somewhere after he had fallen in whilst attempting to cycle on a day of heavy frost. He had managed to drag himself out of the freezing cold water with the help of a few passing students, but the bicycle had sunk to the bottom of the Cam and disappeared in the mud, never to be seen again.

There was an old bench Gabriel hoped would still be there, where he might sit and enjoy the tranquillity of the evening. It was still there, but unfortunately Gabriel had been beaten to it, and a young couple were already occupying the seat. He backed away, desperate not to disturb them, walking with slow, quiet steps towards the cover of the building. Judging by the argument the couple were having, a little louder than perhaps either of them realised, they were not at all interested in Gabriel's figure slipping back into the shadows.

"What do I have to do to prove how much I care about you?" asked the young man in an unbearably whining tone. A lovers' tiff, bless them. It was definitely best to leave them to it.

"Please don't ask me again; I will not marry you!" came

the strong, determined female response. "I can't marry any-one. I'll lose everything."

Worse than a lovers' tiff then, thought Gabriel, feeling a little more sympathetic towards the man. A proposal of marriage rejected. Unrequited love, the staple of every English poet's work for hundreds of years. Gabriel was sure it was a sin to eavesdrop, but he found himself hovering around the corner of the building, out of sight of the young couple, but comfortably within earshot. "You'll regret this, you know," the man continued, the whining tone becoming a little more aggressive. "When you're some faded old blue-stocking, alone with your microscopes and books."

There was the distinctive sound of an open hand slamming against an impertinent cheek, followed by a strangled moan. "If you imagine I'll ever regret refusing you, you're even more arrogant than you look! If I were inclined to marry, it would not be to you. I should have to trust the man for a start."

"I can't believe you're still going on about that! I said I was sorry!"

"The only thing you were sorry about was getting a slap on the wrist for your pains. You'd humiliate me like that again if you had the chance, if you had something to gain from it."

"Daphne, if you're prepared to express an opinion, you should be prepared to see it in print. Don't be such a coward!"

There was a slap, then another sound, something between a gasp and a cry. Gabriel looked out discreetly from his hiding place, concerned for the lady's safety, and caught sight of the man leaping to his feet like a scalded cat. He was clutching his face, and Gabriel could barely suppress a giggle, whispering *Attagirl!* under his breath. The allegedly cowardly Daphne had not required an archangel to protect her from a boorish male and had struck a second time. Gabriel left the two lovebirds to it and slunk back across the road to the chapel.

He ended up spending the next twenty minutes walking up and down the road outside Saint Stephen's to avoid being reported for loitering on college property. It was not the most satisfactory start to his holiday, and he heaved a sigh of relief when he stepped back into the college and noticed people streaming out of the chapel. It was time to rejoin polite society.

Gabriel noticed that Arthur was deep in conversation with a gauche-looking young man, and he suspected that they were not discussing the finer points of the chaplain's sermon. As soon as Arthur saw his friend waiting for him, he broke off midsentence and motioned for Gabriel to join them. "Let me introduce you to my friend Father Gabriel," said Arthur to the young man at his side. "I first met him when he was younger than you."

The young man extended a hand enthusiastically. "Robert Sutton, Father, how d'you do."

Gabriel tried to shake off the invasive thought that young Robert Sutton resembled Bela Lugosi in full makeup when viewed from the right angle. It was not just the billowing bachelor's gown, as that could have a similar effect on anyone; the boy had lank dark hair and coal-black eyes set in a wan, sallow face that spoke of long hours of study and the desperate need for exposure to sunlight. This would have been the moment Giovanna might have started to sing something from *Die Fledermaus*, in a joke only the cognoscenti would get. "How d'you do," echoed Gabriel. "You must be one of Dr Kingsley's pupils?"

"He works in my lab," confirmed Arthur as the three of them walked towards the Great Hall and the promise of a halfway decent dinner. "He should be Dr Sutton in a little over a year, all being well."

"You must tell me more about your work," said Gabriel, then immediately regretted it. They reached the Senior Combination Room, where the other fellows and their guests were relaxing before processing into dinner. Gabriel had the sinking feeling that he was going to spend the evening surrounded by boffins discussing whatever obscure aspect of biochemistry they were working on. It would all be highly intelligent, the way of the future and entirely impenetrable to anyone without at least two degrees in the natural sciences.

Gabriel's thoughts were stopped in their tracks by the sight of an exquisitely beautiful young woman standing near the fireplace, involved in what looked like a politely stilted conversation with a much-older man. It was Atta Girl Daphne, looking endearingly unruffled as she moved towards them, quite unlike the young woman who had just socked a man in the face twice for insulting her.

"You must be another of Dr Kingsley's students," said Gabriel, extending a hand to Daphne, who took it very properly, treating him to an enchanting smile. "How d'you do."

"I'm a junior research fellow," said Daphne, correcting him with deserved pride, "but yes, Dr Kingsley supervised my doctoral thesis. Just a pity that another university had to award me the degree."

"Times are changing, even at Cambridge," Arthur declared, placing a hand on Daphne's arm. "You are in the presence of greatness, Gabriel. Daphne is one of the brightest minds in this university—if not in the country." Daphne blushed and began to shake her head, but Gabriel suspected she was used to Arthur's effusive praise, as she did not appear surprised. Nor did anyone around them, for that matter. "In twenty years' time, when you read that Professor Daphne Silverton has been awarded the Nobel Prize, you will remember this meeting."

"I pray that I shall live long enough to hear about it," said Gabriel, but Daphne's cheeks were flaming red, and she turned to the others for some form of diversion.

"I see you've already met Mr Sutton," said Daphne, physically pulling Robert towards her, as he had shyly stepped away from the group. "Robert likes to hide his light under a bushel. He never talks about his work, but it's very important."

"I never talk about it because no one has a clue what I'm talking about," said Robert with refreshing honesty. He smiled appreciatively at Daphne before adding, "I'm very fortunate to work in Dr Kingsley's lab."

"We make a formidable team," Arthur agreed, signalling for them to move with him towards the hall. "So much in our world is changing, but I hope Cambridge never abandons the Socratic teaching method. Wisdom has been passed from teacher to pupil for millennia. It's the best way."

Gabriel smiled at the sight of Arthur shepherding Daphne and Robert in the direction of the door, through which Gabriel could already smell boiled vegetables and the more delectable aroma of roasting meat. Arthur had borne all the hallmarks of a confirmed bachelor when Gabriel had first met him, his mind and heart entirely preoccupied by the pursuit of science. He had never won that Nobel Prize he had once dreamed of, but he seemed to be doing a good job of trying to create future winners. It seemed to Gabriel that Arthur had found solace in his college community and the intellectual rigour of his department in a similar way that Gabriel had found a home in his abbey. They were both monks of a kind, both fathers to those who needed them.

Gabriel found himself standing at a long wooden table laid out with silverware, fine china plates and empty glasses promising wine and port. The table was on a raised platform at the far end of the hall, giving Gabriel a good view of the long tables with their flickering candles and gowned students standing in rows, waiting for grace. A bell was rung, and the master of college, standing at the head of the table, intoned the words:

Benedic, Domine, dona tua quae de largitate sumus sumpturi.

There was a murmured chorus of amens around the room, closely followed by the scrape of benches being moved and students settling themselves in their places. Gabriel sat down whilst Arthur helped Daphne into her chair. Daphne was sitting directly opposite Gabriel, and he wondered whether the lady's position—with her back to the throngs of chattering male students—was deliberate. On either side of her sat Arthur and Robert like faithful acolytes, but Daphne appeared happily immune to the fuss that was being made of her and showed no sign of any awkwardness at being the only female in an entirely masculine environment. But then,

Gabriel thought that a young woman making her way in the world of science must be quite accustomed to such a scenario.

The company paused whilst uniformed figures moved silently round the table, serving slices of nondescript meat swimming in gravy, new potatoes and a selection of boiled vegetables. Gabriel was aware of his glass being filled.

"Has Cambridge changed very much, Father?" asked Daphne, giving Gabriel a friendly smile. If she did not feel out of place, she might think he did and was sweetly bringing him into the conversation.

"I'm not sure dear old Cambridge ever changes," answered Gabriel, returning her smile. "It's the one fixed point in a tumultuous world."

"I wouldn't be so sure of that if I were you," came a clipped voice to Gabriel's left. Gabriel turned gingerly to face the speaker, a man of around Arthur's vintage with a shock of silver hair and the craggy, lined face of a man a little too fond of his pipe. "It's not so very long ago that the likes of you and dear Dr Silverton here would not have been permitted to grace this table. You are of a Papist tendency, I assume, from your absence at evensong this evening?"

"Let me introduce you to Dr Crayford," Arthur put in tersely. "He was of course at evensong this evening and sang louder and flatter than any other member of the congregation. Being the good staunch Protestant that he is."

"My dear Arthur," answered Dr Crayford in the condescending tone Gabriel suspected he used on his undergraduate students, "I have never claimed to be a Protestant, good or staunch for that matter. I merely seek to conserve the traditions that I believe have served this university well for the past five hundred years."

"By worshipping a God you do not believe in and pledging allegiance to a church you have publicly described as an adulterous king's bastard child," answered Arthur.

Gabriel, never the world's most consummate diplomat, felt the sudden need to change the subject. "Dr Silverton, are you from a family of scientists?" he asked. "Arthur here was playing with petri dishes before he was walking, so I'm told."

Daphne chuckled. "No, my father was a bank manager. I'm afraid he did not much approve of my going to university, but my mother talked him into letting me go."

"A man of good sense, your father," said Dr Crayford, happy to sabotage the harmless conversation, having failed to provoke an argument before. "A pretty little popsy like you ought to be married by now."

"The nuns at Saint Philomena's were very keen to help girls get to university," Daphne continued, ignoring the jibe. "They were quite pioneering like that."

"Is that the convent school in Croydon?" asked Gabriel, and immediately regretted the question. There were plenty of schools called Saint Philomena's scattered around the country.

"That's right," confirmed Daphne. "My father was not desperately keen on convent school either, but my mother insisted. She told him it would be good for my deportment." There was a titter of appreciative laughter. "My family has moved to Oxfordshire now."

"Oh, did your father's bank move out of London during the war?"

Daphne nodded. "In a manner of speaking. Our home was destroyed during the doodlebug raids. Father's bank found him a position away from the city."

Arthur patted Daphne's hand. "Those wretched rockets devastated that part of the country."

"Yes," answered Daphne, her voice suddenly harder, "and the men who built them have been punished for their crimes with jobs in America."

There was an unpleasant silence along their part of the table, no one quite knowing how to respond, whilst Daphne appeared embarrassed by the comment and stared down at her plate. Eventually, Arthur gave a little sigh and declared, "I think we forget how safe Cambridge was during the war. We were spared the fate of other cities."

Gabriel had indeed forgotten the gentleman's agreement between the Luftwaffe and the RAF during the war—the RAF had left Heidelberg alone on condition that the Luftwaffe leave Oxford and Cambridge in one piece. Other cities were razed to the ground with the loss of hundreds of thousands of civilian lives, but the great seats of learning had been spared.

"My family consider themselves quite fortunate," said Daphne quickly. "We all survived the war, and so many didn't. My father was at work and my mother was visiting a friend when the house was destroyed. Many of the neighbours were not so fortunate. My father said, 'One can always rebuild the house but never the person.'"

"Very wise," said Gabriel, but those familiar images of flames flickered through his mind. He busied himself balancing his knife and fork carefully at the edges of his plate while his head cleared. He felt a strong sense of admiration for a young woman like Daphne. She came across as reassuringly down-to-earth for a person who was apparently one of the most brilliant of her age. She was part of the new

32

generation of Britons emerging from the social watershed of the war, the convent-educated girl from a middle-class suburban family, who was navigating her own path through a bewildering world where the dictates of class and sex still barred so many doors.

"Daphne sometimes comes to stay with my parents on her way home," Robert put in. "They live just outside Oxford."

Gabriel pondered the information. "Wouldn't it have been easier for you to study at Oxford then?" he asked.

"The other place?" joked Robert with a look of mock horror on his face which quickly subsided. "I did my first degree at Oxford, but my tutor advised me that Dr Kingsley was the best man to supervise my doctorate. Well, I had to fly the nest sooner or later."

Gabriel thought that Robert looked a similar age to Daphne, but he was some years behind her in terms of his studies. He must have spent at least a couple of years in the armed forces, but the numbers did not quite add up. If he were in his midtwenties, Robert Sutton would have been called up quite early in the war and ought not to have completed his first degree yet. He showed no visible sign of disability, but Gabriel did not dare ask him what had precipitated his discharge from the army. There were far too many young men living with hidden injuries following their time in active service, and it was never polite to ask; the man himself must volunteer the information.

When the meal had come to a reluctant end and the port had been passed faithfully to the left around the table, the undergraduates in their serried ranks were released into the night by the master's recitation of the concluding grace.

Those dining at high table trooped back into the Senior Combination Room. All except Daphne, who complained of a headache and asked to be excused.

Gabriel sat with Arthur, Dr Crayford and Robert smoking cigars by the light of the fire. Or at least, the older men smoked cigars whilst Robert made valiant attempts at drawing in the thick, rough smoke without choking. After two or three puffs, he was so overcome by a fit of coughing that he was forced to step outside to catch his breath. "Poor chap!" exclaimed Gabriel as the men roared with laughter, giving Robert even less reason to return. "At least he did not disgrace himself before his ladylove."

Arthur and Dr Crayford immediately stopped laughing and looked askance at Gabriel. "You don't really think that boy has a pash on Daphne, do you?" asked Crayford incredulously. "I'm not sure he'd have the guts if she encouraged him!"

Now that he had met Daphne, Gabriel had readjusted his understanding of the scene he had witnessed earlier, and he suspected that Daphne might have been repelling the young man near the river because she had set her sights on another. "If there is any feeling, surely it's the other way?" asked Gabriel tentatively. "The way she drew him into the conversation earlier . . ."

"She was being kind to a shy young man," answered Arthur. "She's far too sensible to go chasing after men, especially a man like Robert." Arthur looked uneasily from Gabriel to Crayford and lowered his eyes, realising his mistake too late. "Look here, Gabriel, there is a suspicion that young Sutton may be inclined the other way. One does not

34

speak of such things, of course—it would be the ruin of him—but Daphne is no fool. Women always notice."

"Nonsense!" snapped Crayford, sounding genuinely riled for the first time that evening. "You just don't want your little darling going and falling in love. Can't have her doing the right thing and getting married, abandoning work a man could do better."

At that moment, Robert reemerged, red faced, decidedly out of puff and trying desperately to avoid eye contact with any of them. "Sit down, old chap," said Arthur genially, pouring Robert a glass of water from the half-empty jug on the table. "You'll get used to it. If I were you, I'd smoke a pipe before I tried another cigar. The tobacconist on Trinity Street can advise you on where to start. Gentlemen should always be able to smoke. It's like being able to take a drink without ending the evening legless."

There was more laughter, but Robert busied himself taking sips of water, and before long, the conversation had moved on from Robert's unfortunate inability to smoke a cigar elegantly to the more pressing subject of everything that was wrong with Clement Attlee.

When he finally made it to bed, Gabriel was aware of a pleasantly muzzy sensation encasing his head; he had a nasty feeling that he was a little drunk.

3

Gabriel could not fault the effects of the port, as he slept deeply and dreamlessly that night, waking before dawn feeling rested and rather more alert than was normal for him at that hour of the morning. He quickly realised that his alertness was a form of anxiety. Gabriel had promised to go and see his former in-laws that day, and the very thought of it caused a dull throbbing pain to spread across his chest. He knew he would never go back to sleep now and got up, bracing himself as he threw off his bedclothes and the bitter cold of the room hit him.

It was far too early for the gyp to be up and about, which was a relief to Gabriel, who could not shake off his scruples about being waited on. He grabbed the clean, folded towel that had been left for him and went in search of a bathroom and the means to shave. It was impossible for Gabriel to avoid the thought that parish life had softened him. The college was no more dour than the abbey, but Father Foley's presbytery had been a cosy little place, and he had become a little too used to the creature comforts it offered.

Gabriel distracted himself from the penance of a damp bathroom and the shock of cold water in the basin, with the laying of plans for the day. He would walk to Our Lady's and hear Mass, then perhaps go in search of breakfast. When he was ready, he would go to visit his in-laws. Of course he would go.

Gabriel looked at his face, the lower part covered in shaving foam, and could already sense the creep of procrastination. The very thought of taking that lonely walk down Chesterton Road to the Gervasonis' eccentric little house started Gabriel down a path of excuses not to go at all. He had no business descending upon them unannounced after so long; the shock would be terrible. The mere sight of him would bring back memories so tragic, it was immoral even to contemplate hurting them like that . . . Even Gabriel's decision to walk to Our Lady's for Mass reeked of delaying tactics, since the grand old parish church was on the other side of Cambridge and would extend a fifteen-minute walk from college to the house to a journey in excess of forty-five minutes. In defiance of his need for procrastination, Gabriel left an apologetic note to Arthur pinned to his door, containing his in-laws' address and the suggestion that they meet for lunch at noon if Arthur could spare the time.

Gabriel forced himself to remember them as he made the lonely walk to Our Lady's, past the Round Church, Sidney Sussex, Christ's and the array of closed, silent shops. The streets were eerily empty at that early hour, and the sun was struggling to rise, offering Gabriel few distractions from his thoughts. Giovanna's parents had clung to him during those early terrible days after the fire, but even then, Gabriel had had the sense that they were already drifting apart. He could never be sure if it was his own guilt or genuine insight, but Gabriel had become increasingly convinced that Giovanna's parents were reproaching him for not being there when Giovanna and little Nicoletta had found themselves in mortal danger, that he had not been able to force his way into the flames and smoke and rescue them as a true hero would have done.

Perhaps—and he could hardly reproach them for this—Giovanna's parents had wished that he had been the one to perish in the flames. It would have been easier for everyone if it had been that way round, if Giovanna and Nicoletta had been out for the evening, far away from danger, and he had been the one to die. Her parents could have taken them back into their home and comforted them, helped them to rebuild their lives . . . *I should never have returned*, thought Gabriel. *This is why I have never come back. It does no good!*

They had exchanged letters for the first few months after the funerals. When Gabriel had entered the novitiate, Giovanna's mother had given him a beautiful purple velvet bag that had belonged to Giovanna, containing a few little keepsakes. He had carried that bag around with him ever since, discreetly hidden away, and he had refused to be parted from it. After that, Gabriel had written a couple of times, but he had had precious little to say; and when he received no answer on one occasion, he had taken it as a sign that they wished now to be left alone. The two people who had bound them together were gone.

Our Lady's was a sumptuous if ludicrously incongruous neo-Gothic building on Lensfield Road. When permission had finally been given for a Catholic parish church in Cambridge, following the Catholic Emancipation Act, the university authorities had insisted that the church should be out of the centre of Cambridge, its polluting Papist influence kept away from the university and its august colleges. Such had been the resistance to the building of the church, that Catholic students had taken it in turns to guard the site to prevent vandalism from militant Protestants, but it stood tall and untroubled now, a regiment of gargoyles protecting it from whatever evils might be waiting to invade this hallowed space.

Gabriel immediately felt himself relaxing as he stepped inside, going through the reassuring motions of dipping his hand in the holy water stoup and genuflecting before the magnificent high altar. His memory had served him correctly: Mass was just about to start, and he slipped discreetly into a pew near the back. There was safety here, among the strangers huddled together in this echoing sanctuary. Gabriel could see old ladies kneeling like reverent mushrooms, their hats tilted forwards as they commended their husbands and their children to God; to his left, Gabriel could see a small child, aged perhaps three or four, walking confidently up and down the side aisle, waving at the saints ensconced in the stained-glass windows as though greeting her friends. Gabriel smiled, thinking that those pious figures, standing with one hand raised, probably did look to a child as though they were waving.

It was the sort of thing Nicoletta had done in this vast, ornate playground guarded by angels and friendly saints. The thought of her caused Gabriel to stand up abruptly and move to the side aisle, where he could walk the length of the church without disturbing anyone. Nicoletta's favourite place, the chapel of the Blessed Sacrament, was tucked away in a corner. There was a stained-glass window depicting the martyrdom of Saint Thomas à Becket, which Nicoletta had found alternately fascinating and terrifying. Frozen forever in little pieces of coloured glass, Saint Thomas knelt at the altar, four knights hovering behind him, one with his sword raised to strike. Gabriel was not sure now whether Nicoletta had really understood what was going on in the tableau, but he remembered Giovanna lighting a candle with her and trying to keep her quiet after she had burst out in the shrill voice of an infant: "Look behind you, Tommy! Look behind you!"

Gabriel reached into his pocket for a penny to light a candle. He had tried to develop the habit over the years of praying for people who intruded upon his thoughts—there were many of them—and he took advantage of the opportunity to light a votive candle now. "I hope you're praying for me too, Nicky," he said softly, taking a candle from the box below the ornate metal stand. There was comfort in the mechanical act of holding the wick to one of the other candles that was in the process of burning out and watching the flame catching. As he set his candle carefully on the stand, the bell rang out for the consecration, and he dropped automatically to his knees. *Enough!*

Gabriel felt too jittery to stop anywhere for breakfast, and he walked steadily through central Cambridge, mentally ticking off the different colleges he passed as he went: Downing, Emmanuel, Christ's, Sidney Sussex, Magdalen, before turning to the right onto Chesterton Road. It was a long road with the river to his right, and a series of colourful houseboats became steadily more visible as the morning brightened. Gabriel had never remembered it being so long when he had cycled this way to meet Giovanna after lectures or walked her home after a romantic dinner, but the time together had always passed so quickly.

And there it was, a whitewashed terraced house with a red door, and wisteria twining itself around the front window. The house was set a little back from the road, as Gabriel had remembered, and a man's bike stood propped up against the wall. Just one bicycle—Mama Gervasoni must have given up cycling or been unable to ride anymore. Gabriel was just bracing himself to knock on the door, when he noticed a woman's face staring wide-eyed at him through the sitting room window, and their eyes met. It was Giovanna's mother, of course, unmistakably her, and judging by the look of shock on her face, it had not taken her long to recognise him either.

Gabriel did not knock on the door, since there was no longer any need, and braced himself as he heard a torrent of unintelligible Italian words behind the door, then the scrape and clink of locks being turned. The door slowly opened to reveal Mama Gervasoni standing in the doorway, still looking at him as though he had fallen out of the sky. Gabriel had always known her a handsome woman, and age had lent her an almost regal quality, her black hair streaked with silver so perfectly it could almost have been painted. Her face, thinner than he remembered, was as smooth and delicate as ever.

"Good morning, Mama," said Gabriel. He was sure he had rehearsed what to say the moment the door opened, but whatever tactful line he had memorised on the journey here, it escaped him now.

"*Dio mio,*" whispered Mama, but she held out her arms and pulled Gabriel into an embrace vigorous enough to leave him virtually winded. "Come here, you stupid boy! I want to slap your silly face!"

She did not slap his face, but she bundled Gabriel through the house into the back kitchen as though he were a naughty boy who had come home late from the park with mud all over his clothes. "I'm awfully sorry, Mama," said Gabriel, wanting desperately to tell her to loosen her grip on his arm. She flung him into a chair. "I should have warned you I was coming—it was just that it all happened rather quickly. My friend invited me——"

"You be quiet, you crazy boy," she answered, snatching the kettle from the stove with a violent energy that had always exhausted Gabriel to watch. "My God, all these years and here you are, sitting in my kitchen as though you never left! You became a Benedictine, not a hermit."

Gabriel let Mama Gervasoni's shrill, accusatory voice wash over him with an overwhelming sense of relief. He was home, sitting in a warm kitchen overlooking a vast garden, being chided by his mother-in-law. "I'm sorry. I'm not sure where the years have gone. I stopped travelling when I entered the monastery—well, to begin with, at least. What with the war and all the disruption . . ." Gabriel looked up at the old matriarch, who was pouring coffee beans into a hand grinder. He could not remember the last time he had seen real coffee, and he doubted she was growing it in that kitchen garden she appeared to have cultivated to get her surviving family through the war. "I didn't know what to say to you, Mama. I wasn't sure you'd want to hear from me. You didn't answer my——"

The grinder was shoved across the table to him like a small wooden missile; he took the hint and started turning the handle. She was giving him a job to do, making it clear to him that—whatever had passed between them—he was

43

not a visitor. The fact that they were sitting in her kitchen was a compliment, not that Giovanna's family had ever been known to stand on ceremony. Giovanna had always said that, much as she loved England, she could never quite get used to all the social niceties, the many prim little rules that seemed to govern middle-class life.

"You are my son, *Gabriele*," she said emphatically, taking cups out of the cupboard and laying them down with a clatter as though they had done her a personal insult. "You will always be my son. Why would I not wish to hear from you?"

Gabriel felt the unwelcome prickle of tears gathering beneath his eyelids, and he turned the handle on the grinder with greater energy. He could think of a thousand reasons why his in-laws would not have wanted to hear from him, the many reasons that had gone round his head in the weeks and months and years after Giovanna's and Nicoletta's deaths. Was he really supposed to quote them all to her now? He felt a hand on his arm and stopped moving. "Slowly, slowly," said that singsong female voice. "You do not have to tell me why you have stayed away. We always knew that if you could have saved them, you would have. We never doubted that for a moment, if it helps."

Gabriel let Mama Gervasoni take the grinder from his clenched hands, and he sat in silence as she removed the ground coffee from its little drawer. The only audible sounds were her graceful steps around the kitchen and the sudden whistle of the kettle boiling. "I still think of her all the time," he said quietly. "And Nicoletta. And both of you." He looked around uneasily; there was a pair of men's gum boots by the back door, and he felt a little safer asking. "Where is Papa? I thought I saw his bicycle . . ."

"It has a puncture. He's working this morning. He could not bear the thought of retirement and got himself a position at the post office."

"I'm sorry to have missed him," said Gabriel, truthfully. "I could . . . I could go to the post office and surprise him?" It was a ludicrous suggestion that Gabriel would never have had the guts to see through. Mama gave a hearty laugh.

"Don't you dare—you'll give the poor man a heart attack!" she said. "But you've not missed him. You will see him later." She handed Gabriel a cup of coffee, looking at him expectantly. "Now, how long do you mean to stay in Cambridge?"

Gabriel floundered for an answer. He had forgotten Giovanna Senior's directness. "Well, I was going to spend another night . . ."

"*Va bene*," answered Mama. "You will spend tonight with us. No, no, you will stay with us. You will be a good deal more comfortable in our home than in that draughty old college of yours. You'll get some decent food for once." She sat down opposite him, giving him a smile of pure pride. "We have *central heating*. Can you not feel it?"

Come to think of it, it was warm, but Gabriel had put it down to the heat from the kitchen stove. He had always remembered this room to be cosy and warm, even in the bitterest of Cambridge winters. "I'll have to speak with Arthur Kingsley. I'm sure he won't—"

Gabriel was startled by a sudden, urgent rapping at the front door, so loud and unexpected that it felt like a bomb going off in the quiet of the house. Mama jumped to her feet, storming to the door like an avenging angel, with the words, "Who on earth bangs the door like that?" Gabriel saw her hands tremble as she left the kitchen, and he made

45

to follow her. He doubted that the person attempting to get in meant her any harm, but she must have a lingering horror of an urgent knock at the door.

To Gabriel's astonishment, the door was thrown open to reveal Arthur's stooped figure. The man stood on the doorstep, dishevelled and breathless, snatching his hat off his head in a delayed act of courtesy to reveal hair stuck to his forehead with perspiration. "Heavens, Arthur, what's happened?" demanded Gabriel, relieved that his mother-in-law let the poor man in without a word.

Arthur staggered into the hall, gulping with the effort of calming himself. "Gabriel, please, will you come with me? Something terrible's happened."

"Will you not sit down?" asked Mama kindly, indicating the door to the sitting room, but Arthur shook his head vehemently. "Truly, you should sit down."

Arthur looked desperately at Gabriel. "I'm dreadfully sorry, I would never have burst in on you like this. It's just that, well, you left your address on that note, and I couldn't wait. It's . . . dear God, it's . . . she's dead."

"Dead?" Gabriel instinctively reached out to Mama, but she pushed his hand away. She was not Gabriel's present concern, and she wanted him to know it.

"Daphne. I found her when I went into the lab this morning. The police are there now, but I . . . I need you to . . ." Arthur leaned back against the now-closed door, and for a ghastly moment, Gabriel thought the man was going to faint. Arthur had apparently noted the danger himself, and he began taking slow, deep breaths, forcing himself to remain calm. "Gabriel, it appears to have been an accident, but I shan't be right in my mind until I'm sure."

Gabriel nodded. "Of course." He turned to Mama apologetically, but she patted his arm.

"You go," she ordered him. "I will send a telegram to your abbot to say that you must stay a little longer. Just tell me where to send it."

There was something intensely reassuring about Mama Gervasoni's ability to take charge in a crisis. A lesser woman might have broken down at the sound of savage hammering at the door and the mention—out of the blue—of a young woman killed in an accident, a drama played out whilst she was still getting over the shock of being reunited with her dead daughter's widower. But just like Giovanna had been, Mama was a formidable force of nature, and Gabriel felt able to put all other thoughts aside as he hurried with Arthur across the road and over the footbridge, listening intently to his friend's words.

Like any man in a state of shock, Arthur's account of what had happened came out in a stream of disconnected observations, and Gabriel was grateful that they were crossing Midsummer Common to avoid the busy streets of the town. Apart from the odd bicycle whirring past them, it was quiet enough to have a reasonably private conversation. "I can't understand how such a thing could have happened," declared Arthur, looking fixedly ahead as he spoke. "Of course, terrible accidents do happen—labs are dangerous places—but it's so unlike her to make a mistake like that. So out of character. Daphne was careful about everything; I would have trusted her . . ."

"Arthur, tell me exactly what has happened," said Gabriel steadily. "Go back to the beginning."

47

"It's as I said, I found her dead this morning. She was . . . she was dead . . . she was lying on the floor as if she were sleeping."

"What time did you find her?"

"I went to the lab at around eight o'clock this morning. I knew something was wrong; I can usually hear—"

"Were you the first to arrive?"

"Of course I was, or someone else would have raised the alarm!"

"Are you sure no one else had been in that morning?"

"As sure as it's possible to be. We're not lazy at my lab, you know, but one is either a night owl or a morning lark, and I'm a bit of a night owl myself . . ."

"But are you usually the first to arrive?"

"No, the second. Daphne is usually in very early. I'd join her at a more civilised hour, and the others tend to trickle in afterwards."

Gabriel turned up the collar of his coat. Apart from a row of trees at the far roadside of the green, the whole area was exposed, and the bitter wind stung his face. "All right, you said you knew something was wrong."

"Yes, I've no idea what it was, but the hairs on the back of my neck stood on end. I knew before I let myself in that something was wrong. And there she was, simply lying there." Arthur struggled to a halt as they reached the road, clinging to the low metal railings for support. "Look here, old man, I'm not sure I should be dragging you into all this. The police are sure it was a case of accidental poisoning. I know they're right; it fits with what I saw. It's just . . . well, it's only a gut feeling. One shouldn't get irrational."

"Gut feelings can be important," Gabriel assured him. "I

48

always trust mine. If something does not feel right, it usually isn't right."

Arthur stared down at his clenched fists. Gabriel was aware of the painfully short time that had passed since Arthur had stumbled upon the body of a beloved pupil; it might be hours before the full shock of what had happened began to sink in. "Arthur, perhaps you should go home. I'm not sure—"

"No, I must show you the scene before everything gets moved about," answered Arthur resolutely, moving to cross the road. Gabriel hurried after him. "Frankly, I'd trust you with my dear friend over the police any day." Arthur's fingers strayed to the brim of his hat. "I do hope my gut feelings are wrong on this one, Gabriel. I can't bear the idea that anyone would hurt that girl deliberately."

There it was, the struggle Gabriel had seen before. An apparent accident, a fall in bad light, the muddling of sleeping powders . . . and the nagging thought at the back of the mind that an accident was a little too convenient. "Perhaps you could tell me exactly what happened when you found her?"

But Arthur had slipped into the dark silence that inevitably followed a shock, triggered perhaps by their proximity to the lab. Gabriel's own thoughts returned to the evening before, to the quarrel he had overheard as he had walked through the college grounds during evensong, to the charming young woman he had observed at high table. Gabriel knew that he was able to think through the events of the evening only because he had not yet allowed himself to process what had happened. A young woman who had been on the threshold of a hugely successful life, who had had the love and admiration of so many of her colleagues, was dead. As they spoke, her body was probably already on its way to the mortuary. Gabriel shook his head and turned with his friend down the narrow road that led to Arthur's lab, grateful for the shelter of the tall buildings on such a chill, windswept day.

Gabriel remembered cycling over from his own faculty to have lunch with Arthur when he was in his first year. There was a well-kept garden at the front of the building where it was possible to enjoy a picnic and a cigarette during recreational moments, the different lab teams clustering together to talk about the news or the football, rarely about science. At this hour of the day, the little garden was deserted, except for a policeman standing guard at the door. The policeman moved towards them, then recognised Arthur and touched his helmet in what was almost a salute. Arthur nodded in acknowledgement and led Gabriel quickly inside.

The building was a good deal grander inside than it looked from the garden, with an echoing hall and stairs, doors leading in all directions. He followed Arthur upstairs, noting that faint chemical smell that permeated every part of a building like this. Gabriel was about to risk asking a question when they were greeted on the landing by two more uniformed men. They had obviously been waiting for Arthur's arrival before they could leave.

"We're finished here now, sir," said the older of the two men, a swarthy individual in his fifties who spoke with the respectful tone of an undertaker. "It looks very much like an unfortunate accident. We are unlikely to need to investigate any further, though as you'll be aware, there will have to be an inquest since the young lady died unexpectedly."

"Yes," said Arthur mutedly. "It is my intention to keep the lab closed until I have had the chance to talk to the others. We're all very shocked, as I'm sure you understand. Would you like me to keep the lab locked in case you need to gather further evidence?"

The sergeant shook his head. "No need, sir. We're not treating the death as a crime, so there's no crime scene, as it were."

Arthur nodded, though Gabriel doubted that anything the policeman had said had permeated his friend's confusion. On the other side of the door was the place where Arthur had had the most horrific shock of his entire life, and he was steeling himself to face it. "Why don't we go into your study first?" suggested Gabriel, causing Arthur to step back wordlessly to let him through. "When you're ready, you can take me through to the lab and tell me what you remember."

Gabriel placed a hand on the wooden door and gave it a firm push. He was surprised at how easily the door opened, since it looked a good deal heavier than it was, and he had braced himself for some resistance. He stepped inside and found himself standing in an old-fashioned man's study. It was a smaller space than Gabriel had envisaged, much of the room taken up by two desks—one squeezed into a corner, looking like a late addition to the furnishings, the other a heavy mahogany desk, positioned near the back wall to give a good view of both the door and the small window. The desk had Arthur's fingerprints all over it, every bit the domain of a middle-aged professor. There were the usual trimmings: pens, a bottle of ink, a blotting pad, a myriad of papers scattered untidily in piles. Directly behind the desk, there was a bookcase heaving with volumes of academic journals and other books whose spines Gabriel could not read from where he was standing.

Besides the desks, the only other notable objects in the room were a cupboard and a second door to the right. Gabriel's immediate impression was that this was an unremittingly bleak place in which to work, and Arthur must spend a good many hours of his working week sitting at that desk. It was a shade too dark for comfort, the window letting in very little light, which Gabriel suspected was a result of its not having been cleaned for years. The study also had that musty quality so many such spaces have, smelling of old books and dusty corners and perpetually damp overcoats. Gabriel wondered that the atmosphere could even be bearable with two people squeezed into such a close space, both trying to concentrate on their own work.

Arthur stood in the doorway and looked for a moment as though he were going to go over to his desk and sit down, but he went over to the connecting door and gave it an irritable shove. "Let's get this over with, shall we?" he said. "I'll be easier in my mind when we've talked it over."

The door led through to a generously proportioned laboratory. Gabriel was surprised yet again by how different it looked to how he had imagined it. The lab was poorly lit and cluttered, so much more chaotic than the orderly science lab he remembered from school. It smelt the same, that nondescript chemical smell he had first noticed on the stairs, and there were long wooden tables and objects Gabriel thought he ought to recognise—things in bottles, beakers, bizarre-looking metal gadgets he thought he had had to label in his exercise book once. On another occasion, Gabriel would have asked Arthur to give him a tour of the place so that he could find out the names of all the toys in this scientific playground, but his eye caught Arthur standing in silence, head bowed, staring down at a chair lying on its side.

"Arthur?"

"This is where I found her," said Arthur in a detached monotone. "It took me a moment to spot her because of where she'd fallen. The first thing I saw was her hand poking out from behind that bench there. The empty canister of liquid nitrogen was quite near her body."

The police had been as good as their word, and it looked as though they had moved nothing except for the body, which had been taken away. Gabriel frowned, the upturned chair irritating him unexpectedly. "I trust this is not a foolish question, but if she had knocked over something as dangerous as liquid nitrogen, wouldn't she have made a run for it?"

Arthur looked up at him sharply. "Of course she would have! Any sensible person would have! She must have tripped over that chair and fallen over. Even a short delay would have been enough." Arthur made a sudden bolt for the door. "I need some air," he said over his shoulder, in what would have been bad taste if Arthur had not looked so ashen and breathless. He staggered out onto the landing and stood leaning against the wall, panting as though he had run a marathon. Gabriel observed that he had cleared the room in a little more than three seconds and had had a clear run to the door.

Gabriel followed Arthur out into the corridor. "I'm sorry to put you through all this," said Gabriel apologetically. "I know it's all far too much to take in at the moment. I just can't help feeling that this all looks a little staged. Of course, it may have been an accident . . ."

"It must have been an accident," echoed Arthur, numbly. "Looking at where poor Daphne fell makes it abundantly obvious that it was an accident. If she fell as she tried to escape, she could never have got up. Within seconds, she would have been too breathless and disoriented to move."

But it took you only a few seconds to leave the room, pondered Gabriel, watching the colour returning to Arthur's face, *and you are much older than Daphne. You were not running for your life.*

"Arthur, you should go home," said Gabriel. "You need to be somewhere quiet and safe. Why don't I accompany you back to your rooms?"

Arthur shook his head impatiently. "No. I need to go and see Daphne's landlady. She'll be frantic with worry, and I cannot bear the thought of some policeman breaking the news to her."

"I can go and break the news," volunteered Gabriel, though the prospect filled him with horror. "You must rest. There's just one more question I have for you, if I may; then I think you'd better lock up the lab for now."

Arthur looked warily in his direction, but Gabriel was used to being looked at like that and took no notice. "What is it?"

"Could you show me precisely in what position Daphne's body was when you found her? I know it's hard, but I can't help feeling . . ."

Arthur strode back into the lab without a further word and pointed at the empty space near the chair. "She was exactly there," he said, pointing.

"Facedown? Or on her back?"

"Facedown. Like this." He drew one arm over his face and stretched out the other. "Almost as though she were fast asleep." His voice faltered, and his arms dropped to his sides with a disconsolate slap. "Let's face it, this was a tragic accident. I don't understand why I cannot get this nagging thought out of my head that this is all wrong. All of it. It's not just that I cannot believe she would have been stupid enough to make such a mistake. It would hardly be the first time a very brilliant person has come a cropper in a moment of clumsiness. It's just . . ." Arthur let out a growl of frustration and left the lab, this time not stopping outside. Gabriel heard his steps thundering down the stairs and followed him, pausing briefly to right the toppled chair. A chair Daphne had never dragged down.

4

Gabriel followed Arthur back to his rooms and sat with him until he was sure his friend was calm enough to be left to his own devices. Both men knew that Arthur would not be given a minute's peace over the next few days and that he would have to face the other members of his team before long, but he needed a few hours' solitude before he attempted to speak with anyone else. When Arthur's hands were steady enough to light a cigarette, Gabriel took out a notebook and pencil, laying them on the coffee table beside him.

"Why don't you write down the address of the house where Daphne was lodging?" asked Gabriel. "I'll go and talk to Daphne's landlady while you rest."

Arthur placed his cigarette in the heavy marble ashtray at the centre of the table and picked up the notebook and pencil. "It's a rather nice little house the other side of Parker's Piece. A bit of a walk, but you should have no trouble finding it." Arthur scribbled the address untidily on the paper. "I have to identify the body this afternoon. Seems a little absurd since I found her, but I gather it's necessary." Arthur handed Gabriel the paper and snatched up his cigarette.

"If you'd like me to be there, of course I'll come," promised Gabriel, pushing the paper into his pocket. "I'll return as soon as I can."

Arthur rose to his feet. "It's not that I need you to hold my hand, old man," he assured Gabriel, palpably embarrassed. "I rather thought you might want to take a look at the body yourself, simply to satisfy yourself that there was no foul play."

Gabriel nodded appreciatively, then stepped outside onto the staircase and made his way through the quad to the main gate. The faintest sliver of sunlight was fighting to pierce the monochrome sky as Gabriel passed the Round Church and narrowly avoided a collision with a bicyclist. He was sure he could not remember those gowned figures on bicycles looking quite so batlike when he was one himself, but Gabriel was struggling to collect his thoughts. If he had not been so worried about unsettling Arthur, Gabriel would have asked him rather more questions about Daphne's landlady to prepare himself for the task of breaking the news.

Daphne had only been a lodger, of course, and as far as Gabriel knew, her landlady might not have even known her very well. The very term "landlady" put Gabriel in mind of a fossilised old harpy in a faded housecoat, grey hair in curlers and a much-chewed Woodbine hanging out of the corner of her mouth. Nevertheless, discovering that a young lodger had died out of the blue was going to come as a terrible shock to the stoniest of hearts.

Gabriel walked diagonally across the wide, flat stretch of grass. It was these green spaces that made Gabriel fall in love with Cambridge all over again, much more than the architecture. In better weather, there might have been sports teams out training, students with rugs and blankets enjoying a picnic, men and women out for a stroll, but it was virtually deserted now. Gabriel wondered, as he reached the buildings at the other side of the green, why Daphne had lived in digs when she might have been able to live in halls. The house was a good deal closer to the lab than were the women's colleges, making it a practical choice, or Daphne might simply have desired a more independent life than the rigid timetables and regulations of a women's college.

It might have been plain and simple comfort, thought Gabriel, taking in the neat façade of the house, with its red-painted front door and smooth, scrubbed steps. This looked like a cosy, well-kept house, somewhere a young unmarried woman could find refuge after a long day of squinting into microscopes. The thought caused a dull ache to spread across Gabriel's chest. This was no tawdry boardinghouse, it was a home—and Daphne, he suspected, had been more than a paying lodger.

As if to confirm Gabriel's thoughts, the door opened, and the most atypical landlady imaginable stood before Gabriel. The lady of the house was a well-preserved woman with thick curls of silver hair carefully coiffured in a London salon. Her face was skilfully painted to enhance a pair of emerald-green eyes, and she was dressed in a cream silk blouse and elegantly tailored skirt that spoke of style if not wealth. "Good morning, young man," said the woman, enunciating the words in clear, rounded tones. A shadow passed over her face as she noted Gabriel's attire, but her composure did not flicker. "How may I help you?"

Gabriel floundered for a reply. There was something aristocratic about this woman. Despite her senior years— Gabriel would have placed her in her early seventies—she stood with the poise of a prima ballerina, and he almost felt as though he ought to kiss her hand or do something equally decorous. Instead, he removed his hat. "Good morning," he said. He tried to think of a preamble and quickly gave up. "Do I have the pleasure of addressing Mrs Bellinger?"

Mrs Bellinger narrowed her eyes momentarily. "I should prefer to know whom *I* have the pleasure of addressing, sir," she replied curtly. "Or is it 'Father'?"

"Forgive me, yes—I am a Catholic priest. I . . ." This was going disastrously wrong. It was like trying to explain one-self to a maiden aunt who had the self-assurance of Queen Victoria. "It's about Daphne," he persisted, faltering on Daphne's name. His mind had gone blank; he could not remember her surname, and referring to her by her Christian name alone made it sound as though he knew her personally. "Dr Kingsley asked me to . . ."

There was no need to finish the sentence or to agonise over the possible social impropriety. Mrs Bellinger's impenetrably calm expression was replaced immediately with a look of what was either sadness or fear. "Oh no, that's why they've sent a priest, isn't it?" she said in a tone of desperation. "It's always a priest or a policeman they send. I was going to talk to Dr Kingsley myself. Daphne did not return home last night, you see. I found her bed not slept in when I took her a cup of tea this morning."

Gabriel looked at Mrs Bellinger's worried expression and had his worst fears confirmed. He had no way of knowing how Daphne had viewed the arrangement, but Mrs Bellinger had evidently doted on the girl. "I'm very sorry, Mrs Bellinger," Gabriel said, but the old woman's eyes filled with tears.

"Has she had an accident?" she asked. "Is she in hospital? I shall go directly. She'll want her things, the poor girl."

Gabriel shook his head, causing Mrs Bellinger to turn on her heel and flee inside the house, leaving Gabriel to follow awkwardly, closing the door behind him. "I'm so sorry," said Gabriel to Mrs Bellinger's back as she led him into the drawing room. "Dr Kingsley meant to speak to you himself, but I'm afraid he's rather distressed."

Mrs Bellinger sat herself in a plush tawny armchair near the fire, inviting Gabriel to sit in the opposite chair. "I knew something dreadful had happened," said Mrs Bellinger, still sitting ramrod straight but with the faraway look of a woman who has yet to grasp the enormity of the news. "She's ever such a good girl, you see. A good Catholic girl. She's never out late, wouldn't dream of sleeping anywhere—anywhere but her own bed, if you understand what I mean." The tears glistening in Mrs Bellinger's eyes flowed free. She took a lace handkerchief out of her pocket, releasing a scent of lavender oil as she did so. "What happened?" she managed to ask.

"At the moment, it looks as though the young lady may have met with an accident," said Gabriel as gently as he could. "Her body was found on the floor of her lab, and it appears that she may have upset a canister of liquid nitrogen. I gather that the gas is very toxic and would have caused her to suffocate."

Mrs Bellinger placed a hand over her face and sobbed. Even in the throes of what looked like quite genuine grief, there was something theatrical about the woman's movements, which Gabriel found curious more than anything else. He was certain that Mrs Bellinger had had no idea of the fate that had befallen her lodger, beyond the intuition of a woman who knows that a young person has acted out of character and must therefore have come to harm.

Gabriel looked around, desperately seeking evidence of the presence of others in the house. The drawing room had a bohemian feel to it, suggesting the home of an artist or a musician. There was a piano in one corner with a series of wooden recorders of different sizes hung over it; the paintings on the wall hinted at a family who had travelled extensively before the war years had rendered it impossible. There was a male influence in this house as well: Gabriel noted a man's smoking jacket hanging on a hook on the back of the door, and photographs on the mantelpiece of young faces that were obviously the Bellinger children.

"Madam, is your husband at home?" asked Gabriel. "It might be better for you to call him in."

Mrs Bellinger took a moment to compose herself before giving Gabriel a sad smile. "I'm afraid it would do no good at all to call my dear Eric into the room," she said candidly. "He's been losing his mind for the past year now and seldom leaves his bed. He must have asked for Daphne ten times already this morning. I've no idea how he'll bear it if he ever understands that she is gone."

"Were you both close to Daphne then?" asked Gabriel. Sitting next to the fire had left Gabriel feeling desperately hot, and he realised he had never removed his coat. Mrs Bellinger noted his discomfort and stood up, proffering a hand to take his coat from him. Gabriel scrambled to his feet, struggling in his embarrassment to undo the buttons, but the farcical struggle to extricate himself from his jacket released some of the tension, and Mrs Bellinger snatched away his coat with a weary smirk. Gabriel remembered Father Foley's words of advice when he had first joined his parish, that the recently bereaved need the distraction of mundane tasks. Therefore, if a priest enters a house and the young widow offers him a cup of tea, the answer must always be in the affirmative, even if the priest in question has drunk twenty cups of tea that morning. So, when Mrs Bellinger offered Gabriel a cup of tea, he expressed his delight at the prospect.

Whilst Mrs Bellinger busied herself in the kitchen, Gabriel took the opportunity to survey the room more closely. Photographs always interested him, those little monochrome glimpses into a person's life, though there were certain similarities he had come to notice in personal photographs now. On the mantelpiece, as in so many homes of older people around Britain today, there was a photograph of a young man in naval uniform, the flicker of a smile at the corners of his mouth suggesting an impish sense of humour being restrained. Next to it, there was a young woman every bit Mrs Bellinger's daughter, proudly wearing the uniform of the WAAFs. Unlike her brother, the young girl was making no attempt at a sombre pose and grinned cheekily into the camera, revelling in the excitement of her new life.

Gabriel's eyes drifted towards an oil painting in a gilded frame, hanging like an icon on the wall. It captured a stunningly beautiful Victorian lady whom Gabriel guessed to be no more than twenty. The pose was stiff and formal, but there was no avoiding the sense that this was a woman who enjoyed being on show. She was dressed in a flowing gown, holding a bouquet of roses in her arms, her hair pinned back with what looked like pearls to reveal one of the loveliest faces Gabriel had ever seen. He knew immediately who Mrs Bellinger was.

When the lady herself returned after an interminably long

time, Gabriel noticed that her eyes were swollen from renewed crying, and he hurried forward to help her with the
tea tray. He would never normally have impinged upon the
role of the hostess, but Mrs Bellinger handed him the tray
gratefully and let him set it down on a small walnut table
near her chair. As soon as she was settled, Gabriel retreated
to the other seat and left her to pour the tea. "Do you miss
the stage, Mrs Bellinger?" asked Gabriel, watching as his
hostess poured milk and tea into two fine bone china cups,
her every move deft and elegant.

Mrs Bellinger gave an indulgent smile. "It is many years
since I trod the boards, young man," she answered, handing
him his tea, "and I was Adela Harrison in those days. But
I think you knew that." Her eyes drifted to the painting
on the wall, and she regarded it almost as though she were
observing an entirely different person, which in some ways
she was. "It was a different world, Father, perhaps not a
better world—we all get a little nostalgic as we grow older
—but it was a more hopeful time in which to be young.
We believed we could achieve anything." She took a sip of
her tea, but the action was almost mechanical, a chance to
collect her thoughts. "My husband was a man of science
before his illness; we lived abroad for many years thanks to
his work."

"It must have been hard for you to give up your own
work," said Gabriel.

Mrs Bellinger shook her head. "No. I gave up the theatre
when I married at forty, but actresses are fit for the stage
only in the first flush of their youth. I did well to continue
for so long. And I loved Eric's work. It took us all over the
world." She stared disconsolately into the fire. "Scientists

64

and engineers have wrought so much destruction and death upon the world. That's why Eric loves—loved—Daphne so. He thought a new generation of scientists might employ their intelligence to heal the world."

Mention of Daphne's name brought tears to the old woman's eyes again. Gabriel hesitated, calculating the risk of bringing this stranger into his confidence. She was a highly intelligent and articulate woman, and her love for Daphne was obvious, but the individuals closest to the victim were sometimes the most unreliable, and Gabriel had no way of knowing whether Mrs Bellinger would take his suspicions directly to the police—or worse, to the papers. "I'm so sorry for your loss, Mrs Bellinger. I know that this is very hard for you to take in at the moment, and I am sorry to trouble you further, but I would like to learn a little more about Daphne's life here in Cambridge."

"Why?"

It was a fair question. An elderly lady had just welcomed a complete stranger into her home, he had announced that her much-loved lodger had died in a laboratory accident, and now he wanted to know the story of her life. Gabriel could not quite bring himself to mention his suspicions and changed tack. "She was more than just a lodger to you, wasn't she, Mrs Bellinger?"

Mrs Bellinger's eyes welled up again. "Did you ever meet Daphne?" she asked gently.

"Only yesterday, I'm afraid," said Gabriel. "She seemed to be an exceptional young woman. I'm only sorry that I did not have the opportunity to get to know her a little better."

"Even if you met her only once," said Mrs Bellinger,

"you would have noticed that she was not the kind of person who was *just* anything to anyone. She was the sort of character to whom one naturally warmed. She inspired great affection and loyalty in everyone she met."

"Did you know her before she came up to Cambridge?"

Mrs Bellinger shook her head. "No, and before you ask, I was not in the habit of taking in lodgers. My niece and nephew stayed with us during the war to escape the blitz, since our own children were away. Taking in Daphne was a personal favour."

"Did Arthur—Dr Kingsley arrange things?"

"No, it was another chap. Dr Crayford. He knew Eric from of old. Daphne's father was rather uncertain about his unmarried daughter living far away from home, and he agreed to let her take up her position only if a suitable lodging could be found for her with a respectable family. When she was an undergraduate, she would have lived in halls, of course."

Gabriel nodded. "And the arrangement seems to have worked well."

Mrs Bellinger looked steadily down at her cup as though studying the intricate painted patterns. "Oh yes. She was such a very sweet girl; it was like having a daughter back in the house. And she was so good with Eric. She was the only person I could trust to sit with him when I went out. She used to sing to him to calm him when he became agitated."

"Did Daphne have any enemies?"

Mrs Bellinger looked up sharply. "Of course not. Whatever makes you ask such a question? She was a darling. She hadn't an enemy in the whole world!" She scrutinised him with the merciless gaze of a woman who has seen too much of the world to be easily deceived by it. "You think someone killed her, don't you? How can you honestly imagine such a dreadful thing?"

There had never been a subtle way to bring up his suspicions, and Gabriel did not know the meaning of the word. Faced with Adela Bellinger's piercing, catlike eyes looking across at him, Gabriel knew without being told that he was no longer welcome in the house. As he got up to leave, he could almost see the angry letter on Arthur Kingsley's desk, demanding to know why he had sent a Romish priest to harass a respectable woman.

"Don't worry, old man," Arthur reassured Gabriel as they walked to the hospital. "You did your best."

The only saving grace was that Arthur had far too much on his mind to care a great deal about any response he might receive from Daphne's landlady. The short rest had done Arthur no discernible good whatsoever. If anything, he looked even more haggard than when Gabriel had left him, having had time for the horror of the morning's discovery to sink in. Gabriel doubted Arthur had felt able to eat anything, and there was a distinct smell of brandy on the man's breath that Arthur was trying to hide by smoking his pipe.

"There's no pleasant way to break news like that," said Gabriel, omitting to mention what had actually triggered Mrs Bellinger's indignation and Gabriel's subsequent exit from the house. "Who will speak with Daphne's parents?"

"The policeman I spoke to said that a constable would pay them a visit," said Arthur. "I'd go myself, but her people live in Oxfordshire, and they need to be told as quickly as possible before the story gets into the papers." Arthur flinched at his own words, and Gabriel tried hard not to think of Arthur barricaded into his laboratory by reporters. "Tragic Young Scientist Dead" was the sort of headline that sold papers, particularly as the victim had been so fetching. Things would get a good deal worse if the press received any hints that Daphne's death might not have been an accident.

The walk to Addenbrooke's Hospital took them along King's Parade, past the great iconic mediaeval chapel of King's College. In Gabriel's humble opinion, King's College Chapel was by no means the most beautiful building in the city—he had a particular love for the Bridge of Sighs with its connection to Venice and the tragic final journey of the condemned men of long ago, crossing a covered bridge so that they could not throw themselves into the river in a last act of defiance. King's College Chapel, by comparison, had an empty feel to it, full of memories of mediaeval piety and now mostly full of cultured agnostics who liked a good tune.

The need to keep walking was doing Arthur good, Gabriel could see. It was forcing him to exercise, to take the air and to focus on the small but unavoidable tasks associated with death. "It's frightfully decent of you to come with me," said Arthur as they walked between Corpus Christi and Saint Catharine's Colleges, King's Parade merging effortlessly into Trumpington Street. "I didn't just ask you for moral support, you understand," reiterated Arthur. "It might help to put your mind at rest. I've heard about your detective work."

"I'm not sure I'll be much good in the mortuary," said Gabriel. "I'm not a doctor. But sometimes there's some little detail that makes one think." Gabriel noticed Arthur's strides growing smaller and smaller as they neared the magnificent eighteenth-century hospital building. "It's all right, Arthur, the worst is over."

Arthur did not turn to look at him. "I'm afraid I cannot think of many worse places than a mortuary, identifying the body of a member of my team."

Gabriel jumped at the ping of a bicycle bell close to him as a young man cycled past them at speed, narrowly avoiding the open drain. "What I mean is, the worse thing was finding her on the floor of that laboratory. You had no warning, no idea that anything was amiss until it was too late. You have had some chance to prepare yourself for this."

"In the lab it almost felt like a dream," answered Arthur. "Things like that simply don't happen. Now I know I'm awake, and I know Daphne is dead. If I had a choice, I would remember her cheerfully pottering around my laboratory, not lying cold on a slab."

But there was no way of getting round it; Daphne was dead, and Arthur would never be able to think of her again without seeing her lying in the mortuary the moment the attendant uncovered her body. "It's her," said Arthur in a whisper. "It's Daphne Silverton."

Everything about a mortuary was almost designed to be depressing. There was no way to make a room for the storage of the dead uplifting, unless one saw it as an invitation to live life to the fullest—*carpe diem*. If the attendant had not had to uncover her face when Gabriel and Arthur had entered the room, Daphne might still have been merely sleeping. Her skin had taken on the tincture of death, but with no visible injury, her face looked positively serene. "I want to wake her up," said Arthur. "I feel as though I could give her a nudge, and she'd open her eyes and start apologising for dozing off."

Gabriel looked back at the assistant, who was maintaining a respectful distance. "I wonder if you might give the gentleman a moment?" he asked. The assistant nodded understandingly and stepped outside. Gabriel was struck with an uncomfortable sense of being a voyeur and moved away from the cadaver, leaving Arthur staring down at Daphne's dead face, unable to move. "Arthur," he said gently. "Arthur, is there anything amiss with her? Anything that makes you suspicious?"

Arthur was holding Daphne's right hand as though he expected to find some clue concealed in her clenched fist, but her hand was open, and Gabriel remembered Arthur's comment about seeing her outstretched hand on the floor when he had stepped into the room. Arthur shook his head. "I'm sorry, my dear," he said, placing Daphne's hand across her chest. He turned his back abruptly and moved away from the body, but it was too late. Gabriel saw Arthur's hands folded over his face and heard the rasping sound of sobs being stifled. "This is my fault," he choked out, advancing on the door as though they had been locked in the room and might never escape. "This is all my fault! Please, I have to get out of this room!"

Gabriel followed Arthur at a discreet distance. He knew his friend did not want his company, but he could not risk letting him out of his sight. This was easier said than done, as Arthur was moving through the labyrinth of corridors like a man possessed and did not slacken his pace until they had emerged into the weak light of day.

"Arthur!" called Gabriel, out of breath. Arthur stopped and turned to look at him; he was white and shaking. "Arthur, what on earth is it? What do you mean, it's your fault?"

They were standing in the small garden in front of the grandiose, fortress-like edifice of the hospital. All around them, there was the hubbub of human activity—nurses in their capes and bonnets, walking purposefully in and out, patients being moved in chairs or stretchers—but Arthur appeared oblivious to everything. "Arthur?" Gabriel said again. He looked around for somewhere to sit and noticed a narrow bench to their right. He took Arthur by the arm and led him to it, helping him to sit down as though he were assisting a much-older man. "Arthur, what did you see in there? Why should it be your fault?"

Arthur stared listlessly into space. His eyes were so bleary and swollen that Gabriel could have sworn he had been weeping all day, but Arthur was the sort of man who had probably not cried in public since he was an infant; Gabriel ignored the urge to comfort him. "I saw nothing," said Arthur. "That's why I know it was my fault. Her death was clearly accidental."

"If it was an accident, it was not your fault," said Gabriel.

Arthur's fingers had strayed to the collar of his jacket, and he began twisting it absently. "She was working very long hours, and I'm afraid I encouraged her. She never usually worked late in the evening; she was an early bird. On the rarest of occasions when she did, I was always there. I'm the night owl. But I wasn't there. The one night she chose to burn the midnight oil, and I wasn't there."

Gabriel watched Arthur's fidgeting fingers and felt a knot

of anxiety tightening in his chest. "Arthur, do you know what she was working on? Might there have been some reason she was working so hard?"

"She always worked hard," said Arthur, "but much more so of late. She was excited, said she was on the cusp of a breakthrough. I should . . . I should have told her to slow down!" Arthur had stopped fidgeting and was clenching his fists as though he wanted to strike someone but had no idea with whom he should pick a fight. "She was exhausted; one becomes clumsy when one is overtired. That accident was waiting to happen, and I could have stopped it! I could have told her to make sure she got enough sleep; I could have reminded her of the obligation to look after herself." Arthur looked at Gabriel in desperation. "Don't you see, my friend? She was my responsibility! She worked for *me!*"

There seemed little point in stating the obvious fact that Daphne had not looked particularly tired the night she died. Instead, Gabriel persuaded Arthur to get up and walk with him as far as the nearest tea shop, in the hope that a cup of hot, sweet tea might restore Arthur's nerves a little. There was even less point in reminding Arthur that he had always been in the habit of twisting the collar of his coat between his fingers when he was fibbing—Gabriel remembered him doing that when they were students. However old and venerable he looked, Arthur was as transparent as ever.

5

Arthur was so distracted that Gabriel gave up on the idea of a tea shop and asked whether he would prefer to return to his rooms for a restorative cup of something a little stronger. "I could hail a cab if you're not up to walking," suggested Gabriel, but Arthur declined the offer, and they walked in virtual silence all the way back to college. Gabriel made the most of the silence to think over what he had learnt at the mortuary. It was a tiny detail, but like so many of his apparently inconsequential observations, it was burrowing its way into Gabriel's mind, refusing to give him any peace.

If the news of Daphne's death had not yet reached the ears of the press, it had spread all round the college community by now, and Gabriel could not shake off the unpleasant sense that everyone they passed was avoiding them, too embarrassed or upset to know what to say. Arthur began to relax only when he had locked the doors to his rooms and the two men were seated in gloomy privacy beside the empty grate. "Shall I ask for the fire to be lit?" asked Gabriel, but Arthur shook his head. Gabriel knew that Arthur was freezing cold—he had not taken off his coat—but he did not want to be disturbed by anyone else.

Gabriel got on his knees by the grate and began stacking the fire himself. "Don't bother yourself with that, old chap," protested Arthur, but Gabriel ignored him, absorbing himself in the task of transferring coals from the scuttle to the grate. Arthur was in no position to resist any offer of help and handed Gabriel a box of matches. "I hate to see a guest on his knees . . ."

"It's where I am most comfortable," quipped Gabriel. "You went to the trouble of lighting the fire when I arrived, damp and freezing. Let me extend that courtesy to you now."

"Doesn't fire trouble you?" asked Arthur, watching as Gabriel succeeded in getting the coals to catch on his third attempt. Gabriel suspected that the matches were a little damp but persevered regardless. "I hope you don't mind me asking, but I was thinking about it when you first arrived. Doesn't it remind you—"

"One cannot live without fire," said Gabriel, looking at the pathetic little flames struggling to leap to life. "Sometimes it's the strangest things that provoke an old memory. As you know, I went to see Giovanna's parents today. Well, I saw her mother. The father still works."

"Good, I told you you should."

"Mrs Gervasoni has invited me to stay with them for a few days. I don't think I should; you'll want me here. She'll understand, and it might be easier—less of an imposition on them after all this time."

Arthur got up from his chair and took down a large photograph from the mantelpiece. "No, I think you should go to them, Gabriel," he said, and Gabriel sensed that he was not simply being polite. "I don't want to sound unfriendly, but I'm going to need some time alone to take in what's happened. I'm sure you'll understand with your . . . well, I'm not sure what sort of company I'll be."

"I'm at your disposal," said Gabriel, returning to his chair. The fire was burning brightly, and the faint haze of smoke had cleared from the room. "It's no good, Arthur, I have to ask you this. Why are you telling me that she died in an accident? How can you be sure?"

Arthur looked steadily down at the photograph he was holding. "Look here, Gabriel, I have to be a man and accept my mistake. I didn't want to believe that Daphne's death was an accident—even though the thought of her being murdered is so much more horrific. The fact is, if someone had killed her, I could wash my hands of the guilt, but an accident in my laboratory is my responsibility."

"Arthur, I understand that you'd—"

"I killed her, Gabriel. Let's face it. I was not there when she died; she was working all alone late at night. She was desperately overtired, and I was encouraging her to work those long hours because I was excited by the prospect of her making a breakthrough. A breakthrough for which I could have taken the credit." Arthur slumped back in his chair, apparently exhausted. "You must see, there is no one on this planet who could possibly have wanted Daphne dead."

"Motives are not always easy to understand," said Gabriel, but he knew he was walking a tightrope and was liable to fall. "Most victims of murder—particularly women— know their killers very well, but not always."

Colour was returning to Arthur's face for the first time that day, but only because he was becoming angry. "Look, we're not talking about some poor young girl beaten to death by robbers for her pearl necklace! We're not talking about a little slip of a thing, strangled in an alleyway by some faceless pervert. Daphne died in her laboratory. Are you suggesting that someone took the trouble to get into that building, then found his way through that maze of stairs and corridors on the off chance of finding an unprotected female to attack? Is it any more likely that the intruder knew what liquid nitrogen was, knew where to find it and threw it at her without her noticing that there was anything wrong?"

It was a deliberate caricature of Gabriel's thoughts, but he was embarrassed enough to refrain from arguing. "You're quite right. Put like that, it does sound rather implausible. Why did she paint her nails?"

"What?"

Gabriel had not entirely intended his question to come out like that, but there was no way to prevent its sounding strange, and Arthur's bewilderment was understandable. "Her nails were painted."

"What if they were?" Arthur was not angry now; he was lost. "What on earth has that to do with the price of fish?"

"I'm frightfully sorry, you must think me terribly odd," said Gabriel, ignoring Arthur's snort of indignation. "I just couldn't help noticing in the mortuary, she was wearing pink nail varnish. I somehow imagined that scientists wouldn't do that. Wouldn't it be dangerous? Or at least impractical? You see, her nails looked quite ragged, very scraped and chipped at the ends."

"For pity's sake, pull yourself together, man!" exclaimed Arthur, thrusting the photograph at Gabriel. Gabriel took the photograph in confusion because he was still thinking about Daphne's nail varnish. "That's what you need to see," said Arthur. "If poor Daphne had been murdered, it could not have been a random killing in such a place. There is no one—I repeat, no one—who could have wanted her dead.

Look at all those faces! Those were her friends, her associates, the people she worked with every day of her life. Can you see any of those young men wanting the poor girl dead? They were like flies around a honeypot."

Gabriel knew that Arthur was wrong. Gabriel's loved ones had been killed by hate—Gabriel had always known that—but misguided love, jealous love, frustrated love, controlling love could be a far-stronger motive, and Arthur had just drawn Gabriel's attention to the possibilities.

Gabriel looked more closely at the photograph. It was a formal picture that looked as though it had been taken at the beginning of an academic year: a small group of young students and elderly professors stood together in rows, dressed in their flowing black gowns and looking at the camera—some smiling, some making an effort to look more serious. Daphne was most prominent by dint of being the only woman, but Gabriel recognised a few other faces: Arthur stood to Daphne's side, every bit the benevolent senior tutor, and Gabriel identified Robert Sutton standing the other side of Daphne—standing a little too close to her, Gabriel thought. The gap between them was just that much smaller than between all the others.

"Your department?" asked Gabriel.

"Indeed," confirmed Arthur. "Some of those faces will already be familiar to you."

"I overheard Daphne having an argument with a young man last night while you were all at evensong," said Gabriel, handing the photograph back to Arthur.

"What man?"

"He seemed to be making rather a hash-up of proposing marriage. Got his face slapped for his pains."

Arthur gave a muted laugh. "That'll be Will Valentine. Poor chap, couldn't take no for an answer. He's going to be dreadfully cut up about all this." Arthur looked miserably at Gabriel. "I don't know how I can possibly face them all."

"You're all in the same boat. You have all suffered the loss of someone you loved. You must try to stop thinking that Daphne's death is your fault. Am I right in thinking that if you had been next to her when she upset that canister, you would both have perished?"

"It's possible," Arthur conceded. "Things can happen very quickly, and there might not have been time for either of us to escape. Then again, I might have noticed a moment before she did, and got us both out of the way. Who knows?"

"Precisely. Who knows?" affirmed Gabriel. "Arthur, I tortured myself after Giovanna and Nicoletta's death that if I had only been at the house when the fire started, I could have got them out. I could have saved them. Perhaps the fire would not have happened at all. But it's no good. I was not there, and you were not there."

"I should have been," answered Arthur, in what was almost a whimper. "Logically, you're quite right, of course. But one thing my life as a scientist has taught me is that human beings are not logical. We have to be the least logical specimens on this planet."

Gabriel was saved from prolonging the conversation by a sudden, savage hammering on the door. Both men instinctively shrank away from the sound, but the repeated crash of fists on wood was soon accompanied by the sound of a man's voice shouting. "Dr Kingsley? Dr Kingsley, open up! Please open the door!"

"Oh dear God, it's Robert," groaned Arthur, sounding like an exasperated teacher about to be bored to death by his least promising student. Arthur looked desperately at Gabriel. "What on earth am I going to say to him? He'll be beside himself. What am I to say?"

"You shouldn't have to say anything," said Gabriel, venturing towards the door. "He'll do all the talking. You need only listen."

Gabriel unlocked the inner door, and then the outer door, barely able to step aside before Robert Sutton burst in, breathless and shaking. He was well dressed, having got up that morning in a state of blissful ignorance, but he was visibly sweating around his temples, and his eyes looked wide and glassy with the early signs of shock. "What's happened to Daphne?" he called out. The rest of his words came out in a disordered jumble. "The lab was closed when I got there this morning. I couldn't get in; there was a bobby turning everyone away! Someone said Daphne's killed herself!"

Arthur shook his head. "No, Robert. No."

"It's not true? Please tell me it's not true!" Robert looked from Arthur to Gabriel, awaiting an answer. "For God's sake, is Daphne dead?"

Arthur's mouth opened and shut, but Robert's deranged appearance in his rooms had overwhelmed him. Gabriel stepped forward, motioning for Robert to sit down, but he stepped back, refusing to be placated. "I'm very sorry, Mr Sutton," said Gabriel, "I'm afraid Daphne is dead. It wasn't suicide; she—"

Robert let out an animal roar and staggered back against the wall, leaning forward as though he had been punched in the stomach. Arthur took a step towards him, but Gabriel knew that Arthur was in no condition to deal with a distraught young man and moved between them. "Why don't you sit down, Mr Sutton?" suggested Gabriel. "You've had a terrible shock. It might be better if you . . ."

Robert looked blankly at Gabriel and allowed himself to be led to a chair. There was something about his vacant expression that reminded Gabriel of footage of air-raid survivors staggering through the piles of rubble, bewildered and deafened by the explosions they had so narrowly escaped. "How did she die?" he asked numbly, as though it hardly mattered. It did not change the horrible reality of the situation.

"It appears to have been a tragic accident," said Gabriel. "It looks as though she upset a canister of liquid nitrogen. There's no reason to suggest it was suicide. There was no note or anything like that."

"What reason would she have had to commit suicide?" asked Arthur, finding his voice. He sounded disgusted by the idea. "She had everything to live for. It was an accident. You may take some comfort from that."

"Comfort?" Robert staggered out of his chair and glared at Arthur, causing Gabriel instinctively to stand between them again. "What comfort is there in that? She's dead, isn't she? She's *dead*!"

"I know." Arthur could not look up. "I know; I found her."

"Why should she be dead, of all people?" demanded Robert, taking a step towards Arthur that was unambiguously threatening. "Any of us could have knocked that canister over; why did it have to be her? Why?"

Why. It was the oldest and most desperate of questions.

Of course, Robert was right. Accidents always felt so pointless because they were random. Why did that person step in front of the bus and not the person who had crossed the road three seconds earlier? Why did that man trip on the loose paving stone and break his neck and not the dozens of others who had stepped in exactly the same place?

Gabriel shepherded Robert towards the door. "Why don't I walk you back to your rooms?" suggested Gabriel, grateful that Robert took the hint and moved through the door without any resistance. Gabriel glanced over his shoulder at Arthur—who gave an appreciative nod—before joining Robert outside and closing the door behind him. "Why don't you lead the way?"

Gabriel followed Robert downstairs and across the quad to another, almost identical staircase, but Robert had the luxury of rooms on the ground floor, and Gabriel soon discovered why. Robert's rooms were a great deal more spacious than most sets, and much of his sitting room was taken up by a baby grand piano. "You are a choral scholar?" asked Gabriel as Robert slumped onto a threadbare sofa squeezed into the corner. He did not invite Gabriel to sit down, but the presence of the piano meant that there was an awkward lack of seating, and Gabriel ended up perching on the piano stool as though he were about to treat Robert to a recital.

"It's all right, padre, I won't be needing a lecture," said Robert dryly. "I'd like some answers, but I know there aren't any. Even if you people pretend there are."

"I do not pretend to have answers to every tragedy," said Gabriel, "but if you took the trouble to join the chapel choir, your faith must give you some comfort at a time like this."

Robert looked at Gabriel as though he were the biggest idiot in Christendom. "I auditioned for my choral scholarship because of the pretty music and a better room. There's nothing but the here and now." He stopped in his tracks, staring fixedly down at the warped floorboards. "And Daphne is gone. No flights of angels, no paradise, no hope. A momentary lapse of concentration, and it was over."

Gabriel watched Robert sitting with his head in his hands and stifled the uncomfortable sense of being an impostor, sitting in the room of a virtual stranger while he was reeling from the shock of losing a woman he had admired. More than that, surely . . . loved, despite all the rumours? "Mr Sutton," Gabriel began tentatively, well aware that Robert Sutton had every right to hurl him out of the room whenever he chose. "Mr Sutton—"

"My name is Rob," Robert interrupted impatiently. "Everyone calls me Rob. Everyone worth knowing, anyway."

"Well, thank you—Rob," answered Gabriel, as though Robert had genuinely invited him into his confidence rather than issuing him with a barely disguised rebuke. "Might you want to leave Cambridge for a few days? This will be a very difficult time for anyone who was close to Daphne Silverton."

"Close," echoed Robert bitterly. "I admired her from a distance, Father, but she was never mine. Will Valentine had his eye on her, but she wouldn't have taken him either. She wasn't the marrying kind."

"She was ambitious."

"She was obsessed, Father. Really great scientists have to be," said Robert. "Daphne was great; I'm not. I work as hard as I have to, and I will get my PhD. Then it's very likely that I will leave science altogether. Daphne was never happy unless she was pottering about a lab." Robert fidgeted awkwardly in his seat. The sofa did look incredibly uncomfortable, and Gabriel noticed that Robert kept having to change position to stop himself from sinking through the stodgy cushions onto the floor. "Ironically, if Daphne were going to die anywhere, she would have wanted to die in the lab."

"But I don't imagine she wanted to die at all," said Gabriel.

Robert lent forward as though he were about to start whispering a secret, but his voice was quite calm now. "She didn't kill herself, Father. I don't know why I even believed that rumour when I heard it. She would never have killed herself."

"Many people who have given up on life hide the fact until it's too late," Gabriel reminded him. "Suicide is always a shock when it happens."

"Not Daphne, Father. I'm afraid you're quite wrong if that's what you think. She loved her life. She had every reason to love it. She was at the university she'd fought so hard to get to; she spent all day every day doing work that meant everything to her. She was surrounded by people who would have laid down their lives for her."

Gabriel took his life in his hands and asked the obvious question. "You seem very sure of that. But how well can you really say you knew her? How well does anyone know anyone when it comes to it?"

Robert rose to his feet, which would have looked extremely dignified and masterful had he not virtually had to roll onto the floor before standing up, to avoid becoming entangled in the sofa springs. "I don't expect a man like you to understand what it means to be close to anyone," said Robert scathingly. "One of the wonderful things about Daphne not seeing me as husband material is that she treated me like a brother. She didn't see me as a threat; we talked for hours about all sorts of things she would never have discussed with Dr Kingsley or even Will. She was honest with me because she didn't have to impress me."

Gabriel stood up, sensing Robert's desperation for him to go, but there was so much more he wanted to ask, and he searched for a delaying tactic. Near the piano, wedged into an alcove, stood an ornate nineteenth-century desk. Robert must have rarely worked in his room, as the desk did not look especially well used—a little too tidy, the pens and pencils and blotter pad barely touched.

There were also relatively few photographs, only one in the whole room as far as he could make out. Gabriel risked taking a closer look at the image of a young woman look-ing coyly into the camera. The girl did not appear to be a blood relation of Robert's; even with the photograph's sepia tones, she had a darker complexion and her features were stronger and sharper, her face dominated by large almond-shaped eyes and a shock of unruly dark curls.

"Is that your girl?" asked Gabriel, indicating the picture.

Robert gave a hollow laugh. "Absolutely not, Father. She was an evacuee. My parents are farmers—lots of people in our village took in evacuees, and we got Sarah. So no, she wasn't my girl. She ended up being . . . a bit like Daphne, I suppose. A sister."

"It was good of your family to take her in," said Gabriel admiringly. "It must be quite difficult to open one's house to a complete stranger like that." Very difficult, and yet thousands of families in rural England had done just that to save children from the horrors of the blitz. Not that anything could have been worse than to be a wartime mother, putting a child on a train and waving good-bye, not knowing who would care for him or when he would ever return. "It's fortunate that she found a happy home."

"Best thing my parents ever did, going to the railway station that day to pick up a stray," said Robert, smiling warmly for the first time. "She found it hard to begin with —the local children made fun of her accent—but one did not come across many outsiders in those days. She fitted in with the family perfectly. Within six months, we couldn't imagine what life would have been without her. And at the end of the war, she decided to stay with us."

"Is she still living with your parents?"

Robert shook his head. "She took ill last year with the flu. She had always suffered with asthma, and it hit her hard. We lost her just before Christmas."

The news struck Gabriel like a punch to the chest. He was not sure he was being entirely logical, but it felt like an injustice that a girl should have survived the blitz only to die in peacetime. "I'm so sorry," he said. "I hope you won't think I'm interfering, but wouldn't it be better to go home for a few days? It's hard enough to bear one death, but two . . ."

"This is my home," said Robert, moving towards the door in such an obvious gesture of boredom that even Gabriel noticed it was a little rude. "I'll have to bear the grief wherever I am; there's no point in running away." He placed his hand on the doorknob but made no effort to open it. "At least I have the comfort of knowing Daphne didn't suffer and nobody hurt her. Sarah did suffer; it made it harder to bear."

That much was true, thought Gabriel, as he descended the stairs. The loss of a loved one was unbearable, but it had been the constant thought of what Giovanna and Nicoletta's final moments might have been like that had haunted Gabriel for years and still caused him to wake in a cold sweat. The thought of them trapped in the house with the flames licking the walls, the choking fumes, the fire . . . the fire creeping up on them . . .

Arthur was sitting in his room when Gabriel returned, still looking at the group photograph. He did not look up when Gabriel stepped inside, and jumped out of his skin when Gabriel greeted him. "Is there somewhere you could go?" asked Gabriel, seating himself opposite his friend. "Somewhere away from Cambridge, I mean. I was just saying the same to young Mr Sutton. You could always come back with me to the abbey . . ."

Arthur shook his head impatiently. "I'm not the sort of man to hide away from the world," he said, and Gabriel was not sure if the insult had been deliberate. "I can't leave now. There's always so much to do after a death; that's the horror of it. All one wants to do is to lock oneself away, but there are all the practicalities: sorting through Daphne's work, arranging memorial services and writing obituaries. There'll be an inquest. I'm not much of a shoulder to cry on, but poor old Robert Sutton will not be the only young man to go to pieces in the coming days."

"I'll stay in Cambridge as long as you wish," promised

Gabriel, getting up and moving towards an elegantly carved cabinet he had noticed in the corner. "You need a drink, Arthur."

When Arthur made no answer, Gabriel took a crystal decanter out of the cabinet and poured Arthur a large brandy. "Pour yourself a drink while you're at it," said Arthur, taking the glass a little too eagerly. "This has hardly been the most pleasant of holidays for you, has it? All those memories."

Gabriel poured himself a small shot of brandy. He had temporarily become a little too fond of it after Giovanna's death, and he took care even now to avoid overindulgence. "I cannot pretend that the sudden death of a young woman has not opened a wound," said Gabriel frankly, "but I'm grateful to be here with you at a time like this. I was grateful for friends when I needed them."

Arthur drained his glass in three gulps, which made Gabriel shudder; it was completely out of character for a man as painfully well mannered as Arthur to guzzle anything, especially alcohol. "I've suffered loss before," said Arthur, his voice hoarse from the brandy. "I felt angry and guilty last time as well, but the deaths never seemed ridiculous then. Friends killed on the front line. I suppose the deaths may have felt like a waste, but I never remember thinking them pointless. I can't get over how Daphne died. Part of me wants to give her a good shake for being silly enough to knock over that canister. Another part of me wants to punish myself for not taking better care of her. It wasn't just the long hours, Gabriel; she was worried."

Gabriel tried hard not to look too intrigued, but he found himself sitting up in his chair all the same. "Worried? Was it a man problem?"

Arthur gave a rueful smile and shook his head. "Daphne was not the sort of girl to worry about men, I can assure you. Most of the time, I'm not sure she even noticed we existed. It was her work that was worrying her."

Gabriel suppressed the urge to fidget that always came to him when he had an awkward question to ask. "Arthur, you mentioned before that she was on the verge of something, some breakthrough. What was it?"

Arthur looked away. "I'm afraid I can't tell you that; it was highly confidential. I was the only person who was allowed to know what she was doing. One can't keep secrets from a lab head. But it was groundbreaking work, and she had a conscience. We used to talk late into the evening about the atom bomb and Dr Mengele's experiments in the concentration camps. All those terrible revelations rather haunted her, I'm afraid. But it haunted all of us. All scientists have had to consider the moral boundaries we've crossed in the name of progress, but she was very young to have to consider all this."

"Arthur . . ." But Arthur had risen to his feet and was distracting himself by rinsing his glass in the sink. "Arthur, is there anyone you can think of who would have been threatened by Daphne's work? It seems somewhat coincidental that a young scientist, who was known to be brilliant, should die out of the blue like that. I know it's hard to consider, but—"

Arthur spun round with visible impatience. "My dear friend, I've no doubt you mean well with all this, but Daphne's death was clearly an accident. There has been so much violent death in the world, it's easy to see malice in every tragic death. But Daphne's work was so secret, I could count on one hand the number of people who knew what she was doing, and I was the only one in the department who knew. The only reason the sensitivity of Daphne's work was important is because I know it kept her awake at night. If she was not sleeping well and she was working long hours, she was a candidate for a nasty accident. And I could have prevented it."

It was too late for Gabriel to extract any further information from his friend. Arthur was slipping into the soporific state of grief—helped along, no doubt, by the brandy—and Gabriel quickly realised that he was surplus to requirements. After making Arthur promise to come and find him at the Gervasonis' house if he needed anything, Gabriel let himself out of the room and walked down the stairs into the darkening quad.

6

Gabriel would not be easy in his mind until he had put things right with Mrs Bellinger. He suspected it was just what his director of studies had once called "an unfortunate tendency to worry a thought to death", but he had never lost the habit. In any case, Gabriel thought, it was one thing to criticise a student for worrying a philosophical point to death, but he was not sure it was possible to worry too much about another human being's welfare.

Before leaving college to make the journey to the Bellinger house, Gabriel went up to his room to pack his knapsack. He knew something was wrong before he had reached the top of the stairs. He felt that sense of uneasiness that so often crept over him before he received some nasty surprise or other, but it was only when he had a clear view of the door to his room that his pulse began to race. The outer and inner doors were both open, warning him that someone had entered the room without his permission. He stepped cautiously a little closer and heard the muffled sounds of footsteps padding lightly over warped floorboards.

Gabriel froze, torn between the need to confront the intruder and the voice of common sense that told him not to face a burglar alone. He tried to judge the sex of the intruder, but whoever it was appeared to be treading with a deliberate lightness which confused Gabriel. Unable to contain himself any longer, Gabriel flung himself into the room, shouting, "Who goes there!"

At a later hour, Gabriel was prepared to admit that it had been a ridiculously melodramatic choice of words, but his entrance had the desired effect of causing the intruder to back into a corner. And scream at the top of her voice. Standing in the corner with her back against the wall, her hands clenched in defensive fists, stood Gabriel's mother-in-law. As soon as she realised that she was in no danger, Mama Gervasoni's panic transformed immediately to anger and then relief. Before Gabriel could splutter an apology, she had stomped forward, tapping Gabriel lightly across the ear with the flat of her hand. "You crazy boy! You crazy, crazy boy! You gave me a heart attack!"

Gabriel burst into embarrassed laughter and embraced her, overcome by relief. She had been a reassuring presence during those heady days of courtship and marriage, and he felt an old sense of security returning. "I'm so sorry, Mama," he said, lapsing into Italian for the first time in years. "I'm all on edge at the moment. I thought you were a burglar."

"My, my, you're in trouble," she said with a sigh, nudging Gabriel into a chair. "You have the devil at your heels. I'm just packing your things. You come home with me, away from this draughty, pokey little room."

Gabriel glanced at his bulging knapsack and suppressed a squirming feeling of mortification. It was not just that his mother-in-law had handled his underwear, which was enough to make any man blush—she must have seen and packed his purple keepsake bag. *There's nothing to be ashamed of*, he told himself. She might be touched to know how much Gabriel still thought of Giovanna, but it was like one's mother reading through old love letters—harmless and completely wrong.

"Mama, there's someone I have to see before I come to you," said Gabriel, rising from his chair. "I'm afraid I made rather an ass of myself earlier, and I need to apologise or I shall worry about it all night."

Mama Gervasoni smirked knowingly. Gabriel had many gifts, but tact was not one of them, and she spread her hands in acknowledgement. "Don't let me ask how," she said. "I will take your bag home, and you go and make peace with this person, whoever he is. It is still early. When you get home, we can have something to eat."

Gabriel picked up the knapsack, trying hard not to think of food. He had not eaten a thing all day. "I wouldn't dream of letting you carry my bag all the way to your house," he said. "I'll take it with me. I shan't be long. At least I hope I shan't."

"You look like a wayfarer," said Mama Gervasoni as they walked together through the college. "How does that song go? 'My knapsack on my back.'"

"I am a wayfarer now, Mama," said Gabriel. "It's my calling."

Mama Gervasoni regarded him sadly. It occurred to Gabriel that she must often look sad, but he had not noticed it earlier. "Well," she said in a considered tone, "you come and rest in my home while you can. We all need shelter from the storm."

Gabriel pondered glumly, as he crossed Parker's Piece again, that Arthur had no place to shelter from this storm. However many friends Arthur had gathered about him in the course of his work, Gabriel was one of the few he could

93

really talk to, and Arthur had not even chosen to confide in him. Where would Arthur shelter during the tempestuous days to come, when grief and anger and misery would engulf him? Who would cook him dinner and distract his troubled mind?

That Arthur was a man in torment was beyond question, but Gabriel was more troubled by the thought of how much Arthur was hiding. Did a man as intelligent as Arthur honestly believe that Daphne's death had been an accident? If her work was so secret and so morally ambiguous, was something on his own conscience that he desperately needed to share?

Gabriel found himself standing outside the Bellinger residence again and knocked on the door, taking several steps back in anticipation of an unfriendly response—wisely, as it turned out. The door opened with the same quiet grace as its owner, and Mrs Bellinger stood in the doorway with a look so glacial across her face that Gabriel shivered visibly. "I have written a letter of complaint to the police," she said sternly, standing in front of Gabriel like a sentry who has been commanded to guard the garrison with his life. "I intend to post it first thing in the morning. One should always allow time to calm oneself before taking action, do you not agree?"

Gabriel nodded appreciatively, trying to ignore the obvious threat. The letter had not been sent yet—it might not be sent if he behaved himself—but he had no idea how he was supposed to help the woman other than to make himself scarce. "Mrs Bellinger, I came to apologise for my words earlier today," said Gabriel, pleased that the speech he had rehearsed in his head came out so coherently. "It was very wrong of me to ask such questions. I thought I should tell you that there is no suggestion that Daphne's death was anything other than an accident. I'm afraid I couldn't help thinking—"

"You couldn't help thinking," Mrs Bellinger put in, "that Daphne must have been murdered because you take pleasure in playing the detective. I've heard of your exploits."

Gabriel flushed; the woman had the ability to make Gabriel feel like a six-year-old schoolboy who had inadvertently said a naughty word in front of the class. He should have written her a grovelling letter and had done with it. "It was the shock of her sudden death, that was all. I should have kept my thoughts to myself."

Mrs Bellinger looked piercingly at Gabriel. She did not speak and made it abundantly clear that she did not expect to be spoken to, and Gabriel knew that a thousand thoughts were settling themselves in her mind. Mrs Bellinger had the intense look of a woman who thought deeply about everything, who noticed everything but seldom gave anything away. "You should perhaps have kept your thoughts to yourself," she said after what felt like an interminable time. "And if you had, I should not have thrown you out of my house. But then I should not have had time to think over what happened to poor Daphne in recent weeks."

To Gabriel's surprise, Mrs Bellinger motioned for him to come in, and he stepped across the threshold of her home in a state of confusion, unsure whether the more polite action would have been to demur. "I really oughtn't to trouble you again, Mrs Bellinger," he began, but he was silenced by Mrs Bellinger's smirk.

"Yes, yes, yes," she said dismissively, helping him off with

95

his coat, "I have never had a great deal of time for social niceties. If I invite a person into my house, I expect him to enter. In your case, I have invited you into my house because I have something I wish to say to you. Now, be a good boy and take a seat in the drawing room while I make some tea."

More tea, more fireside chat, and this time Gabriel could not relax in the slightest. He was terrified of putting a foot out of place but also felt a shred of hope that he might have an ally in Mrs Bellinger after all. He might not be the only crackpot in Cambridge to think that Daphne's death was not an accident.

The word "crackpot" clattered awkwardly around Gabriel's head when Mrs Bellinger followed him into the sitting room, carrying a large, cumbersome box which she set on the floor before him. "You may wish to make yourself familiar with these items while I make the tea," she said, turning her back abruptly and leaving Gabriel in the company of the box.

Gabriel got on his hands and knees to inspect the box. The sudden change of position made his head swim momentarily, but he forced himself to examine the exhibit he had been given. The tantalising question of whether Gabriel's hostess would provide biscuits hovered for a moment at the forefront of Gabriel's mind, before his eye noted that the box was well looked after. There were no traces of dust or cobwebs on it, but Gabriel wondered, as he pulled out a stack of papers, why Mrs Bellinger did not store her things in a more suitable vessel—a filing cabinet, perhaps, or the drawers of her desk. He soon began to see why the materials were concealed as they were. This was the sort of box that probably lived under a bed or was buried at the bottom of a wardrobe, somewhere where the contents could be kept carefully hidden from respectable eyes, like a stash of dirty magazines or a box of contraband sugar.

The first bundle Gabriel removed contained multiple copies of the same leaflet, neatly tied up with string: *Atom War*. He knew that it was a detailed denunciation of the atomic bomb before he had taken the trouble to remove one of the leaflets to read. Some anonymous pacifist had been kind enough to post a copy of the very same leaflet to the presbytery just a few weeks before.

Below the layer of leaflets, there was a handmade banner, the letters inexpertly painted: "War Is a Crime against Humanity." Like an archaeologist, Gabriel had the sense —as he reached the next layer in the box—that he had finally reached the most revealing artefacts. He unrolled posters dating back from the war years and the decade before, containing such unpopular messages as "War Must Be Renounced as Well as Denounced" and "War Is Futile." One poster filled Gabriel with an overwhelming sense of sadness: "Who Wants War? Nobody! Then Help to Abolish It by Joining the Peace Pledge Union! We Say NO to War." It dated back to those last desperate days of appeasement, when Neville Chamberlain had waved his infamous paper from the steps of the plane and declared, "Peace for our time."

Gabriel sat back on his heels and let out a long sigh. He had never accepted the legitimacy of outright pacifism, even though one of his uncles had been imprisoned as a conscientious objector during the first war, but he had lost what vestiges of respect he still had for pacifism when Mahatma

97

Gandhi had instructed the British people to surrender to the Nazis, to give up their homes, their lives, the safety of their women and children . . . and not just the British. He had also told the Jews to offer only nonviolent resistance to the Nazis as they were being persecuted and disenfranchised and ultimately murdered in their millions. Gabriel could almost hear Abbot Ambrose's sardonic tones on the subject. "I see Mr Gandhi is in favour of the use of force against the British for the sake of home rule in India. Pacifism is all very splendid, as long as someone else's country practises it."

Beneath the posters, there were copies of the Peace Pledge Union's newspaper *Peace News*, which Gabriel did not bother to open. He looked back at the poster that demanded to know "Who wants war?" *No one does!* thought Gabriel. *Except perhaps a small number of war profiteers, and they did not bring Hitler to power! Who on earth in his right mind ever wants there to be a war for any reason?* He knew, of course, that this was not entirely true—or at least had not been true in the past. Gabriel was old enough to remember the cheering crowds after the declaration of war back in 1914, all those desperately excited young men champing at the bit to go to war and give Kaiser Wilhelm a bloody good thrashing. But he did not recall anyone thinking that way when the last war had been declared, Chamberlain's famous speech being greeted by silence and not a few tears. "We are at war with Germany." Mercifully, the world had moved on, but this group was fighting yesterday's battles with alacrity.

"I trust you are suitably appalled," declared Mrs Bellinger. Gabriel looked up to see his hostess advancing towards him with a tea tray, so imperiously that she might have been Boudicca striding out to meet the Roman army. He could well imagine her leading a protest march or standing on her soapbox at Hyde Park Corner, demanding that the nations of the world lay down their arms. "Yes, I suspected you would be. Hence my unwillingness to let you into my little secret. Not that it is much of a secret, you understand."

"Pacifism is not a crime," said Gabriel. The image of his uncle in prison uniform flickered before him like Banquo's Ghost. "Not at present, anyway."

"There were rather more of us during the Great War," said Mrs Bellinger, placing ironic emphasis on the word "great". "There were more still during the twenties and thirties. But then war came again in spite of our efforts, and many gave up. They bought the lie that might is right."

"Like your children, Mrs Bellinger?" asked Gabriel, hoping he did not sound cruel for mentioning the two proudly uniformed young people whose photographs adorned this very room. "Did they buy a lie when they chose to serve their country?"

Mrs Bellinger rolled her eyes impatiently, busying herself with the act of pouring the tea before answering. "Unlike you people, I believe in freedom of conscience."

"As a matter of fact, we believe—"

"They sincerely believed that Hitler could be stopped only through violence, and they took their places as cogs in the great war machine. I brought them up as pacifists, but I also bought them up to follow their own conscience. I could not be a hypocrite and cut them off for doing just that." Mrs Bellinger handed Gabriel a cup of tea like an olive branch, and Gabriel rose to his feet to take it from her before seating himself in an armchair. He felt a little glow of delight at the sight of two biscuits carefully balanced on the

99

saucer. "They are my children, after all. One can disagree profoundly with a child's actions and love him with all one's heart."

"That is certainly true," Gabriel agreed, glancing down at the papers he had laid out in piles near the box. "Did you get Daphne caught up in all this?"

"My good man, you make it sound as though I lured her into the coven of the Peace Pledge Union! I merely discussed the subject with her. You can surely not disapprove of that?" Gabriel shook his head. "She was a brilliant young woman —but you know that, of course. With Eric sedated in his bed by eight every evening, I rather enjoyed my conversations with Daphne. We often talked late into the night about all sorts of things—philosophy, politics, religion. Naturally, with my interest in pacifism, we often discussed the subject of war and the armed forces."

"And she was in agreement with you?"

Mrs Bellinger took a sip of her tea. "Not entirely—not to begin with, anyway. She was one of those rather wishy-washy young people who thought the war was a frightful thing and all that, but she took the lazy line that war is sometimes inevitable. She was dead against the atom bomb, of course. It angered her that science is so often used in pursuit of destruction rather than the preservation of life. That was how she came to take the first step towards my position. Before I knew it, she was addressing a public meeting at the Quaker chapel."

"I'd imagine she spoke very well," said Gabriel.

"She was marvellous, such an inspiration when the group was so demoralised. She spoke eloquently, without notes, for half an hour, and one could have heard a pin drop. There was no coughing or fidgeting; everyone in the room hung on her every word." Mrs Bellinger sank into silence, and Gabriel knew she must be thinking what a loss Daphne's death had been, for her cause if not for science.

"You must have been very proud of her," said Gabriel, but Mrs Bellinger needed very little prompting to continue.

"Oh, I was! Daphne carried so much more conviction because she was a scientist and a member of the new generation. She gave us hope somehow that, if the brightest and the best could turn against war, there truly might be a way to bring about peace on earth." Mrs Bellinger put down her cup with a jarring clang that made Gabriel jump. Her tone was suddenly brisk. "But then, of course, that wretched professor heard about the meeting and stopped her from involving herself any further with our cause. Claimed it would ruin her career, cause her to make a fool of herself for associating with cranks and fascists, as he called us. Daphne cried her eyes out when she told me about it. I think she was rather frightened of him."

Gabriel resisted the urge to protest. The professor he knew was not remotely intimidating; a more mild-mannered, affable fellow could surely not be found on the streets of Cambridge. But, almost as quickly, the thought came to Gabriel that he had only ever known Arthur as an equal. They were two men working in different fields, members of the same generation, even if Arthur had been older than Gabriel. The relationship must have been quite different to Arthur's relationship with Daphne, a young woman, a pupil, a subordinate, even if Arthur had not seen it that way. And

Gabriel had never seen Arthur at work. Perhaps in his lab there had been another side to him that Gabriel had never seen and would never see.

"Hard as it may sound to hear, Mrs Bellinger, he may have had a point," Gabriel ventured, aware that he was sailing very close to the wind. "However unfair it was, your organisation was perceived as pro-fascist before the war, and it may not have been good for Daphne to be associated with——"

"It was completely unfair! We weren't traitors; we were patriots! If you had seen what the last war had been like, you would understand that. We loved our country so much that we did not want to see another generation dragged through such destruction."

"I was not entirely oblivious to that war myself," Gabriel began, but he stopped before Mrs Bellinger could talk over him. She was not remotely interested in his experience.

"You were a mere boy," she said dismissively, flapping an impatient hand in his face. "I drove ambulances. I saw with my own eyes what wars do to people, what wars do to the young. If you'd only seen them."

"I did."

But Mrs Bellinger was in full flow, addressing him as though she were addressing a union meeting. "Young men with their limbs blown off, their faces smashed in. Boys who should still have been playing cricket at school writhing in agony, crying for their mothers. Men who'd been gassed. You cannot imagine the horror of a young man slowly choking and burning from the inside out. Even Wilfred Owen did not do that abomination justice! The fascists did not want a war because they wanted to unite with Hitler. We did not want war because we detest violence."

"Mrs Bellinger, how would you have stopped Hitler? It's surely not an unreasonable question. It's all very well to detest violence, but what would you have done to beat back the panzer divisions, the Luftwaffe? If the Nazis had been triumphant, think of the millions who would have died."

"Millions did die. Do you suppose that the inhabitants of Hiroshima cared less about dying than we did? Do you suppose they were desperately pleased to be blasted off the face of the earth in the name of liberty?"

"That's not what I'm saying," said Gabriel, relieved that they were actually having a conversation now, rather than Gabriel finding himself the unwilling audience to a strange woman's rantings. "I suppose I'm wondering how important liberty is to you, whether you believe it worth fighting for."

"I daresay you have already guessed the answer," Mrs Bellinger retorted, but there was an acidic edge to her voice now. "I value liberty, but not enough to see other people die for it. And during this last war, that is precisely what happened. I was never going to be in the firing line. I had no right to expect young people to fight a war I was not prepared to fight myself."

Gabriel was about to respond when the conversation was brought to an abrupt end by an almighty thundering noise directly above their heads. Gabriel instinctively leapt to his feet, but Mrs Bellinger put out a hand to reassure him. "What was that?"

"Don't trouble yourself; it's my husband."

Mrs Bellinger rose as though intending to go upstairs, but she was too late. There was the uneven patter of a man hurrying unsteadily down a flight of steps, and an elderly man appeared in the doorway, gasping for breath. He was virtually bald apart from a smattering of white, straggly hair, and he was dressed in faded pyjamas, barefoot and carrying a walking stick which Gabriel suspected the old man saw as a weapon rather than an aid to mobility. A more unlikely husband to the elegant, beautifully groomed Adela Bellinger was difficult to imagine. "Where is she?" bellowed the man, far louder than Gabriel would have thought possible from such a frail-looking individual. "Where's my girl? Where's Daphne?"

Mrs Bellinger walked slowly towards him, as though any sudden move might alarm him. "Eric dear, come back to bed," she said in the coaxing tone of an Edwardian nurse-maid. "Let's go back upstairs to bed."

Eric took a swing at his wife with his walking stick, missing her by a fraction of an inch. Gabriel instinctively dashed forward to protect her, but Eric caught sight of him and recoiled, letting out an unearthly cry. "You took her, didn't you?" he raged at Gabriel, resisting volubly as his wife stepped behind and took him by both arms, nudging him backwards out of the room. "You took Daphne, didn't you, you monster?"

Gabriel was astonished at how easily Mrs Bellinger was able to encourage Eric out of the room and up the stairs, when just moments before, Gabriel had seriously feared for her safety. Eric staggered up the stairs, clinging to the banisters as he went, shouting at the top of his voice, "Give her back! Give her back! I can look after her. Why must everyone interfere!"

There was a lengthy interval whilst Gabriel stood in the middle of the sitting room, uncertain as to what he should do. Above his head there was the stamp and creak of bodies moving about the room as Mrs Bellinger encouraged Eric back to bed. So many couples had been denied the chance to grow old together, but Gabriel was struck by the tragic reality of this marriage and what it had become. They must have been a handsome couple once, cut quite a dash in London society. They had, unusually, been equally successful in their chosen professions, raised children who had wanted for nothing—only for the frailty of old age to descend on a fine man without warning and turn him against the woman he most loved in the world.

Mrs Bellinger returned to the sitting room, looking deceptively unruffled, but Gabriel noticed that she struggled to make eye contact with him as she sat herself down. Her cheeks were flaming red with the humiliation. "It's all right, Eric is settled now," she said quietly. "I'm afraid I have locked the door. It seems awfully cruel, but sometimes it is a little safer for me that way."

"Mrs Bellinger, oughtn't your husband to be in a home," asked Gabriel, "for your own safety? He's a good deal bigger than you."

"It is his lifelong wish to die in his own bed, and I will honour that," said Mrs Bellinger, with renewed strength. "I swore to love my husband in sickness and in health, and I will not abandon him to a glorified asylum because he has become troublesome. It was easier when we had Daphne with us. I often wondered why she had not chosen to read medicine rather than the natural sciences. She would have made a superb doctor, so brilliant, so gentle."

"Why did your husband think I had done something to Daphne?"

Mrs Bellinger blushed a little deeper. "Put those words out of your mind, please, Father; he didn't know what he was saying."

"Did anyone ever visit Daphne at this house?" Gabriel pressed. "Perhaps someone with whom she quarrelled?"

"Father, please believe me, he accused you because he had no idea what he was saying. He probably thought you were Frankenstein's Monster or something as ridiculous as that."

Gabriel helped Mrs Bellinger pack up the box, unwilling to leave her with a floor covered in curled posters and bundles of leaflets. It gave him just enough time to ask the question he had been about to ask earlier. "Mrs Bellinger, you said that you had had time to think after I left," he began, aware that he was taking his life into his hands. "Is it your belief that Daphne's death was not an accident?"

"Naturally," said Mrs Bellinger, looking him steadily in the eye.

"Then do you believe that her death was connected with her work for your organization?"

"Why would I have brought up all this if I had not thought so?"

Gabriel screwed his nerve to the sticking point. "If you think she was murdered, who do you think did it?"

"Dr Kingsley, of course," she answered immediately. "No need to look so shocked. He's clever enough to kill a woman and make it look like an accident."

"But why? He adored her. Why would he do such a thing?"

"Most men who kill believe themselves in love with the victim. And most women who are killed know the killer.

Surely you must know that by now?" Mrs Bellinger's face was thunderous; Gabriel commanded himself not to show any further emotion, even if she was accusing one of his oldest friends of cold-blooded murder. "He wanted to control her every move; he saw her as his own personal property, like so many teachers do. But she had a mind of her own. Sooner or later, he was always going to make her pay for that."

Gabriel took his leave as soon as he could, unable to bear the thought of spending another minute in Mrs Bellinger's presence. She was lying about Eric's outburst, she was obviously lying to him, and even a consummate actress like Adela Bellinger could not hide it. Gabriel hurried through the dark streets, aware that the minutes were ticking away and Mama Gervasoni was waiting for him with dinner. For the first time in so long, Gabriel felt the thrill of having a family of his own to which he could return, and he was overwhelmed with gratitude for it.

"Are you forgiven, my son?" asked Mama Gervasoni as soon as she opened the door and saw Gabriel standing there. "It must have taken some time."

"I'm sorry, Mama," said Gabriel, stepping inside and removing his hat. He had stridden through the streets of Cambridge as fast as he could, meaning that he was perspiring in his coat in spite of the cold weather and felt quite out of breath. "'Fraid there was a bit of a scene, and I didn't want to leave the lady until all was well."

Mama Gervasoni helped Gabriel off with his coat and led him into the dining room, where a man was laying the table. He was stooped forward, setting out knives and forks, giving

Gabriel a perfect view of his familiar shiny bald head. At the sound of two sets of footsteps, Papa Gervasoni looked up, his rugged swarthy face breaking into a warm grin. "Well, if it isn't the Archangel *Gabriele*!" He stepped round the table and embraced Gabriel in a bear hug that fairly squeezed the breath out of his body. "My boy, I thought you would never return!"

Before he could start issuing more apologies, Gabriel found himself seated at a table heaving with home-baked crusty bread, a vast tureen full of steaming vegetables, and a leg of lamb that smelt gloriously of wine and rosemary. Gabriel dreaded to think of the number of coupons they had used up to get hold of the lamb, and he suspected they would not eat meat again for weeks. Sensing Gabriel's discomfort, Papa Gervasoni carved Gabriel a thick slice of meat and dropped it onto his plate. "Don't worry, son, we have saved the fattened calf for you. We have precious little reason to celebrate these days."

"Gosh," was the best Gabriel could manage, but he was heady with the aromas of food after a day of hunger, and he offered no resistance as his mother-in-law heaped his plate with beautifully seasoned vegetables, lightly roasted, just as he liked them. "This is marvellous! But I hate to think of the two of you eating bread and dripping for the next month."

Papa Gervasoni chuckled. "No, no, no, son. Our ration books were not hurt by this joint, I assure you." Gabriel's alarm only made him laugh more heartily. "No need to look so mortified, my little angel. A farmer owed me a favour, that's all. I did some work for him; he paid me with the leg of lamb. After your little visit this morning, my lovely wife hurried over to the post office to send a telegram and to tell me to call in the favour immediately."

"It really is most kind of you both to welcome me back to your home like this," said Gabriel; he felt the words choking in his throat. "I really am most . . . most obliged to you both. I thought perhaps it might be hard . . ."

But he could not go on. Papa Gervasoni filled Gabriel's glass with wine and touched his wrist affectionately. "No need to be brave, son. There's no need for the stiff upper lip here."

Gabriel's hand went his face, but to his horror he realised he was already weeping. He heard the sudden scrape of chairs and felt Mama's arms around his shoulders, pulling him to her. It had been such a very long time since he had been so close to anyone that his head swam with emotion. But then, it had been a long time since he had cried, and all his defences were crumbling. He knew only that he was loved, that he was welcome, that he was forgiven.

"We're only glad to have you home," said Mama when Gabriel was calm enough to say grace so that the three of them could eat. "When we lost our daughter and granddaughter, it felt almost as though we'd lost you too. Giovanna would never have wanted you to be so alone."

"You must stay as long as your friend needs you," said Papa. "You know better than most how he must be feeling after such an accident. If you want to bring him here, we'd be happy to—"

"It wasn't an accident. She was murdered," said Gabriel quickly, before he could regain the urge to suppress his suspicions. "That young woman was murdered, and her death has been made to look like an accident. I'm sure of it now."

The Gervasonis looked nervously at one another before turning back to Gabriel for some kind of explanation. Gabriel had taken a large bite of bread to stop himself from having to speak any further. "Why do you say that?" asked Papa. "I heard it was an accident, and everyone thought it was an accident. Even the police—they think it was an accident. Didn't she knock over some chemicals or something?"

"Back in Italy, did you ever come across an accident that was a little too convenient?" asked Gabriel. "You know, where you felt sure that someone was being silenced?"

Papa nodded reluctantly. "I know what you're saying, and yes, I once knew a policeman who suffered a nasty fall off his balcony. Smashed his head on the pavement below. And everyone knew that he had been pushed. Except for the law, apparently."

"But this woman was just a young girl, surely," Mama put in. "What reason would anyone have to kill her?"

Gabriel threw up his hands in surrender. "There you have me, I'm afraid. Everywhere I turn, I am told that Daphne Silverton was loved by everyone, that she hadn't an enemy in the world. Everything points to her death having been an accident, except that it *doesn't*. Everything about that scene felt fraudulent to me. Take the place where she was supposed to have died. Nothing was in disarray at all, except for one chair that had been overturned, and even that chair seemed to me a little too far from the body for Daphne to have knocked it over herself. Surely, if she had been flailing, trying to escape death by suffocation, she would have pulled the contents of the bench down with her?"

Gabriel did not notice the absolute silence at the table. His in-laws were no longer even eating; they were looking at him fixedly, having been listening carefully to his every word. But it was his turn to fall silent, because a troubling thought that had irritated him since he had first stepped into that lab was finally making sense. "No, I'm wrong," he said slowly. "She wouldn't have flailed, pulling everything on top of her—she would have bolted straight for the door. It's the door that is wrong. The bench where Daphne died was the closest to the door. The second she realised the danger she was in, she would have made a dash for it and got herself to safety almost immediately."

"Might she have locked herself in?" suggested Papa. "Perhaps if her work was very private, she did not wish to be disturbed. She may not have had time to unlock the door."

"But her body was nowhere near the door. If she'd made it as far as the door, then realised that she'd locked it, she might have collapsed up against it, in the act of trying to turn the key." Gabriel got up from the table. "I'm sorry, Mama, but I must go to Arthur. I have to speak to him."

Mama intercepted Gabriel at the door and shooed him back to his seat. "Not tonight, you crazy boy," she chided, placing a hand on his shoulder, as though she expected him to make a break for it. "It's late. The poor man may already have retired for the night. You mustn't trouble him with this now; there's nothing he can do about it."

"But he'll be able to tell me. He'll know if I'm right."

"*Certamente*, but it would be better to think a little bit before you go rushing to your friend with your theory. If that poor girl really was murdered, you will need better evidence than a hunch about a door."

Reluctantly, Gabriel agreed. Mama was right. It was late, and Arthur might already be in his bed, having chased away his troubles with a stiff drink and a couple of sleeping pills. Even if he were awake, it would only infuriate him to be pestered by Gabriel when he was just staggering to the end of what was quite possibly the worst day of his life. Gabriel returned to his meal, but he ate unconsciously, preoccupied with the task of piecing together Daphne's last minutes.

"Might I have a piece of paper and a pencil?" asked Gabriel when Mama reached over to collect his empty plate. "I should like to write down a few things."

Mama mumbled something to her husband in Italian which Gabriel did not quite catch. By the time she had retreated into the kitchen with the dirty plates, Gabriel's father-in-law had taken him by the arm and led him into their modest sitting room, where coffee and cigarettes quickly arrived, along with a bottle of Papa's homemade grappa. It was a lurid green colour, like the remnants of a nuclear experiment.

Gabriel sat down on the lumpy sofa, waiting whilst Papa left the room and returned with a notepad and pencil, which looked rather like the sort of object a housewife might keep on her kitchen windowsill to write down the shopping list. "*Allora*," said Papa, pouring the coffee and a thimbleful of the grappa. "Are you writing a note to yourself to ask your friend about the door?"

"The door, yes, the use of the chair as a clumsy prop. The problem of the nail varnish."

"Nail varnish?"

"This may seem a rather absurd detail under the circumstances, but when I viewed the girl's body in the mortuary, I couldn't help noticing that she wore nail varnish." Gabriel put a hand absentmindedly on the coffee cup, registered that it was too hot and drew back. "I thought it an odd thing for a scientist to wear. I mean, scientists use their hands all the time and must be constantly washing their hands. It didn't seem very practical."

"Ladies like to look nice," said Papa with a shrug, pouring himself a considerably larger glass of grappa than he had risked giving Gabriel. He took a noisy gulp. "There's nothing surprising about that, surely?"

"The varnish was very chipped about the ends," Gabriel explained. "That's hardly surprising in itself, but the young lady appears to have been quite fastidious about her appearance. I noticed it at dinner, how well groomed she was. Not the dishevelled, unkempt academic one might expect. She didn't have a hair out of place. I couldn't help thinking that if she had chipped her nail varnish, she would have repainted her nails as soon as she could, or removed the varnish, which means that the damage must have been done quite soon before she died."

"If she were scratching about, trying to escape the room, I'm sure she would have chipped her nail varnish. People have been known to break their own fingers trying to get out of a locked room."

"Exactly!" said Gabriel triumphantly. He took a sip of the grappa—it really was only a sip—and felt a small volcanic eruption taking place on his tongue. He swallowed with a supreme effort and felt the inside of his mouth and throat being immediately anaesthetised. It was some time before he could speak again, causing Papa to burst into gales of laughter.

"*Che vergogna!*" chuckled Papa, handing Gabriel his coffee. "You know, I think it will be cool enough to drink now if you sip it gently. Not that I think you're in a position to do anything else."

The coffee was still quite hot, but it had the effect of loosening up Gabriel's vocal cords again, and he looked gratefully at Papa through his watering eyes. "Thank you," he said ruefully, keen to move the conversation away from his ineptitude with potent alcohol. "Of course, you're right about the chipping nail varnish, but that's surely the point, isn't it? Everything about the death scene feels wrong, and the sight of Daphne's chipped fingernails only confirmed that to me. Nothing about the position of the body made sense, and it wasn't just what I could see in that room that felt wrong. It was what I couldn't see. Either she was so completely taken by surprise that she had no time to struggle or escape . . . or she did not die in that room."

"And if someone did move her body, you know it was definitely murder," said Papa gravely.

"Or someone else blamed himself for her accident and tried to cover it up by moving her," suggested Mama, stepping briskly into the room. "It might still have been an accident. Perhaps she was working in a different lab when the accident happened, and whoever she was with moved her body so that nobody would suspect him."

"I think they always work in the same lab," said Gabriel, but he faltered. Now that he thought about it, he had no idea how scientists conducted their day-to-day experiments. He had assumed that if a person was a member of a lab, he would work only there, in the one place with the same colleagues. But he had no way of knowing if this was correct.

"Arthur said that Daphne was working on something very secret," said Gabriel, letting the notepad and pencil fall idly into his lap. "If it was secret, perhaps she had to work elsewhere sometimes, simply to be out of view. If that were the case, whoever else worked in that lab would have a reason —a very good reason—to move her body, or it might raise questions as to what she was doing." Gabriel's head was starting to spin. He was sure it had nothing to do with one mouthful of Papa's homemade grappa, even though he suspected it contained more alcohol than the ethanol in Arthur's lab. "I have to speak to Arthur. It all comes back to Arthur."

"I wonder whether you should be a little careful about involving your friend," said Mama, pouring herself a coffee. Sensibly, she ignored the alcoholic chaser. "How can you be sure that he is innocent? If you really think the girl was murdered and you have no idea who did it, could it not have been this man? This Arthur?"

Gabriel was horrified and shook his head frantically. "Oh no, no, I don't think that at all possible," he said, but even he realised that he sounded a little too hasty. "He really did seem absolutely devastated this morning, and it takes a lot to ruffle a man like Arthur Kingsley. Even he couldn't hide his emotions. He had everything to lose by Daphne's death; he believed she was destined for greatness. With Daphne being a member of his lab, I'm sure Arthur would have received a great deal of the credit for anything she achieved. I cannot see that he had any reasonable motive."

"Not all motives are reasonable," said Mama, spooning a trickle of honey into her coffee. The shortage of sugar must be quite a penance for a sweet-toothed woman like her.

"She was like a daughter to him," Gabriel put in. "He has no relatives of his own. He seems to have cared for the young people in his lab as though they were his family. It can happen like that."

"Yes, and most murders happen in families," added Mama, but she sensed Gabriel's distress at the direction the conversation had taken and gave him a reassuring smile. "My dear, why don't you try to forget about this for now, or you will never sleep tonight? It's the first time the three of us have been together for such a very long time. Let us talk of happier things."

7

Mama had insisted upon Gabriel retiring early for the night, though the Gervasoni definition of early was markedly different to Gabriel's, and it was nearly eleven before Gabriel found himself safely ensconced in his room. The Gervasonis had not been insensitive in billeting Gabriel in this particular bedroom—as he recalled, the house had three bedrooms, one a loft room converted many years before to give the tiny house some much-needed extra space. It was just so strange to find himself bedding down for the night in his late wife's childhood domain.

The room had barely changed since Giovanna had last occupied it: the curtains were of a soft rose material, just the sort of dusky pink Giovanna had loved; the walls were covered in floral print wallpaper, showing bunches of rosebuds and primroses against a cream background. On the bookshelf, there was a collection of novels to suit the tastes of a girl in late adolescence, as well as some childhood favourites —*The Wind in the Willows*, *Alice in Wonderland*, a collection of stories by Angela Brazil. There were the well-thumbed-through anthologies of poetry Giovanna must have studied at school and a beautifully bound *Little Ones Missal* which had no doubt been a First Communion gift.

Little of what hung on the walls would have given much indication of the character of the girl who had slept here, as the pictures and icons could have belonged in any Catholic home: a statue of the Sacred Heart on the windowsill, an icon of the Blessed Mother positioned so that it would be the first thing the occupant of the bed would see when she opened her eyes in the morning. Near the window, there was a print of a dramatic mountain scene, a detail of the lush, mountainous region of northern Italy where the Gervasoni family had once lived.

Gabriel had prepared for bed mechanically, hurrying across the small landing to the bathroom to clean his teeth before returning to the bedroom to change and say his prayers. The three of them had snuggled up in this room when they had come to visit the house, Gabriel and Giovanna and Nicoletta, his infant daughter tiny enough to sleep in a makeshift cradle in the corner. Gabriel never usually felt lonely when he got into bed at night, but on that evening he felt the absence of a warm human presence and lay awake, half expecting to hear the gentle, almost comical snores of his baby girl.

Arthur had arranged a small gathering of Daphne's friends for a private memorial in the college chapel at eleven o'clock next morning. It felt absurdly soon to start commemorating Daphne when she had not yet been buried, but Gabriel suspected that Arthur was rushing to bring Daphne's friends together to get the ordeal over with. Gabriel had not been invited, but he endeavoured to sneak into the narthex, or whatever Protestants called it, to see what he could learn.

Gabriel was back to the problem of Arthur again. He was already wondering whether he had been too aggressive in his defence of his old friend when Mama had asked an entirely reasonable question. It was beyond the breadth of Gabriel's imagination to think of Arthur Kingsley committing a pre-meditated murder. Contrary to the received wisdom, the murders Gabriel had encountered in his unexpected career as an amateur detective had always been about hate, not love. But how did he really know that Arthur was incapable of such a crime? What did he really know about his friend after all these years? They had been friends in another world, when they were young and unburdened by life—or so it had seemed at the time—when the world was still convincing itself that Europe's fragile peace would hold. What did he know about the sort of man Arthur had become in the intervening years? For that matter, what did Arthur really know about Gabriel? Gabriel's life as a Benedictine must surely be as bewildering to Arthur as Arthur's distinguished scientific career was to Gabriel.

At some point in the early hours of the morning, the small quantity of grappa Gabriel had been coaxed into drinking hit him like a sledgehammer, and he fell into a deep, dreamless sleep. He was so soundly asleep that he did not notice the slivers of sunlight shimmering through the gap in the curtains, nor the sounds of the other two occupants of the house getting up and tramping round the kitchen, nor the smell of coffee wafting up the stairs.

Gabriel did not even hear the door open or Mama's tuneless singing as she stepped into the room, bearing a breakfast tray. Gabriel was suddenly aware of being gently but determinedly shaken awake. In his bleary confusion, he felt as though he were drifting on a life raft in the middle of the ocean, with a crushing weight bearing down on one side, threatening to capsize him. He clung to his bedclothes in desperation.

"Wakey, wakey!" called a singsong voice Gabriel immediately recognised. "Wakey wakey, sleepy head!" It was his mother-in-law, and Gabriel was lying in bed in Casa Gervasoni. He had a nasty feeling he had overslept.

"What time is it?" he mumbled, rubbing the sleep from his eyes. "Have I missed the memorial?"

"It's all right, son, you've still time," promised Mama, helping Gabriel sit up, then taking the trouble to plump up a large pillow behind his back. Gabriel blushed. He hated the thought that he was being pampered, even though he was rather enjoying the experience of being looked after so affectionately. Mama handed him a cup of strong coffee with a knowing smile and a large, sticky-looking pastry. "You looked so exhausted and sad last night, we both thought you needed a good sleep."

"Thank you," said Gabriel gratefully. He sensed Mama wanting to see him eat, and he took a bite of the pastry, which had a fruity, syrupy taste that was quite overpowering first thing in the morning. Not that it was first thing in the morning, thought Gabriel guiltily, stifling the urge to cough as the syrupy sweetness hit the back of his throat. He took another sip of his coffee, which tasted as bitter as gall after the pastry. "It's awfully kind of you."

Gabriel's own mother had died years ago from a sudden stroke as she had pottered about the garden. The stroke had rendered her unconscious, and she had slipped away in a state of happy oblivion just four days later, long enough for the family to assemble at her bedside and ensure that she was comforted by the rites of Holy Church. It had been a good death, all told, but she had been only sixty at the time, and it had meant that she had missed many of the events of Gabriel's adult life. It felt strange to be mothered again, and Mama noted his bewilderment. "It's all right, Gabriel. A priest deserves the love of a mother. You will always be my son."

Gabriel's eyes began to water. He stared ahead of him, knowing that blinking would release tears, and he could not bear the thought of blubbing all over his mother-in-law a second time. To his relief, she stood up and made for the door. "I had better leave you to get ready," she said brightly. "You don't want to be late."

Gabriel nodded, waiting until he was alone before wiping away his tears with an impatient hand. He had no reason to be so maudlin about everything. He was sitting up in a more-than-comfortable bed, eating a delicious if unusual breakfast in a home where all were good to him. He refused to think of what the day might hold as he finished his coffee and got out of bed. He was sure Mama must have put something restorative in the coffee—his headache had completely disappeared, and he felt perfectly calm as he washed and dressed. There was even hot water—oh joy of joys—and he bade good-bye to the Gervasonis on his way out of the house with a sense that he was ready for anything.

Gabriel crossed over the road so that he could walk a little closer to the river and admire the houseboats. In a flat, colourless landscape, the houseboats in which intrepid little families lived created welcome splashes of red and green and blue along the bank. They were always prettily painted with gingham curtains in the windows and usually flags flying from the flat roofs. Gabriel was just admiring a vessel named *The Winnie and Clem* when he noticed a small dark figure on the other side of the river. He was hurrying across the common, waving extravagantly in Gabriel's direction.

The man—he could just make out that the figure was wearing a flat cap and a black suit—gestured for Gabriel that he should wait for him before dashing out of sight. Gabriel realised that the stranger was going to attempt to intercept him by crossing the footbridge, but even if he hurried, it would take him at least five minutes to double back on himself, cross the bridge and weave through the side streets onto Chesterton Road.

Gabriel waited, loitering awkwardly by the black metal railings until a breathless figure came dashing down the road, holding his hat. As the young man drew closer and staggered to a halt, Gabriel recognised him as the poor unfortunate he had overheard arguing with Daphne the night she had died —the man Daphne had refused to marry and had treated to not one but two slaps in the face. Gabriel had not managed to get a close look at Daphne's suitor on the night in question, but on closer inspection, Gabriel could see that the man was no Adonis. Though not at all handsome, he had a striking-enough face, incredibly thin, with every tiny undulation of bone sharply visible. Gabriel could just make out curls of red hair protruding from beneath his hat.

"Will Valentine," said the man, holding out a hand eagerly. "You were the clerical chappie who was snooping when I was in the garden with Daphne."

Gabriel blushed deeply, thrown by Mr Valentine's directness. It had not occurred to Gabriel that he had been spotted, and he was not going to lie and deny that he had ever been there. "I'm frightfully sorry, I was just stretching my legs before dinner—"

"Don't give it another thought! I caught sight of you only as you were walking away," said Will, and he seemed at pains not to cause Gabriel any further embarrassment. "Shall we walk? We don't want to be late—we're going the same way, I presume?"

They continued down the long, wide Chesterton Road together. "I'm so sorry for your loss," said Gabriel automatically. "Am I to understand that you and Daphne were walking out together?"

"Well, as you probably gathered from our conversation —assuming you heard the entirety of it—I regarded the relationship as a little more permanent than Daphne did. God rest her soul."

"You are a Catholic?" asked Gabriel, at the sound of those telltale four words.

"Not quite. I had an Irish nanny." He gave a wry smile at Gabriel's flushed face. "No need to look so sheepish, Father. I noticed that you were snooping only because I'm the one who usually does the snooping. I'm a reporter with *Town and Gown*. I don't much care who heard what I had to say; I wish only that my last conversation with Daphne had been pleasanter."

Gabriel nodded sympathetically. "If we could only know that there would never be another conversation, how different our words would be! But perhaps it's better that we never know." He glanced sideways at Will Valentine and noticed how haggard he looked. Unlike Arthur, Will was sufficiently young and skinny that the ravages of shock did not show so keenly, but Gabriel could see the grey smudges beneath Will's eyes and the pinched look about his mouth that suggested the constant clenching and unclenching of teeth. "It's always very hard when someone we love dies in an accident," Gabriel continued. "I do know how that feels. If I can do anything to—"

"Daphne's death was not an accident, and if you're half as shrewd as I hear you are, Father, you already know that."

"Indeed."

"Let me cut to the chase," said Will, having brushed aside the awkward business of figuring Gabriel out. "We don't have very long, and once we're at the memorial, we'll be unable to speak privately. I've heard about your sleuthing activities—that's why I found out where you were staying and watched the house from a distance until I saw you leave."

Gabriel stifled a shudder. "You're good."

"I know my job, and I owe it to Daphne to encourage you to do yours. If I need a priest's ministrations, I'll go and pester old Gilbey down at the chaplaincy. I need a detective today."

"Why do you think Daphne was killed? I think she was, but I didn't know her."

Will's voice dropped a notch. "Because ambitious women in crusty old institutions like this always make enemies. I can't tell you who did it—if I knew that, I'd be plastering the name all over the front page—but I do know that someone had a reason to silence her permanently."

Gabriel could not quite hide his surprise at Will's reasoning. "I'm sure a woman as brilliant as Daphne Silverton ruffled the feathers of a few old chauvinists, but enough to provoke murder? It seems a little farfetched."

"Don't be fooled by this university's genteel appearance," Will continued conspiratorially. "Academia is filled with violent rivalries and jealousies. There are men here who would do anything to hang on to their reputations, believe you me. They're little better than dockside thugs in gowns, the lot of them."

I spy a clever young man who was denied the chance to go to university, thought Gabriel. He said, "That's quite a statement to be making, Mr Valentine. I can't think of many dons who would murder an innocent woman over an academic disagreement."

"Is this your first time here?" asked Will.

"No. BA honours degree in Classics, Saint Stephen's College." It was the first time Gabriel had ever felt the urge to pull rank, and he was going to do it properly. "First class."

Will blushed. "Sorry. I should have known, what with you being friends with Dr Kingsley."

"What about you?"

"Had to drop out after a year to go and fight Jerry. By the time I got back from the war, I needed to earn a living. I'm hoping to get a job on a paper in London." He lowered his eyes, his confident tone slipping. "I'd . . . well, I'd hoped to take Daphne with me."

"But she would have had to leave Cambridge and her research."

"I could have made it worth her while. She would have had a good life with me."

Gabriel suppressed a smile at the man's arrogance. It did not seem to occur to Will Valentine that a young woman as brilliant as Daphne Silverton could never have been satisfied with a university dropout like him; there was nothing he could have offered her that would ever have rivalled the opportunities and intellectual stimulation of Cambridge. As though reading his mind, Will persisted, "Look, Father, you strike me as one of those modern types. It's all very well being a bluestocking when a girl's young, but if she's to have a lonely old age, what good is all that learning in the end? Have you ever seen the PhD library? All those endless papers, miserably gathering dust, that only five people in the whole world have ever read! And each of those papers represents years of a person's life. I shouldn't have wanted Daphne to waste her life like that, peering down microscopes to get her name on papers no one ever reads. With me, she could have lived."

She could have lived, thought Gabriel as the two men glanced at each other, silenced by the unfortunate choice of words. *If she had not been here, in this place, at this university, in that particular laboratory, at that particular moment, Daphne Silverton would certainly have lived.* But that was not what Will had meant. "Mr Valentine," Gabriel began cautiously, "I've heard it said that Daphne was on the verge of a breakthrough, a discovery of some sort. Had you heard anything about that?"

Will puffed out his cheeks in a manner that irritated Gabriel. "She'd not told me anything about that, and she might have mentioned something if she was trying to put me off. It's what she would've said, isn't it? 'I can't marry you, darling Will; something wonderful is about to happen! My life is about to change . . .' Oh, I don't know if I'm making any sense. I suppose all I'm saying is, I don't know anything about that."

They were getting close to the college now, and Gabriel noticed little groups of students moving in the direction of the college entrance, no doubt gathering for the same purpose. Gabriel knew that they might be being observed already and that any conversation about Daphne's death should come to a close before they were within earshot of any possible eavesdropper. "If it wasn't because of Daphne's work, why do you believe she was murdered?" asked Gabriel softly. "We may not have much time."

"I told you, someone was jealous of her. Someone resented her, felt threatened by her. That's all I can say, but I mean to find out more." Will gestured for Gabriel to walk past the college entrance so that they could stand on the bridge that crossed the Cam. Gabriel watched as Will leaned against the metal railing, his face whitening at the thought of attending Daphne's memorial. He needed a moment to compose himself before they stepped into college. "Is this normal, Father?" asked Will. His hands clutched the railing and he looked out at the river, to all intents and purposes as though he intended to throw himself in. "One moment I'm having a perfectly sensible conversation with you about Daphne and her work and all that; next minute, I feel as though I'm going to be sick. I feel . . . I really do feel quite faint, Father."

The young man was trembling from head to foot. Gabriel put a hand on his shoulder. "It's all right, my son; this is perfectly normal. You're grieving. There will be many moments like this in the weeks and months to come, but it will get better in time."

"Do you know that?"

"Oh yes, very much so. You will never stop missing her, but the pain you're feeling now will recede in time. You'll be able to remember your happy memories of Daphne."

"I will find out who did this to her," said Will. "I'll find out why she was killed and who did it. And God help him when I do."

Gabriel glanced over his shoulder to ensure they were not being overheard, but the few passers-by who walked behind them showed no interest in the conversation. "Perhaps it would be better if you were to take a little rest, just to give yourself time to come to terms with what has happened. It mightn't be healthy for you to be rooting around—"

"I need to be useful, Father," said Will emphatically. "I need to feel that I'm helping Daphne somehow, even if it's too late to save her."

Gabriel saw a familiar figure out of the corner of his eye and touched Will's wrist in warning. There was nothing unusual about what Will was saying—it was the sort of pronouncement any man might make in such a situation—but Gabriel was sure Will would rather not be overheard.

"Thank you for coming," said Arthur, when Gabriel turned round to greet him. "It's awfully good of you."

Arthur looked every bit like a man trying desperately to affect an air of professional detachment: he had dressed carefully for the occasion, down to the black tie Gabriel could see protruding from the top of his long black overcoat, but Gabriel noted that Arthur was clasping his hands behind his back, no doubt to prevent anyone noticing that he was shaking.

Arthur glanced at Will Valentine, making no attempt at hiding his disgust at the sight. "I hope you don't mind me attending Daphne's memorial," said Will, in a humble tone that did not become him. "I should like to pay my respects."

Arthur looked away as though it were beneath him to make eye contact with a little man like Will. "It's a free country," said Arthur coldly. "But if all Daphne's failed suitors decide to attend, we'll need to adjourn to a larger chapel."

Will winced visibly, but he knew better than to pick a fight at such a moment, and he slipped away from Arthur and Gabriel, walking alone into college. "Be kind, Arthur," urged Gabriel, as Arthur glowered in the direction of Will's receding back. "He's only a boy."

"He's a grown man, and he has a damned nerve turning up here. If there is an afterlife, Daphne has every right to come back and haunt him. Wretched little man."

"He wanted to marry her, Arthur," said Gabriel, taken aback by his friend's animosity to a young man who appeared relatively harmless. "He must be awfully cut up."

"That little pipsqueak? Marry Daphne?" exclaimed Arthur, a shade too loudly. A number of heads turned to look at them. "Not fit to loosen the strap of her sandals! I would never have allowed it if she had been foolish enough to accept him. He would have ruined her life."

The two men walked briskly into the college, making their way to the chapel. If they had not been on their way to the memorial of a young girl, the conversation would have been almost comical. Arthur was behaving like a Victorian patriarch, the type who might have gone after an inadequate young man with a horsewhip for daring to claim his daughter. But this was twentieth-century Cambridge, and Daphne had not been Arthur's daughter, however much Gabriel suspected his friend might have wished otherwise. Nor had Daphne needed a father figure to see off her suitors, from the way Gabriel had seen her behave in the last hours of her life.

"He's a worthless little tick," muttered Arthur, slowing down for a moment to compose himself before the ordeal of facing his students. "He hurt her very deeply. Far more than you know. It's an insult to Daphne's memory that he should be here."

"I'll be waiting for you outside," promised Gabriel, saluting Arthur as he strode alone to the chapel door. A moment after Arthur had disappeared inside, Gabriel saw three young women—Girton College girls, Gabriel assumed—walking together to the chapel, weeping quietly. Gabriel was reminded that Cambridge was a tight-knit community, and a tragedy like this would send shock waves throughout the university. Long after Gabriel had returned to his home, Daphne's close friends would have to deal with the sight of her face staring out at them from the pages of the newspaper or the college bulletin board, endlessly reminding them that she was gone. And if Daphne's death really had not been an accident, the story would not die quickly.

Gabriel heard a bell ringing and the sound of a hymn he recognised as "Abide with Me", famously sung by Edith Cavell on the night before her execution. *Fast falls the eventide . . . the darkness deepens . . .*

Gabriel turned his back and began to walk across the college entrance, with the idea of making for the riverbank again. He had not gone far, however, when he heard the patter of footsteps crossing the cobbled path behind him and his name being whispered. He turned around to see Robert Sutton lurching towards him. It may have been simply his lanky stature, but Robert Sutton gave the impression that he was constantly on the verge of falling over, and Gabriel held out a hand like a traffic warden to indicate that he should slow down.

Robert took the hint and staggered to a halt, bending forward a little to catch his breath, but he was not out of breath from running. Gabriel could hear the wheezing tones of a man racked by sobs he was desperately trying to suppress. Gabriel took a step towards him. "The memorial's a little too much then?" asked Gabriel gently.

Robert nodded, running a hand over his eyes. "It's that wretched hymn," he said in a voice so deathly quiet that Gabriel struggled to hear him. "I couldn't bear to hear any more." He walked unsteadily beside Gabriel, back towards the porter's lodge. On any other occasion, Gabriel might have taken the poor boy in the direction of a tea shop, somewhere warm, dry and anonymous where he could get the man to soothe his nerves over a cup of Darjeeling, but Gabriel knew he could not stray far from the chapel when he had promised Arthur that he would wait for him. There was a good view of the chapel door from the window of the porter's lodge, and Gabriel would be able to keep a lookout for Arthur whilst hopefully calming Robert down a little.

Robert appeared too dazed to express any opinion and trotted meekly along into the porter's lodge, where Mr Derrick sat behind the counter, leafing through the morning papers. It was not the most perfect choice for a private conversation, as the porter's lodge was something of a thoroughfare, students popping in and out to check their pigeonholes and to beg the porter for the master key whenever they locked themselves out of their rooms. In the absence of an alternative, it would have to do.

Mr Derrick took one look at the pair of them and motioned for them to come with him, lifting a portion of the counter to let them through. "Dear oh dear, you look like death warmed up, young man," he said to Robert, taking in the boy's wan, sunken face and swollen eyelids. Gabriel suspected that Robert Sutton had always been of a sickly pallor, but the shock of Daphne's death had left him looking one step away from death's door. Mr Derrick instinctively knew that the boy needed to be away from prying eyes, or he would never have permitted the two of them into the hallowed ground of the porters' own territory. "You were friends with that poor lassie, weren't you?" asked Mr Derrick, arranging two wooden chairs for them. "I saw you both at dinner together. What a terrible business."

"I don't suppose he could have a glass of water?" asked Gabriel quickly. Robert was looking so glassy-eyed that Gabriel feared he might faint.

"Hot sweet tea is what he needs," declared Mr Derrick. "What you both need by the looks of you. You're looking none too chipper yourself, Father, if I may say so."

Gabriel wondered, as Mr Derrick went off in search of the necessary tea things, whether death always cast a particular pall over anyone who had known grief before. It was said that there was a clearly defined difference between a soldier who had killed and a soldier who had not killed; perhaps the same might be true of grief. Those encountering grief for the first time could be marked out as different from those for whom grief was a well-worn path. "They sang that hymn at Sarah's funeral," Robert explained finally. "I always think of her when I hear it. Strange, really, since she wasn't a Christian, but none of us knew how to arrange a Jewish burial, and we thought she probably wouldn't mind."

"Your evacuee friend?" asked Gabriel, relieved that Robert was at least talking.

"My evacuee *sister*," Robert corrected with the faintest of smiles. "Please don't mistake me, I feel terrible about what's happened to Daphne. Of course I do, but her death has made me think so much of Sarah. It still feels so fresh. I'm sorry, I'm not making any sense. You must think me heartless, grieving for the wrong woman. I'm not; it's both of them. I'm not sure where one grief ends and the other begins, if you know what I mean."

Gabriel did know what he meant, even though Robert was rambling hopelessly. That was what Gabriel had meant by the well-worn path. Walking it again inevitably brought back memories of the previous journey. Whatever the rumours, Gabriel had no doubt that Robert had been at least a little in love with Daphne, even if it had been the desperate love of a socially inadequate young man who knew he would never dare tell the girl in question what he thought of her. It struck Gabriel that this young man was a quite different character to Will Valentine, who evidently had a very high opinion of himself. Robert was all too aware of his own inadequacies, his lack of charm and wit, perhaps even his lack of good looks. It was quite possible that Daphne would have overlooked any of these failings if she had found in him a soul mate who was her intellectual equal. Robert may well have been that, though it scarcely mattered now.

"I can't stop thinking about how they both died, Father," said Robert listlessly. "How much both deaths feel like my fault."

"I thought Sarah died of pneumonia," said Gabriel. "Surely you can't blame yourself for that? It's a terrible illness, but it can happen to anyone. Even a strong young woman."

"I've always thought she died of a broken heart," said Robert. "I know it's sentimental, but I've always thought she might have survived if she hadn't been so sad. I took her to the pictures, you see, and they showed a newsreel of the liberation of Belsen. There were soldiers placing hundreds of skeletal bodies into a long mass grave. When they started burying them, Sarah was screaming so much I had to take her out. Everyone was very kind about it, but she wouldn't calm down, and I had to take her home. She cried about it for days, and then she took ill. They were her people, Father. What a terrible shock it must have been, seeing all that death. After that, it was as though she just faded away. She didn't want to live in such a terrible world anymore."

Gabriel winced, wondering how many thousands of people—including many children—had been unsuspectingly exposed to those terrible images of torture and death in picture houses all over Britain. It had never occurred to him to feel any great concern for them, since many more thousands of people had witnessed those horrors firsthand, either as innocent bystanders or as the victims themselves. The full horror of a young Jewish girl seeing the tragedy of her people's destruction in those shadowy black-and-white pictures hit him like a slap in the face. But there was another broken heart in his care for the moment. "Mr Sutton—Robert—you know you mustn't blame yourself. She would have found out sooner or later. The news was all over the wireless and the papers; you could hardly have hidden it from her. Even then, you've no way of knowing why she succumbed to her illness. You mustn't blame yourself for Sarah's death or for Daphne's."

Robert opened his mouth to respond but stopped himself at the sight of Mr Derrick appearing with two steaming mugs of tea. "There you go, this one is for you," he said, placing a blue-and-white enamel mug into Robert's hands.

"I hope you don't mind, but I've slipped a bit of something special in there to calm your nerves. Helps me every time."

Robert gave a weak smile of thanks and raised the mug to his lips. Gabriel took his rather-more-conventional tea from Mr Derrick, and they exchanged a conspiratorial glance. Gabriel was not sure how "little" a drop of something special Mr Derrick had placed in Robert's tea—he could smell the Scotch whisky from where he sat. "Thanks awfully, Mr Derrick," said Gabriel, but Derrick was already retreating away from them, distracted by the sound of the door opening.

"Take your time," Derrick said over his shoulder as he went.

"I wonder if you should see a doctor," suggested Gabriel to Robert's bowed head. "He could at least give you something to help you sleep at night until you start feeling a little better. The exhaustion won't be helping."

Robert raised his head very slowly and stared incredulously at Gabriel. "I assure you, Father, no drug in this godforsaken world could possibly give me rest. I have been careless with the life of a woman I loved, for the second time. I should have stopped Daphne going to the lab after a late dinner. She was far too tired to be working at that time of night."

"You had no way of knowing she was going to the lab," said Gabriel, recalling Daphne's departure that evening and the ripple of disappointment among the men it had caused. "She said she had a headache; she gave every indication that she was going directly home."

"Precisely!" Robert spluttered, almost choking on his own words. "Daphne never gets headaches; she never gets ill! I've never known her get a headache, even when she'd been hard at work for fourteen hours! I should've known it was a pretext to slip away, but she never works late at night. She's an early bird. She was. *Was*." A pathetic moan escaped Robert's throat, and he forced down a mouthful of tea as though deliberately trying to choke himself.

Gabriel's ears pricked up at the suggestion that Daphne had acted out of character. He was clutching at straws—but then he often was, in these situations—and possibilities were forming in his mind. *Did someone send her to the lab on some pretext? Did someone send her there knowing that she would be all alone in that building and completely vulnerable? Had she arranged to meet someone?* He tried to think through the events of the evening, wondering whether anyone present had slipped her a note or whispered a few private words in Daphne's ear while they had been all together, but Gabriel quickly realised it was impossible to know. There had been many different conversations around that table, and at the height of the evening, the dining hall had been quite noisy. Anyone before or during the dinner might have suggested such a course of action to Daphne—well before the dinner, for that matter. Might Will Valentine have found some way to convince Daphne to meet him after dinner on the pretext of patching up their feud?

Robert was looking a little calmer now and glanced awkwardly at Gabriel. "I'm awfully sorry to have burdened you with all this," said Robert haltingly. "It's not at all like me to get into such a state, but it's hard to know whom to talk to. I suppose I just wish there were something I could do to make everything all right. That's the problem with death—it is all so final. It's not like a person getting ill and having the chance to nurse him back to health. Once he's gone, he's gone."

"Mr Sutton," said Gabriel cautiously. He was not sure about the ethics of asking such a question to a troubled man like Robert; but, like Robert, Gabriel could think of no one else to ask. "Might I ask—"

"I do wish you'd call me Rob, or at least Robert," said Robert a little more brightly. "'Mr Sutton' feels wrong somehow. It would be like being called 'sir' by my father."

Gabriel groaned at the thought of how irredeemably ancient he must appear to a man like Robert Sutton, but he decided to take the invitation as a compliment. "Robert then. I have a question about liquid nitrogen."

Robert's back stiffened. "Father, this is in awfully bad taste."

"There's method to my madness, I promise. I need to know, could anything else cause a person to suffocate that way?"

"Another chemical, you mean?"

"Not exactly," said Gabriel, feeling as though he were walking on tiptoe across a minefield. "There's no reason why anything other than liquid nitrogen should have been used. It's just . . . well, I'm sorry, I know this is in bad taste, but for example, if someone had smothered her with his own hands, would the effects have been the same?"

Gabriel suspected that Robert would have jumped to his feet if he had had the energy to do so, but he simply blinked as though Gabriel had hurled the contents of his teacup into his face. "Father, Daphne's death was an accident. I hope you're not suggesting anyone actually hurt her. Why on earth would anyone do that?"

"But if someone had, could that empty canister of liquid nitrogen have been a smokescreen, so to speak?" Another ghastly choice of words, but Robert did not appear to have noticed.

"I can't see how," said Robert with a tone of weariness creeping into his voice. "If someone had suffocated her with his bare hands—as you put it—there would be signs of pressure, bruises around her nose and mouth. And if she'd been strangled, there would have been marks on her throat."

"What if something had been used to avoid making any marks? A pillow or blanket, for example?"

Robert squirmed at the thought. "Look here, I'm not a pathologist myself, so I can't be sure, but I'm fairly certain that if a person had placed a pillow on her face, there would still be evidence. There might be fibres . . . oh God . . ." Robert closed his eyes and appeared to be silently counting to ten.

"I'm sorry, this is wrong," said Gabriel quickly. "Forget I asked; forget all about this."

"No," said Robert with unexpected firmness, though his eyes remained tight shut. "We're both in the same boat; neither of us has anyone else to talk to. You can hardly ask Dr Kingsley a question like that in the state he's in. Believe me, he's in an even worse way than I am, even if it doesn't show." Robert swallowed hard and opened his eyes to look directly at Gabriel. "You've no idea how he doted on her, Father. I cannot imagine how he's going to go on without her. You mustn't do anything to unsettle him."

"Of course not," promised Gabriel, ashamed that Robert had felt it necessary to say as much. "Of course not . . . and

. . . and I should not have said as much to you. You're suffering too."

Robert shook his head impatiently. "Whom else will you ask? It's a reasonable enough question. But you can put your mind at rest on that point. If she had been killed in the way you suggest, there would still be signs, and even if there was nothing on her face or in her nostrils to suggest she had been smothered, it's likely she would have marks elsewhere on her body. Unless she had been completely taken by surprise, she is very likely to have put up a fight."

"She was quite slightly built," ventured Gabriel. "A strong man . . ."

"Even if she had been quickly overpowered, there would probably still be marks—on her arms perhaps—where she'd been held down. That's what makes liquid nitrogen so dangerous—it acts so very quickly. Smothering a person would take longer, long enough for the person to struggle at least. She would have struggled."

Gabriel saw a stray tear slide down Robert's cheek and noted with relief that Mr Derrick was hovering as though awaiting instructions. "They're coming out of the chapel now," he said, in the reserved tone of a policeman bearing bad news. "Why don't you leave Mr Sutton to me. I'll take care of him and see he gets safely to his rooms."

Gabriel stood up, turning to look at Robert before he left. For the first time, he noticed a red rash on the palm of Robert's left hand, which made him think instinctively of stinging nettles, though he had no idea where Robert would have come into contact with such a plant in central Cambridge. Gabriel thought he really ought to try to persuade

Robert to see a doctor. The gaunt, weary look might well be grief, but those little red spots must surely be something more serious.

"Mr—Robert," said Gabriel, placing his empty mug on the chair he had recently occupied. "May I come and visit you again later today? I should like to see that you're all right."

Robert made no answer and did not look at Gabriel as he slipped away. Ordinarily, Gabriel would have reported his suspicions to Arthur on the grounds that the one person Robert might listen to was Dr Kingsley, but he could not trouble Arthur with his worries now. Gabriel watched from a respectful distance as Arthur stepped out of the chapel, surrounded by a group of students. There were hushed conversations, the shaking of hands, all the little rituals one usually associated with a funeral, except that in this case the body had yet to be released for burial.

Arthur was as much a father figure now as he had been in the Senior Combination Room, seated proudly with his academic children, but this was the side of family life most people preferred to ignore. Arthur glanced across the quad and noticed Gabriel standing in the shadows waiting for him. He nodded and began to take leave of the young people around him. Gabriel was about to signal to Arthur not to hurry, but he quickly realised that Arthur was desperate to escape, and Gabriel stepped forward to meet him. A number of the students looked askance at Gabriel as though they found the idea of Dr Kingsley fraternising with a priest unconscionable, but Arthur made a great show of greeting Gabriel warmly and walking away with him out of the college.

"Thank you, old chap," said Arthur. "They're a good crowd, and they're all very distressed, but I've taken about as much sympathy as I can bear this morning."

As they passed the porter's lodge on the way out of college, Gabriel glanced quickly inside and noted with relief that Mr Derrick was chatting easily with Robert Sutton, who appeared to be relaxing for the first time. The whisky was no doubt taking effect. "You should eat something," said Gabriel solicitously. "I'll wager you haven't eaten anything all day."

"I can't say I have, I'm afraid," Arthur admitted, shaking his head. "I didn't get a wink of sleep last night, then I felt too queasy for breakfast. To be honest, I couldn't face the buttery this morning. I'm finding it rather difficult to face college at all."

"Has anyone been unkind to you?" demanded Gabriel, turning to look at his friend, who was staring down at his boots as though feeling the need to inspect the ground very carefully with every step. "If they have, you know, you could always—"

"No, no, everyone's being terribly kind. It's just the sense of being noticed—singled out, I suppose. Everywhere I go, I feel as though someone's whispering. It may be in my mind, of course, but it's hard to shake off that feeling of being under constant observation."

They walked in the direction of King's Parade, where Fitzbillies and the Copper Kettle and other assorted tearooms were to be found. There was a queue of students outside Fitzbillies, so they ducked into the Copper Kettle, taking a seat upstairs on the grounds that they were less likely to be disturbed there. Unfortunately, it was lunchtime and the tearooms were busy, but Gabriel preferred the smokescreen of background noise at moments like this.

"I have a proposal for you," said Gabriel when they had removed coats, gloves and hats and were settled comfortably. "When the brouhaha is over, come and spend some time at my abbey."

Arthur gave a sardonic smile. "I'm not sure a cross old atheist would be particularly at home in your hallowed walls," he said.

"No one is turned away, I assure you," said Gabriel. "Everyone deserves some peace and quiet to recover."

Arthur gave a long sigh. Like Robert, Arthur looked desperately weary. "I never thought I'd be tempted to disappear into a Babylonish community, but the thought is quite appealing at present. Anything that takes me away from that lab."

A freckle-faced waitress appeared at their table, so quietly that she might have been transported there by magic. "Good afternoon, gentlemen. What can I get you?"

Arthur picked up a menu, looking up at the young woman in apparent confusion. "Well, I'm not sure. Gabriel, what would you like?"

Gabriel smiled at the waitress. "How about some cucumber sandwiches?"

"Certainly, sir," she said cheerfully, scribbling in a notepad. "Sandwiches for two then. Would you like a pot of tea with that?" Gabriel nodded. The waitress noted Arthur's mourning clothes for the first time and gave him a sympathetic smile. "I tell you what, I've some very nice rock cakes baked only this morning. Want me to bring you a few of those as well?"

Gabriel nodded enthusiastically, though he had a personal dislike of rock cakes and would have to cut them up into small pieces before daring to eat them. One of his brothers had had the hilarious idea, when they were children, of baking a rock cake with a real rock inside it for him. The end result had been that the five-year-old Gabriel had lost two teeth, and his brother Ignatius had avoided sitting down for a week. The fact that the lost teeth had been milk teeth which would have fallen out anyway did nothing to lessen his father's wrath, and Gabriel somehow felt responsible for his brother's screams, though he could never quite work out why.

"I'm sorry things have turned out this way," said Arthur, as though he had just gone through the worst emotional crisis of his adult life with the intention of wrecking Gabriel's holiday. Gabriel's mind was still on his big brother's tears, and he took a moment to return to the troubles of the present. "I'm not sure even a trip to a monastery could stop me being haunted by Daphne's death. I shall always wish I'd been there."

Here we go again, thought Gabriel. Guilt was so fickle, such a poor judge of the severity of a sin or even the presence of a sin. He had noticed in his years as a priest that people could be crushed with the most terrible weight of guilt for an event that had nothing to do with them or of which they were only tangentially responsible, but then could just as easily feel no sense of guilt or shame at all about a premeditated act of cruelty. "Arthur, you know it was not your fault," he said slowly and deliberately. "I cannot take the grief away from you, I cannot take away the loss, but I can tell you not to blame yourself."

"Daphne's parents blame me," he said matter-of-factly, "and they're not the only ones. Daphne's mother was kind enough to send me a telegram as soon as she had been told the news, to inform me that her daughter's blood was on my hands."

Gabriel thought of how completely Giovanna's parents had absolved him of any blame for their beloved daughter's death; he thought of the unconditional love and affection they had shown to him in the immediate aftermath of that tragedy and in the short time since he had arrived back in Cambridge—the way they had welcomed him into their home, embraced him, extended hospitality to him and called him their son. And here was Arthur having his worst and most misdirected beliefs confirmed by an angry mother. "She is beside herself with grief," said Gabriel. "She's only just heard about the loss of her daughter, it may be many months before she can think clearly about what has happened. She'll see it all very differently one day."

Arthur reached into the inside pocket of his jacket and pulled out a folded piece of paper, opening it slowly on the tabletop. It was the crudest scare tactic in the world, but some anonymous person had cut out letters from newspaper headlines and stuck them onto a piece of notepaper to form the word MURDERER. A moment later, Arthur was snatching the paper up and cramming it back into his pocket as the waitress appeared, carrying a large tray containing a round-bellied teapot, cups and a jug. The two men sat in silence as she laid out the tea things, promising them as she moved away that she would return directly with the food.

"When did you get that?" asked Gabriel, but Arthur had sunk into silence, saying nothing as the waitress returned with plates of sandwiches and rock cakes. Wordlessly, she poured them both a cup of tea. Gabriel noted the absence of a sugar bowl with not a little regret, then told himself that the continuing sugar shortage was good for his teeth.

"Arthur, when did you get that?"

"Someone slipped it under my door early this morning," said Arthur tonelessly. "I heard a rustle, but I couldn't bring myself to get up. If I had, I might have run after the messenger and found out who he was. Or she. But I doubt a woman could have got into college at that hour."

"Does this have to be about Daphne?" asked Gabriel, hoping it did not sound like a silly question. "I mean, has anything like this happened before? Scientists are sometimes targets for such behaviour."

Following the dropping of the atomic bombs on Hiroshima and Nagasaki, Gabriel imagined that attitudes towards scientists might have taken a turn for the worse, particularly in a university town. Particularly in a town with a very active pacifist organisation at work . . .

"I had nothing to do with the Bomb," said Arthur emphatically, "but yes, I've had all manner of leaflets and anonymous messages sent to me since the war. People are so ignorant; they don't know one branch of science from another. All scientists are evil; all scientists are responsible for the uses to which their inventions are put. I had to stop dear Daphne getting caught up with those cranks. They had their hooks in her quite badly at one point."

Gabriel had some pressing questions on that subject for Arthur, but he had the good sense to see that the man was in no mood to be questioned about anything. He needed to talk, and he needed a friend to listen to him. Gabriel sat back and ate, letting Arthur lead the conversation in whichever direction he chose.

"She soon saw sense, of course. They really are ridiculous people. Why go after scientists anyway? It's the politicians who make the decisions; it was President Truman who gave the order to drop the Bomb on Hiroshima. It was his responsibility."

"Arthur, I know you had nothing to do with the Bomb, so I'm sure you won't mind my asking," said Gabriel, "but is what you say really true? Surely the scientists who developed the Bomb must bear some share of the responsibility for what happened. Without the weapon, President Truman would have had no—"

"Oh, come now, Gabriel!" snapped Arthur, showing more energy than he had since he had hammered on the Gervasonis' door the previous day. "You're an intelligent man, an educated man, not like those idiots with their banners and slogans. Those people would have left this country to burn if they had had their way! They would have forced us to sit back and let the Germans tear our country apart, abolish the world's first parliament, tear up the Magna Carta. They would have stood on the streets singing their pretty little songs whilst innocent people were hanged in the Market Square, whilst children were gunned down in the street! They would have averted their eyes whilst Jews and Communists and . . . and . . . well, people like you, my friend . . . were sent to death camps. The scientists who built the Bomb had more moral credibility than those cretins."

Gabriel took a little longer than was strictly necessary to swallow the soft white bread in his mouth before attempting

146

a riposte. "Arthur, I'm not sure it's a fair comparison. One need not be a pacifist to oppose nuclear weapons."

"Oppose them by all means, but don't blame the creators of those monsters! If America hadn't got there first, Hitler may well have. The technology itself is not to blame."

"Arthur—"

"Is the man who invented the first gun responsible for the deaths of every single man, woman and child to have been shot dead over the past four hundred years?" Arthur demanded, causing the figures seated at the neighbouring tables to turn and look at him. "Be reasonable, man!"

Gabriel waited until they had ceased to be the centre of attention before attempting to continue the conversation. He knew that there was no point in trying to argue with Arthur in such a state; he would only become progressively more and more irrational until he lost his temper and walked out. And Arthur needed to remain friends with those closest to him.

"Arthur, what was Daphne working on that was so important?"

"You wouldn't understand; there's no point trying to explain," answered Arthur with the effortless arrogance of a man of science talking to a man of the cloth. He looked sheepishly at Gabriel. "No offence, old man, but unless one works in the field, it's difficult to explain. But yes, it was important. That was why my first reaction was to think she'd been killed, but I realise now I was being melodramatic."

"I was always told to trust my instincts," said Gabriel, pushing the plate of food towards Arthur. He was guiltily aware that he had been eating whilst his friend had barely touched a crumb. "What was it really that made you think it was murder?"

"Nothing!" answered Arthur abruptly. "That's the point. I was being irrational; I was frightened and upset. Because of Daphne's work, I suppose I thought there must have been some malice involved, but there was really no reason to believe it was anything other than an accident. I should never have put the idea in your head. You're never going to let it go now, are you?"

Gabriel was not going to lie to Arthur and pretend that he would forget all about it. When a nagging truth had burrowed its way into Gabriel's mind, he was completely incapable of letting it go, and his every instinct told him that Daphne had been murdered. For her sake and for his own sanity, he knew he could not stop looking, even to placate a distraught friend. "Why don't you eat something, old chap? You need your strength."

With the utmost reluctance, Arthur picked up a neat, crustless, triangular sandwich and began to eat, whilst Gabriel topped up his teacup. A sudden idea struck him. "Look here, Arthur, why don't you come home with me this evening? The Gervasonis won't mind one more round the table. It will do you good to have some company and good food."

"I can't possibly impose on complete strangers like that, uninvited," Arthur began. "It would be appallingly rude."

"They don't stand on ceremony like us," promised Gabriel. "I wouldn't suggest it if I thought they'd mind."

Arthur shook his head. "It's a very kind thought, old man, but I need to be alone. We can meet again tomorrow, take a nice long walk along the Backs, have a chat about old times."

"I'd like that. Are you sure you'll be all right, Arthur?

I hate to think of you sitting all alone in those rooms of yours."

Arthur smiled wearily. "I'm used to being alone, Gabriel —a little like you, I suppose. My head hasn't stopped spinning since I found Daphne's body. I need some peace and quiet to think."

"I understand."

When they parted company at the doorway of the Copper Kettle, Gabriel watched his old friend walking along King's Parade with a sense of gnawing anxiety. He knew Arthur was lying to him again; he had known the man far too long to fail to notice his evasive behaviour, and Arthur had been a hopeless liar even when they had been students. It was just that he was not sure whether Arthur was lying to Gabriel or to himself. He might simply want to believe that Daphne's death had been a tragic accident in the way any man might wish that there had been no malice intended to a close friend, that there could be no one on this planet who would want to hurt a woman so dearly loved.

He would take that walk with Arthur the next day, and they would try to speak about happier times, but Gabriel knew he had to try to persuade Arthur to be honest with himself about what had happened. The journey to the truth was always easier in company.

8

Gabriel sat on the low wall outside King's College and waited a discreet ten minutes before getting up and moving back towards college. If he had been of an ironical character, Gabriel might have given a hollow laugh at the thought that this short holiday had been Abbot Ambrose's attempt at distracting Gabriel from the terrible situation in his parish. Walking alone down Trinity Street, his host bereft by a catastrophic personal loss, Gabriel might also have been forgiven for packing his bag and hurrying directly to the railway station.

But the Gervasonis had invited him to stay until the whole business was cleared up, and Gabriel thought that perhaps they, like him, had the sense that there was justice to be done in the town before he left. He entered Trinity Street post office and sent a telegram to Abbot Ambrose, trying hard to avoid the telegraph operator's incredulous look as he dictated his message:

> **GIRL MURDERED STOP MUST FIND**
> **KILLER STOP HOME SOON STOP**

"Is it a code?" asked the operator as she took his money. Gabriel was distracted by the chain attached to the woman's reading glasses. It was one of those annoying beaded numbers, but it had snapped, and she had tied it together in an ungainly knot just below her left ear. "Well, is it?" she persisted when Gabriel failed to answer. "Or one of these daft games the students are always playing? You look a little old to be indulging in behaviour like that, if I may say so."

It was the first time in his life Gabriel had almost said the words, "I'm a detective", but it sounded pretentious and possibly not true. The lady might think he was a policeman in disguise or something . . . and what would Inspector Applegate say if he heard him use that hallowed term, all because he had stumbled upon a few murderers during the past year? Gabriel smiled at the woman, took his change and left with all possible speed. It was only as the bell chimed over the door, signalling his exit, that Gabriel remembered that Mama Gervasoni had already arranged for a telegram to be sent to his abbey. Abbot Ambrose would think him stark staring mad, if he had not already formed that opinion.

Gabriel knew he ought to check up on Robert Sutton, having left him in the capable care of Mr Derrick, but when he reached Robert's rooms, the outer door was locked. Gabriel hurried back to the porter's lodge to find Mr Derrick in his usual place behind the counter. "No need to fret," said Mr Derrick before Gabriel could ask the obvious question. "One of the dons took him out for a bite of lunch. Seemed the best place for him in the state he was in, poor boy."

Gabriel's curiosity was piqued. "Oh? Which one? Dr Kingsley was with me."

"Dr Crayford. He was Mr Sutton's supervisor when he first arrived. Mr Sutton changed his mind about his studies and moved to Dr Kingsley's lab, but there were no hard feelings."

"That was very kind of him," said Gabriel before taking his leave. He was guiltily aware of having made an unpleasant judgement about Dr Crayford, mostly because of his disparaging comments about Daphne. It had not occurred to Gabriel that a person as apparently cold as Dr Crayford would be so considerate as to come to the aid of a distressed young man, but if he had been Robert's supervisor, it would be quite natural to come to his assistance now.

Gabriel would have liked to have gone back to the lab to take a better look at the place where Daphne died, but it would be impossible to gain access without Arthur's help, and he knew better than to pester Arthur when he had asked so emphatically to be left alone. Instead, he walked back through town and crossed Parker's Piece, in search of the next best thing: the place where Daphne had lived and where he could talk to a woman who did not need convincing that Daphne's death had been murder.

Mrs Bellinger was all of a flutter when Gabriel knocked at the door. She managed to look strikingly regal even in black, but she was not the sort of woman who would have let her sense of style slip even in a time of tragedy. She was dressed in a carefully tailored black velvet gown, her customary string of pearls substituted with a black beaded choker cut from some precious stone Gabriel would never have recognised. Gabriel suspected that Mrs Bellinger had been crying, but her carefully applied makeup concealed any evidence of her loss of control.

"I wondered when you would return," said Mrs Bellinger with a pert smile, standing aside to let Gabriel in. "I rather hoped you would."

As he stepped into the hallway, Gabriel was aware of the

faint aroma of a floral scent. He suspected that Mrs Bellinger had spent the morning distracting herself with some light spring cleaning, not that Gabriel could imagine the lady in a pinny with her sleeves rolled up. Mrs Bellinger put a finger to her lips and indicated the open door of the sitting room, where an elderly man dozed in an armchair. "Best not to wake him," whispered Mrs Bellinger, motioning for Gabriel to step through the door a little farther down the hall to the right.

They were standing in a dining room, laid out as though awaiting the imminent arrival of a large group of well-heeled guests. There was a crisp white damask tablecloth draped over a long table surrounded by ten mahogany chairs, with ten places laid out in immaculate squares, not a dessert fork out of line, with every napkin skilfully rolled into a well-polished silver ring. It was the sort of dining room Miss Havisham might have had in her home if she had employed a good housekeeper whilst keeping her home frozen in time.

"I know how it looks," said Mrs Bellinger apologetically. "You must think me quite batty. We haven't entertained in years, what with the war and Eric's illness. I'm afraid I felt the urge to do something that used to make me happy, and I laid out the table. We had some marvellous dinner parties here, you know."

Gabriel realised where the scent was coming from. The napkins had been sprinkled with it so that guests would be treated to the sweet smell as they opened them up. "It's a beautiful room," said Gabriel awkwardly, wondering how long the pair of them were going to have to make conversation, standing in the corner of this museum piece. "If this is a bad moment, Mrs Bellinger . . ."

"Not at all," she answered immediately. "The fact is, performing a mundane task settles the mind. The only thing I can think about is Daphne. I kept thinking all morning that I really ought to clear out her room. Her family will want her things, and it would be ever so cruel to ask them to do it; they may not even wish to come to the house." Mrs Bellinger looked almost imploringly at Gabriel. "It's hard to think of touching anything. Her room's just as she left it; I could almost imagine that she will come back again. And I thought you might wish to see it anyway."

"I should like that, if you don't mind," said Gabriel. "It might help. You see, I'm quite at a loss as to understand why she was killed at all. I have a hunch, but it's not much to go on."

Mrs Bellinger smiled, and they walked back into the hallway together, treading as softly as possible so as not to disturb the sleeping Eric. When they had reached the top of the narrow stairs, Mrs Bellinger said, "A hunch is a good place to start."

They were standing in front of a magnolia-painted door. Mrs Bellinger placed her hand on the doorknob but was hesitating to open it. Gabriel had not experienced such a moment after his own loss, as there had been no home to return to, but he knew the torrent of emotions she must be experiencing. "Why don't I go in first?" suggested Gabriel, waiting for Mrs Bellinger to step away from the door before moving forward. He opened the door very softly, as though afraid to wake the occupant of the room.

The first thing Gabriel noticed when he stepped inside was that Daphne was a predictably tidy person. The room was immaculately clean and orderly, almost as though she had anticipated a complete stranger walking in to inspect her belongings. Gabriel had always thought that one of the worst things about murder was the way the victim was granted no privacy whatsoever—all the dark corners of their lives had to be exposed to the penetrating glare of the police, their personal effects rifled through, their friendships analysed and dissected for clues, the most intimate aspects of their lives discussed and judged by strangers. Ordinarily, Gabriel doubted that even Mrs Bellinger would have ventured into this room without knocking first and awaiting an invitation to enter, but there they both were, standing in the middle of a spacious female domain like two amateur burglars.

The room was pleasantly airy with a large window near the bed which overlooked a walled garden. Everything in the room was as colour coordinated as the landlady herself; the bedclothes—counterpane carefully pulled back, sheets smooth and unruffled—were the same buttercup yellow as the wallpaper, whose yellow-and-white stripes gave a Victorian feel to the place.

"I had the room redecorated before Daphne's arrival last summer," Mrs Bellinger explained. "I wanted her to be very cosy here, seeing that she was far away from home."

"I'm sure she was," said Gabriel. He noted the bookcase, laden with novels, hefty scientific tomes and cardboard folders of what he assumed had been Daphne's study notes. "Were those the notes for her current work?" asked Gabriel, pointing at the folders.

"I don't think so; I believe they were the notes from her undergraduate studies. I'm sure I remember her saying that they were not allowed to take their lab books home with them."

"Did she keep a diary?"

Mrs Bellinger shook her head. "I don't think so, not the sort of diary you mean. There's probably a diary in the drawer of her bedside table with her appointments and suchlike, but she was not the sort of girl who would have kept a journal. Far too self-effacing."

Gabriel swallowed his embarrassment and got on his knees to open the drawer of Daphne's bedside table. There were various objects that he might have expected to find: a copy of a novel Gabriel had never heard of, quite newly published; a bag containing what looked to Gabriel's untrained eye like a set of curlers and a hairnet; and an expensive-looking edition of the New Testament, leather bound with gold-edged pages. Gabriel guessed it had been a confirmation present.

He opened it and noticed an inscription on the flyleaf. Not a confirmation gift then, a school prize. Top of the class in divinity, June 1934. "Was Daphne a religious girl?" asked Gabriel. "You called her a good Catholic when we spoke before."

Mrs Bellinger shook her head. "Her mother was a Roman Catholic and I believe tried to raise her Catholic. She was ever such a good girl, but I don't recall that she was particularly religious. She rarely attended church."

"Yes, I wondered since she appears to have won a divinity prize."

Gabriel became aware of extraneous material slipped between the pages of the book and barely heard Mrs Bellinger's comment: "Whatever Daphne did, I daresay she liked to come first." Daphne had used the book as an unofficial scrapbook. There were dried rose petals pressed between two pages, a postcard from an English seaside resort and a folded newspaper cutting. He had barely unfolded it before Mrs Bellinger chimed in with, "Oh no, why on earth did she keep that? I told her to throw it away the day it was published!"

The headline read "Pacifism and the Modern Scientist". Daphne had cut out a substantial article which must have taken up most of one side of a page, but instead of the reporter's name, the words "Staff Reporter" were printed underneath the headline. The article was an interview, beginning with the question: "Can scientists be trusted in the atomic age?" Gabriel skimmed past the opening paragraph, written in a sensationalist style to draw him into an article he had every intention of reading. He slowed down only when he saw the words "Daphne Silverton".

"Why on earth did she agree to be interviewed by a local paper on such a contentious subject?" mused Gabriel out loud. "The interview is very recent. She must have spoken to this journalist after Dr Kingsley had warned her against her involvement with the Peace Pledge Union."

The interview certainly left little to the imagination, and the Daphne who emerged from it was both strong-minded and eloquent, showing all the boldness and imprudence of youth but also all its fire. "The public have every right to be suspicious of us if we're not honest about our activities. We have rightfully lost respect with our moral equivocation on matters of life and death. If we scientists allow ourselves to become dealers in death, we misuse the power our knowledge gives us. It is not enough to blame politicians for the atrocities committed in time of war if we are their willing pawns. No scientist was forced at gunpoint to work on the Bomb; they chose to use their knowledge to wreak destruction and death upon thousands of innocent lives."

"She had no idea she was being interviewed, Father," Mrs Bellinger explained. "She said she was having a nice, relaxed chat with a friendly journalist. He never said to her that he would be publishing her words. It was grossly unfair. The first thing she knew about it was when she opened the newspaper and read her name. She was distraught."

"What did Dr Kingsley say?"

"It wasn't so much what he said that troubled her." Mrs Bellinger pulled out the chair from Daphne's desk and sat down, apparently exhausted. "Daphne was scared to death; it was the first time she ever went to work late. She said she just couldn't face him, and she came home very early, absolutely beside herself."

"Had they argued?"

"Daphne said that Dr Kingsley had been in an absolutely foul temper; she had never seen anything like it from him before. She said he was kicking furniture and throwing things about; she was terrified. She could hardly remember everything he'd shouted at her afterwards. She said she'd actually thought he might hurt her."

"He would never have done that," Gabriel protested. The man he knew would never harm a woman, even in the foulest of tempers. Gabriel was not sure Arthur would even have been capable of thumping another man in a row. "I don't doubt that Daphne must have been very frightened. I have never seen my friend behave like that before, but that doesn't mean it didn't happen." Gabriel was struggling to make any sense; he had been thrown by the very notion that Arthur could have frightened anyone so badly. "I . . .

I don't suppose it is of any consequence now, but I'm certain he would never have done her any harm, however angry he was."

"Then why is she dead, Father?" asked Mrs Bellinger, looking forlornly at him in a way that made Gabriel feel partially responsible for Daphne's fate. "She made someone angry enough to kill her; why should it not have been Dr Kingsley? She defied him twice."

This was not a crime committed in passion, thought Gabriel as he took his leave of Mrs Bellinger and began the long cold walk back to Chesterton Road and the Gervasonis. Whoever killed Daphne planned it very carefully, in cold blood. Could Arthur have done that? Would he have been foolish enough to draw Gabriel's attention to the possibility of murder when the death was so clearly intended to look like an accident? Or was that a highly intelligent man's idea of a double bluff?

It was already dark as Gabriel made his way through town. Parker's Piece felt exposed rather than spacious with the biting Cambridge wind snapping at Gabriel's face and not so much as a tree to shield him. He remembered that piercing cold from his student days, the wind travelling to them unhindered all the way from Siberia, or so the popular wisdom claimed. Gabriel was sure he remembered some smart alecks (of which there were many) debunking that particular theory, but Gabriel had still been left feeling as though he were about to tramp across the frozen wastes of Red Russia when he had been woken on a frozen winter morning.

When he reached the road, Gabriel could see clusters of gowned students walking back to their colleges, in a relaxed mood, happy after being released from their various super-visions and lab practicals. It may have been his imagination, but Gabriel could have sworn that he heard Daphne's name whispered as he walked along; but it would be strange if the death of a researcher were not a topic of conversation. His own thoughts returned to the words he had heard Will Valentine throw back at Daphne as they had argued in the college grounds: *Daphne, if you're prepared to express an opinion, you should be prepared to see it in print. Don't be such a coward.*

The more Gabriel thought about it, the more he thought what monumental cheek Will Valentine had had, proposing to a girl he had double-crossed in such a dastardly way. Gabriel had very little time for journalists as a rule—he had read quite enough sensational nonsense after the death of his wife not to trust a reporter to have any moral bound-aries whatsoever—but reporting words spoken in a private conversation seemed particularly cheap.

Gabriel would have to talk to Will Valentine again, but for the moment he had more pressing concerns. He stepped through the entrance to Saint Stephen's, making directly for Arthur's rooms. The outer door was locked, but Gabriel could see a light shining feebly under the door and knew that Arthur was within, albeit determined not to be disturbed. Gabriel knocked gently on the door. "Arthur?" he called, too haltingly to be heard through two thick wooden doors. Gabriel knocked much louder. "Arthur! I know you're in there! Why don't you let me in?"

Gabriel pressed his ear to the door, catching the sound of a chair scraping against the floor and the thud of something hard hitting a table, then nothing. "Arthur, please let me in. You don't have to lock yourself away from an old friend."

There was a further protracted silence, punctuated finally by the sound of footsteps, but Gabriel quickly realised from which direction they were coming and spun round in time to see Mr Derrick approaching him. Gabriel cursed himself for flinching, but for a moment the old man had looked quite alarming. There was something about the stealthy way in which he had advanced up those creaking stairs, so stealthily in fact that Gabriel had heard him only when he was less than a yard away. It did not help that Derrick's black clothes—rather like Gabriel's—gave him the lugubrious air of a vampire at the best of times.

"I thought I saw you crossing the quad," said Derrick, apparently not noticing Gabriel's flustered appearance. "Thought I'd come on up and see if I could be of assistance."

"That's very decent of you, Mr Derrick," said Gabriel, trying and failing to sound convinced. There were occasions in his life when the ability to be very slightly deceitful would be useful. "I came to see how Dr Kingsley was faring. He did not seem well when we lunched earlier."

"If you're worried, I can fetch the master key," said Derrick. "I don't like to go barging in unless it's strictly necessary, but I can always——"

There was a clatter as the inner door was thrown open, just giving Gabriel and Derrick time to scramble backwards before Arthur opened the outer door with a violent shove. "You've absolutely no need to invade my rooms, I assure you!" Arthur blurted out, glaring at Derrick as though he were confronting a burglar. "Can a man not be granted an hour's peace and quiet at such a time?"

Derrick stepped back to indicate that he had no intention of proceeding any further. "Begging your pardon, sir," Derrick began. "It's just, I noticed out the win—"

"It's all right, Arthur, it was not Mr Derrick's fault at all," Gabriel put in hurriedly. "I came to find you, and he happened to see me dashing across the quad. I must have looked as though I were in difficulty."

Derrick nodded quickly. "That would be it, sir. I weren't meaning to interfere."

Gabriel gestured to Derrick that it was safe to leave, and he gave a little bow before turning on his heel and hurrying down the stairs, leaving Gabriel to face a thunderous Arthur. "For pity's sake, man, will you leave me in peace!" came Arthur's predictable admonition. "I can't see anyone today, not even you."

Gabriel glanced warily at Arthur. Every time he had set eyes on him since Daphne's death, Arthur had appeared more sickly and haggard. This time, the cause of Arthur's red, clammy complexion was obvious from the unmistakable odour of whisky on the man's breath. "Arthur, come with me," Gabriel pleaded. "You shouldn't be alone at a time like this. My in-laws won't mind at all; they'll be happy to welcome you."

Arthur shook his head, but everything about his demeanour looked exhausted to the point of death. "Do you remember how you felt when your wife died? The first thing you did was to disappear into a monastery. Don't deny me my need for solitude now."

"Arthur, that's not entirely fair," Gabriel began, but he could already see Arthur's eyes glazing over. "I was homeless; my home had been burnt down. I went where I was made welcome, and so should—" The door closed with a quiet but determined thud, leaving Gabriel standing stupidly on the landing. He waited a moment on the off chance that Arthur would change his mind, then walked slowly down the stairs and out into the cold, dank air.

Of course the poor man had a right to his privacy; Gabriel remembered the overwhelming urge he had had in the weeks and months that followed Giovanna and Nicoletta's death, simply to curl away in his room and hide from the world. It was true that he had gone to live in a monastery very soon after the tragedy. He had been a teacher at a Benedictine school in London, and the community had invited him to stay with them, partly because he really was homeless and had nowhere else to go, but also because they had known —as Gabriel now knew—that a man struck down by an unexpected tragedy should not be left to his own devices.

There were many areas of human existence that lay outside Gabriel's realm of experience, but not this. He knew something of what Arthur was going through; he knew the guilt that was tearing him apart. Gabriel knew, more than anything else, that he would have to persuade Arthur to trust him if he was ever to find out who had killed Daphne. Did Arthur know? Or worse, had Arthur's initial claim—that Daphne's death had not been an accident—been a clumsy attempt at a confession? Gabriel turned onto Chesterton Road and walked home with the greatest sense of relief.

Home. It felt very like home now.

9

It was dark when Gabriel awoke, but the days were still so short that he was used to rising in what felt like the middle of the night. He was not sure how much he had actually slept, despite being sent to bed after a good dinner and more grappa than he dared contemplate, but he had drifted in and out of sleep for hours. He did not remember that the Gervasonis had ever been early risers, and there was certainly no other sound in the house as he washed and dressed, apart from a light scratching emanating from the loft, which he suspected to be mice.

The sound of Papa Gervasoni's tuneful snoring reassured Gabriel a little as he tiptoed across the landing and down the stairs, as the house felt quite forlorn without the bustle of human activity. Gabriel hesitated at the kitchen door, wondering whether he should make himself some breakfast, but a nagging sense of urgency sent him straight to the coat stand and the rituals of preparing to face the outside world. Before leaving, he tore a piece of paper off the notepad he found taped to the table next to the telephone and scribbled a quick memo, saying that he had been called away urgently but would return by the evening.

It felt rude, as though he were using his mother-in-law's house as a free hotel; Gabriel stifled the sense of guilt rising in him with the thought that Arthur's comfort was surely more important, and the Gervasonis would understand that. Every inner voice had told Gabriel not to leave Arthur on his own last night, but Arthur was a grown man, and Gabriel could hardly have forced him to come to a place of safety with him. Even so, Gabriel could not be easy in his mind until he had spoken with Arthur, though he doubted whether his friend would thank him for waking him at such an hour.

Gabriel could feel the morning mist condensing on his face as he walked down the road in the dim light, the clip-clop of the milkman's pony echoing in the funereal quiet. The town was not as dead as it looked; Gabriel could see lights flickering through the cracks in sitting room curtains and was aware that households all around him were beginning to stir. A solitary angler sat on the riverbank, dangling his line in the water as though he had never caught a fish in his entire life and was not about to get his hopes up now. The old man's position, so close to the foot of the bridge, made Gabriel think of the Three Billy Goats Gruff; and he stifled a nervous giggle, hastily quickening his pace when the angler looked round.

The terrible thought had haunted Gabriel from the moment Arthur had first told him that Daphne's death was all his fault. Gabriel could not avoid the possibility that Arthur might have been stating a simple truth. It might not be that he felt guilty for working Daphne too hard so that she became tired and clumsy; it might not even be that he had pushed her too far, had placed such high expectations on her shoulders that—unbeknownst to him—she had taken to working late into the night to hurry up her results. He might really have killed her. Not through carelessness or overambition—he might be Daphne's killer in the most literal sense of the word.

Arthur could never have done that, said Gabriel, then checked himself. How many men of his generation could honestly say that they had never killed anyone? Most of them had been soldiers, even if for a short time, and had to accept the possibility that someone had died at their hands. During the first war, hand-to-hand combat had been less frequent than civilians fondly imagined, but soldiers had still ended lives —enemy troops mown down advancing into machine-gun fire or blown to bits by grenades. Men just like them with families and loved ones and plans for the future. If a man had been trained to kill in one context, might he not be capable of the same outrage in another?

It's not at all the same thing! Gabriel raged internally. Daphne was a civilian, a young woman, and she was known to Arthur. But even that excuse lacked conviction in the knowledge that most women are killed by someone they know. Daphne would not have thought twice if Arthur had come into the lab and started fumbling about with a canister near to where she was standing; by the time he had bolted for the door, it would have been too late.

The college was as quiet as the grave, and Gabriel almost tiptoed across the quad and up the stairs to Arthur's room. To his surprise, the outer door opened easily when he tried it, and Gabriel stepped inside, calling Arthur's name softly in case he had fallen asleep in his chair, too distressed to get up and lock the door. "Arthur, it's me," he said quietly, switching on the light. The tiny sitting room was empty. Gabriel's eye was drawn to the coat stand, and he noticed that Arthur's coat, hat and boots were missing. He knocked on the connecting door to Arthur's bedroom, opening it almost immediately, as he knew he would not get a response.

The bedroom, too, was deserted. Arthur's bed was neatly made, the counterpane carefully folded back, and a man's blue-and-white-striped pyjamas placed in a neat pile on the pillow. The one aberration was Arthur's key, which lay on the bedside table, forgotten about by Arthur in his distracted state. In every other detail, he had gone through all the rituals of the morning that he had learnt at boarding school, but he had done so a few hours earlier than usual. Gabriel turned on his heel and hurried out of Arthur's rooms, taking the stairs two at a time. He could see a light on in the porter's lodge and dashed across the quad, praying that the ubiquitous Mr Derrick would be in residence.

"It's ever so early!" exclaimed Derrick when Gabriel burst in. "I've only just arrived meself."

That much was evident, as Derrick had not yet removed his coat and was still catching his breath from the walk. "I know this sounds mad," Gabriel said, certain he could see the flicker of a smile on Derrick's face. "It's just that I need to see Dr Kingsley rather urgently, and he seems to have left already."

Derrick shrugged. "He were never such an early bird before that lass of his died," he said, stepping behind the counter and disappearing from view. "Not sure he's sleeping at all. Not that I can blame him."

"Well, yes . . . ," Gabriel began, but he could not remember what he had intended to say and trailed off. "Yes."

Derrick reappeared, holding a kettle. "Would you like a cuppa?"

Gabriel shook his head. "No, I must go to the lab and see if I can find him there." He remembered what he had been going to ask. "Mr Derrick, do you have the master key to the lab?"

Derrick shook his head emphatically. "No, no, I'm strictly a college man. Labs and lecture halls aren't my business." He seemed to notice Gabriel's disappointment. "Not to worry, though. If Dr Kingsley's not there and you need to get in urgently, I can show you a way in."

Gabriel nodded in thanks before heading out into the street. It was a measure of how much Mr Derrick trusted Gabriel that he was prepared to make such an admission; any way he had of getting into a laboratory containing dangerous chemicals and valuable equipment was almost certainly illegal.

Gabriel was not the world's most accomplished cyclist, but he would have been grateful for the loan of a bicycle. The walk took no more than fifteen minutes at a brisk pace, but it felt interminable with his thoughts racing. Gabriel checked his watch but realised that he had forgotten to wind it—it had stopped at nineteen minutes past two. He could hear a bell chiming from the direction of Our Lady and the English Martyrs Church. Instinctively, he began praying the Angelus.

> The angel of the Lord declared unto Mary,
> And she conceived of the Holy Spirit . . .

Gabriel was in luck for once. As he hurried down the little side street where Arthur's lab was situated, he noticed lights on at the top of the building. But his momentary sense of relief quickly evaporated as he drew nearer. At the top of the steps the main door hung open, and Gabriel could hear the faint sounds of a commotion somewhere deep inside the building. He broke into a run.

There were two male voices clamouring for attention, a younger and an older, neither of which was immediately recognisable to Gabriel . . . except that the older voice was definitely not Arthur's. Gabriel tore up the stairs, giddy with the exertion, almost colliding with Will Valentine when he reached the landing. He was too anxious to stop and ask Will what on earth he thought he was doing and pushed past him to the doorway of Arthur's study.

Dr Crayford and Robert Sutton were on their knees, huddled over a prone figure. Gabriel did not need to be able to see the man's face to know that they were trying to revive Arthur. Gabriel's eye caught the grotesque remains of a noose hanging from the beam above his head. "Has someone called an ambulance?" asked Gabriel desperately, but he could feel bile rising in his throat and clutched the lintel for support. He wanted to push the other men away, he wanted to kneel by his friend's body and hear him breathing, feel a pulse in his neck, know for certain that Arthur's colleagues had arrived in time to save him.

"The ambulance is on its way," said Dr Crayford, "but they're on a fool's errand." Gabriel saw Crayford grasp Robert's wrist. "Leave him, old chap. He's not going to wake up."

"I thought I saw his lips move," said Robert pathetically. "I did, I'm sure. He can't have been hanging long before we came in; he'd only just arrived. We both heard him come in."

Crayford stood up slowly, his knees creaking with arthritic

pain, before taking Robert by the shoulders and coaxing him to his feet. "We've no idea how long he was hanging there, old man. He was almost certainly dead when we brought him down. It's a quick method; he knew what he was doing."

Gabriel knelt down beside Arthur's lifeless body, frantically pressing his wrist in spite of himself. Arthur was clearly dead and, as Crayford had hinted, had probably been dead for several minutes before he was found. It was not for nothing that hanging was the chosen method of execution in this country; it might be a humiliating way to die, strung up like a carcass in a butcher's shop, but it was quick, and Arthur would have lost consciousness within seconds. Even if he had had a sudden, last-minute loss of nerve, he would have been unable to call for help.

"Oh Arthur, I'm sorry," said Gabriel out loud. He could see the abrasion snaking its way around Arthur's neck and throat, and a small cut beneath his left ear. It was no surprise that Arthur had cut himself shaving, given the distress he had been in, except that that cut had not been there when Gabriel had seen Arthur on the previous night, and he had clearly not shaved that morning, if the light shadow of stubble on Arthur's face was anything to go by.

"Come away, Father," said a voice behind him, and Gabriel turned around to see Robert looking sadly down at him. "I'm sorry, I know he was your friend too. But we should probably leave him now. The ambulance is here; they want to . . ." His voice cracked, either through grief or embarrassment. Gabriel could see two men carrying a stretcher between them, attempting to enter the tiny room. Gabriel nodded and grasped Arthur's cold hand as though taking leave of him. There were ink stains on Arthur's fingers, and two of his fingernails were broken and bloodied, as though Arthur had indeed had a sudden change of heart at the last second and struggled in vain to free himself from the noose that was strangling the life out of him. Gabriel was sure he had heard somewhere that even the most determined of suicides always struggle at the last.

As Gabriel rose to his feet, he noticed ink stains on the floor and splattered against the wall opposite the desk. He avoided looking at the desk, knowing that Arthur must have used it as a platform to reach the beam. He asked, "Did he leave a note? He was writing something."

Robert went over to the desk and picked up a folded piece of writing paper. "Do you want me to read it?" he asked tremulously.

Gabriel removed the paper from Robert's hand and opened it. Arthur's normally elegant, well-crafted handwriting looked rather shakier than Gabriel ever remembered, but it was unquestionably his. The note read:

> I am a murderer. I have innocent blood on my hands, and I cannot live with myself. I know that this may appear to be the cowardly way out, but I believe that sacrificing my life is honourable, perhaps the only honourable act I have ever committed. I cannot face the future burdened with the knowledge of what I have done, nor do I have any right to enjoy my life. I pray that my friends and my students will find it in their hearts to forgive me, but I truly believe that the world will be a better place without me.

Gabriel's eyes began to swim. He felt someone gently but firmly removing the paper from his fingers and placing it back on the desk, then Crayford's voice saying, "You'd better leave that there, Father. The police will need it for evidence. There will have to be an—"

"An inquest," finished Gabriel quietly. "I know."

"Would you like me to walk you home?" asked Crayford. "You're in shock."

Gabriel was about to decline the offer when Crayford made a bolt for the door and stormed out onto the landing, shouting, "Get out! Who let you in here? *Get out!*"

"Take your hands off me. I'm only doing my job!" It was Will Valentine. In all the drama, Gabriel had forgotten that he had seen Will skulking on the stairs. "I've every right to be here!"

"You've no right whatsoever, you repulsive little weasel! Are you a member of this department? I do not recall that you were a member of Dr Kingsley's team."

Gabriel's mind snapped back into focus, and he listened intently to the row going on a few feet from him. He leaned heavily against the lintel of the door again, not quite able to stand unaided.

"Look, I've got an editor to please. I'm not interfering."

"You most certainly are interfering! How dare you come sniffing around here? A man is dead, for pity's sake!"

"I know; what do you think I wanted to write about?"

Gabriel heard the thud of a fist hitting flesh, and a body hit the ground heavily. He stepped out onto the landing to see Will Valentine sprawled ignominiously on his back, with Crayford standing over him and Robert making pathetic attempts at restraining the far-larger man from thumping Will a second time.

At the sight of Gabriel's pale face staring at them, Crayford shook Robert off irritably and backed away from the cowering reporter. "Just go," he said coldly, glaring down at Will. "If I catch you in this building again, I'll have you arrested."

"How did you know he was dead?" asked Gabriel softly. "I didn't know he was dead when I passed you, and these gentlemen had only just discovered him. How could you have known that Dr Kingsley was going to die this morning?"

Will scrambled to his feet, dusting down his rumpled jacket in a desperate attempt at looking nonchalant. "I . . . I didn't. I mean, I didn't know he was dead when I arrived here."

Crayford's cold glare turned into a sneer. "So, a busy reporter just happened to come to the lab at this ungodly hour on the off chance that someone might top himself?"

Will shook his head frantically. Crayford was the sort of man who might have enjoyed an illustrious career in the KGB by the effect his question had on Will. The boy—and he did look very like a young boy on the receiving end of Crayford's anger—stood with his shoulders drooping and positively stammered his answer. "I . . . I wanted to get an exclusive. I went to Dr Kingsley's college last night to try to talk to him, but this awful porter kicked me out and told me not to come back."

"Good man," answered Crayford.

Will ignored him. "I didn't dare go back to college again so I thought if I came here very early, I might catch Dr Kingsley on his way into his lab. I thought I could persuade him to give me an interview about the dead girl. It would have been a scoop."

Crayford's right hand had curled itself into a fist again, but Will was already backing away in the direction of the stairs and freedom. "Journalists really are parasites, aren't they?" observed Crayford to Gabriel, though the only person with whom he was trying to communicate was Will, who had had the sense to hurry down the stairs before he could be asked any further awkward questions. To Gabriel's surprise, Robert went after him, but he doubted Will would be in any imminent danger from Robert. "Parasites!" hissed Crayford again. "If that little twerp had thought to knock on Arthur's door, he might have stopped him committing suicide."

But Gabriel's thoughts were taking an infinitely darker turn. He stepped back into Arthur's study and looked at the ink stains on the floor and wall, then back at the desk. "I wonder why he smashed the ink bottle after writing the note," he mused out loud.

Crayford looked askance at Gabriel. "What has that to do with anything?"

Gabriel searched the desk unsuccessfully for an ink bottle, then looked into the wastepaper basket. To Crayford's evident disgust, he stuck his hand in and pulled out two halves of a broken bottle of India ink. "It seems a rather odd thing to do, don't you think?"

Crayford groaned in exasperation. "Father Gabriel, suicide is a rather odd thing to do, don't you think? The man was not in his right mind. If he hurled that bottle across the room in frustration, who could blame him?"

Gabriel shook his head resignedly. "I daresay you're right. My mind tends to become a little obsessed with details when I'm unsettled. Forget I asked."

Crayford gestured to Gabriel to follow him out of the room. "Are you staying in college?" asked Crayford casually. "This is going to sound awfully callous, but you may have to move if you were a guest . . ."

"I have family here in Cambridge," Gabriel cut in quickly, unable to bear the thought of what Crayford was about to say to him. "They are very kindly looking after me."

Crayford raised an eyebrow. "I was unaware that Roman priests had families."

"They are my late wife's parents," Gabriel answered, trying hard not to enjoy the thought that he had confused Crayford even more with the explanation. "I hope you won't mind me saying this, but I couldn't help thinking you were a little harsh with young Mr Valentine. I don't approve of his behaviour either, but I daresay he has a job to do. It must be rather daunting to have to keep finding stories to satisfy a demanding editor."

"Spare your sympathy for the people he's hurt," snapped Crayford, making for the stairs. "If he doesn't get his story, he simply makes it up. He is a liar, a barefaced liar, like all journalists." Crayford seemed to notice that he was raising his voice and swallowed audibly. "Look here, I hardly need tell you what two deaths in one department will mean for us. It will take months to pick up the pieces. The last thing any of us needs is that little worm wriggling about."

Gabriel cleared his throat. "Dr Crayford, Arthur was my very dear friend. If there is anything I can do . . ."

Crayford shook his head briskly. "The best thing you can do is to leave, Father. I don't mean to be unkind, but there really is nothing to be achieved by staying here and moping."

"I thought perhaps I might——"

"I've heard that you fancy yourself as something of a Sherlock Holmes," said Crayford, "but there really is nothing to investigate here. If anyone was responsible for Daphne's death—directly or indirectly—that man is now dead by his own hand." Crayford began to walk away, and Gabriel knew he was expected to follow, but he remained where he was. After a few steps, Crayford turned to ensure that Gabriel was walking behind him, noted Gabriel standing stolidly some way from him and gave an exasperated smile. "If you leave your address at the porter's lodge, I will ensure that you are informed of the funeral arrangements. I daresay you will want to pay your respects."

"Thank you," said Gabriel, still not moving. "It's quite all right, I can find my own way back to my lodgings. I know Cambridge very well."

Crayford took the hint and walked away a little too abruptly, leaving Gabriel in much-needed peace. Gabriel knew Crayford's type. Dr Crayford had spent much of his adult life living amongst those who were, in the most part, weaker than he. He was not used to being crossed or even challenged, but Gabriel luxuriated in the blessing of being an outsider. He did not have to worry about losing his position if this man took a dislike to him.

He did not die by his own hand, thought Gabriel, returning slowly to Arthur's room. *That much is abundantly obvious to anyone who knew him.* The trouble was that the police had not known Arthur Kingsley, and they would be told merely that he was a lonely old man reeling from the shock of a dear pupil's death. And why wouldn't such a man be driven to end it all? A team of policemen would arrive shortly to make a cursory examination of the place of death. They would take note of the crudely manufactured noose and the scribbled suicide note before filing away Arthur's death as a suicide. *But this was not suicide*. It was not just Gabriel's fear for his dear friend's soul that convinced him. Any doubts he had had over the circumstances of Daphne's death had been swept away by Arthur's obvious murder.

Gabriel tried desperately to pray: *Eternal rest grant unto him, O Lord . . . perpetual light . . .* But the sight of the noose fluttering lightly in the draught started a pulse hammering in his neck. He simply could not accept that—just minutes before —his frightened, desperate friend had been strung up like a criminal and had died the most terrifying and humiliating of deaths, struggling to release himself from the ever-tightening grip of a rope as it crushed his windpipe and choked him.

Let perpetual light . . . he plunges at me, guttering, choking, drowning . . . Let perpetual light shine upon him . . . guttering . . . choking . . .

Gabriel tugged at his hair, the words of the old prayer merging with the more macabre words of a soldier-poet. Why should any man hurl an ink bottle against the wall in a fit of anger after writing a confession so replete with sorrow and resignation? If Arthur had only been a better shot, he might have hit the man at whom he had flung that bottle, bought himself a few seconds to escape or—at the very least—marked out his killer in indelible ink. Arthur would have had a few seconds' grace after writing that final word of dictation. His killer must have momentarily lowered the knife he had held to Arthur's throat, cutting him slightly in his determination to force Arthur's cooperation. Perhaps he had heard a noise or feared that he was about to be disturbed and moved to the door, giving Arthur a moment to act . . .

Gabriel's thoughts were interrupted by the sight of a small wet patch on the floor directly underneath the noose. He felt his temper rise. As so often happened when a man died that way, Arthur had lost control of his bladder as he had dropped down. It was a bizarre detail to cause such stirrings of rage in Gabriel, but the indignity of Arthur's death hit him like a blow to the face. *I will find out who did this*, thought Gabriel. He had not felt anger like this since his wife's death. *Whatever you did in life, whatever you were trying to confess to me —even if it was the death of your pupil—you did not deserve this.*

Gabriel walked out of the room and did not stop until he had reached the welcome anonymity of the bustling market square.

10

When Gabriel arrived back at the Gervasoni home, he was surprised to find Mama clearing away the breakfast things. He had got himself out of bed, washed, dressed, walked to college and then to Arthur's lab, discovered his friend dead and discerned that his suicide had been murder . . . all in the time during which most people in this town had been gently waking to greet the day, getting up and enjoying a leisurely breakfast.

Mama took one look at Gabriel's pale, thunderous face and ushered him indoors without a word. Whatever questions she might have had as to what on earth he had been up to at the crack of dawn, she clearly knew better than to ask them. Wordlessly, she helped him out of his coat and hat. Gabriel could smell coffee and toast, mingled with the scent of rosewater Mama had sprinkled liberally on herself that morning. Somewhere at the end of an invisible tunnel, he heard Mama speak for the first time. "Whatever have you got on your jacket?"

Gabriel looked glassily in her direction; she was pointing at the coat she was now holding over her one arm. About three-quarters of the way down the side of Gabriel's coat, a couple of tiny rose-pink slivers of colour flashed at him, lurid against the black wool. He stared down at them in confusion before feeling the old flash of anger again. "Does it matter? It's only a coat!"

Mama patted his arm. "You sit down and pour yourself some coffee. There's some in the pot. I'll clean this for you. I'm sure I have some varnish remover upstairs."

Gabriel managed a smile as he stepped through to the kitchen before returning abruptly to the hall, his brain snapping into focus. "Varnish remover? *Nail* varnish remover?"

Mama held up the coat. "Yes, that's what it looks like. I can't think how, but you've got a spot of nail varnish on your coat. If I dab it a little, it will come off, I'm sure. Unless . . ." She scraped her nail against the mark, which came away from the surface of the coat with relatively little effort.

"But where on earth . . ." Gabriel saw himself back in Arthur's room, leaning repeatedly against the lintel of the door to stop himself falling in his distress, his coat rubbing against the wooden door frame. He looked down at Mama, but her face blurred and swirled before his eyes. "He did kill her. It wasn't an accident. It wasn't negligence. He killed her in that room and moved her body."

Gabriel was aware of Mama dropping the coat and propelling him into the kitchen, where the warmth of the stove enveloped him like a tender embrace. "Sit down," said Mama determinedly. "What are you talking about?"

Gabriel placed his head in his hands as though he could forcibly stop the dizziness that was overtaking him. "Daphne Silverton's nail varnish was on the doorframe. That's how it ended up on my coat. I noticed in the mortuary that she wore nail varnish—I remember thinking it strange that a scientist would paint her nails at all—but her nail varnish was chipped, as though she'd dragged her fingernails against something hard."

"I thought the young lady died in her laboratory?"

"It's what we were all supposed to think. I thought she'd been moved, but I couldn't be sure from where. Her body might simply have been moved to a different part of the lab. But the gas was released in the study—it can't possibly have been an accident because there would never normally be chemicals lying about in a room like that. Daphne tried to get out of the room; she should have been able to get out. The door opened easily for me—I remember that it opened easily—but she was trapped. She spent her final terrified seconds trying to get the door open whilst someone on the other side held it shut."

Mama sat down at the table beside Gabriel and held his hands. "Do you want that I call the police?"

Gabriel shook his head. "They'll never believe me; it sounds too farfetched. They believe that Daphne Silverton had a nasty accident whilst working late in her lab, that she knocked over that canister and poisoned herself. Now they will believe that Arthur Kingsley blamed himself for her death and killed himself."

Mama jumped back as though he had electrocuted her. "You didn't tell me—your friend? Your friend whom you came to visit?"

"He was found hanged this morning. There was a note. It looks so very much as though he hanged himself because he felt responsible for that girl's death. He didn't commit suicide, but the police will not believe that either. As far as I can see, either Arthur really did kill Daphne and could not live with the consequences, or someone killed them both."

Mama got up and poured Gabriel a cup of reviving coffee, placing it in front of him with a plate of small round rolls.

"Fortify yourself," she said—and it was not a suggestion—"and let's work this out together. If two people have been murdered in this little university, it cannot be so very hard to work out who did it. Who would want to?"

"That's the trouble," said Gabriel, taking a gulp of the coffee. "There are people who *might* have done it, but there is no obvious reason why any of them *would* have done it."

"Let's start with those people, shall we? Then we worry about why."

Gabriel shook his head. The rolls sat in an inviting little circle on his plate, but he had no appetite whatsoever. He picked them up one by one and, much to Mama's stifled indignation, began placing them in a row on the scrubbed tabletop. "Mrs Bellinger was Daphne's landlady. She was distressed to hear about Daphne's death and appears to have treated her more like a daughter than a lodger. She recruited Daphne into the Peace Pledge Union and probably felt very disappointed and betrayed when Daphne was talked into severing her links with that group. But I find it hard to imagine a pacifist killing two people on those grounds."

Gabriel nudged a larger, fatter roll into line. "Then there was Dr Crayford. I get the impression that he had very little time for either Arthur or Daphne. He had easy access to the building in which they both died, and he was present around the time at which Arthur died. I'm not sure, but I'd imagine that it would have been relatively easy for him to slip into Arthur's office on the night of Daphne's death and set that trap for her."

"Is he a man who could murder?" asked Mama.

"Anyone might murder under the right circumstances, but I can't see a reason other than jealousy . . . though men have murdered for less than jealousy. If he knew that they were about to make some major discovery—I was told that Daphne was very close to something—I suppose that might be a motive. But then, the only person he seemed to want to murder this morning was Will Valentine."

"Who's he?"

"Reporter on a local newspaper."

Mama Gervasoni gave a snort of contempt, and Gabriel immediately regretted mentioning Will Valentine's name at all. Following Giovanna and Nicoletta's death, the Gervasonis had gone into hiding to avoid the whispers and rumours that had found them even in Cambridge. If Will Valentine had been the victim, Gabriel was not sure Mama would be giving him quite so much encouragement to investigate. Gabriel placed another roll in the line. "I'm worried about that young man," he conceded. "His profession is his business of course, but he was skulking about the lab at a most convenient time, and I know Daphne had rejected a proposal of marriage from him."

Mama cackled knowingly. "A crime of passion—that sounds much more likely. But in Italy jealous lovers usually stab people; they don't take quite so much trouble about it."

"Quite. But I wouldn't put Will Valentine down as an impulsive type. Beware the wrath of a patient man." Another roll, the smallest of the lot. "Then there's young Robert Sutton."

"Another lover?"

"Hardly, he bats for the other side. Let's call the relationship fraternal. He had already lost an adopted sister, and he may have seen Daphne as a substitute of sorts."

"Because of the war?"

"Pneumonia. But for all his apparent grief, Robert Sutton may not be beyond a little jealousy himself. It's not easy working in the shadow of greatness, and he was quite obviously in Daphne's shadow. Dear old Arthur made very little attempt at hiding his preference for Daphne."

"It's very bad to have favourites, like having a favourite child," said Mama. "We do not speak ill of the dead, but it was foolish of your friend to favour one over the other. Especially a woman. Men are very jealous creatures."

Gabriel winced, wondering if she was right. Her comment certainly made him realise momentarily what it might be like to be a woman, constantly on the receiving end of sweeping generalisations about being the weaker sex and the like. He hesitated, the final little roll suspended between his thumb and forefinger. "It feels like the worst disloyalty to say it, but Mr Derrick knew Arthur and Daphne very well. He knew their movements; he knew where they worked. He told me himself that he could get into the lab if he needed to. But why?"

"Are you going to eat the food I put before you or not?" demanded a shrill female voice. Gabriel looked blankly at Mama, who was standing over him like a slighted hostess. Which of course she was. As he had been taking himself through the list of possible suspects, he had failed to notice that his mother-in-law was becoming more and more irritated by his use of her cooking as investigative props. Meekly, he took a bite out of one of the rolls, signalling his immediate approval. Mama looked so very like Giovanna when she was cross that he wondered whether his wife would one day have looked like that, if her black curls had been permitted to turn a delicate silver and her face had lost its girlish roundness. Giovanna still had dimples at the time she died. He struggled to swallow but finished the roll and started on another. Mama topped up his coffee again.

"I can't seem to find the why," said Gabriel. "For the first time in my life I wish I had studied science."

"Their work might have had nothing to do with it," suggested Mama. "Can you even be sure it is one of those people? Could not someone have walked in off the street and killed them?"

Gabriel shook his head. "I suppose it might be possible, but this feels too deliberate. Whoever did it would have had to have at least some knowledge of science."

"Some knowledge only. It's not just professors who know about poisons. Anyone can learn about such things."

"The killer would have had to gain access to the lab."

Mama was beginning to enjoy herself. "If that man you mentioned said he could get in, anyone could find a way. This reporter man got in too, didn't he?"

Gabriel could feel himself being painted into a corner. "The death was out of the ordinary. There was no robbery," he ventured. "Daphne was not . . . well . . . not violated, I mean. It seems to me that whoever did this was someone very close to both of them. Women are almost always killed by people they trust." *Not my wife, not my daughter*, thought Gabriel, praying his mother-in-law would not draw attention to this obvious fact. *They were killed by some crazed mob, and the police never found out who started the fire.*

"If your friend killed this Daphne but did not kill himself, then his killer must have found out what he did to Daphne and killed him."

187

Gabriel dropped his head onto the table, exhausted. He wondered whether wartime codebreakers had felt like this. "I'm not even entirely sure how the blasted murders happened!" he wailed, not lifting his head. "Did one person kill them both? Were there two killers? Did Arthur kill Daphne and get treated to a dose of rough justice? Have I missed a variable somewhere?"

Mama had lost the thread of Gabriel's ramblings and smiled at Gabriel's bowed head. "What are you going to do?" she asked. "You know you can stay here as long as you need."

Gabriel sat up slowly and took Mama's hand again. In that tantalising moment, his life at the abbey seemed light-years away, just the whisper of a past existence. He was where he was always meant to be, sitting at the family table in his wife's childhood home, enjoying the generous hospitality of one of the only family members he had left. He forced the thought out of his mind and answered, "*Grazie, Mama. Lo so.*"

Gabriel felt so emotionally and mentally exhausted that part of him wanted to stay where he was—warm and safe— until the storm had passed, but he stood up reluctantly. He knew that he would never untangle the web into which he had fallen if he did not act before the killer had the chance to cover his tracks. "There are some people I need to talk to," he said, gulping down the rest of his coffee and hoping he did not seem rude. "May I give this address to my abbot when I send him a telegram? I'd rather no messages came for me at college. I can't be sure . . ."

"Of course you can; you needn't have asked."

Mama helped Gabriel into his coat, but he noted her hands

trembling and turned to face her, just in time to witness her wiping tears from her eyes. "Mama? What is it?"

"You will be careful, won't you, my son?" she whispered. "I know I'm being silly, but I don't like this. You have the devil at your heels again. *Non mi piace*. You will be careful, won't you?"

It had not occurred to Gabriel that anyone would think he was in any kind of danger, but he embraced her. "It's all right, Mama. There's nothing to worry about. Everyone thinks that this was a tragic accident followed by a suicide."

"Someone else knows that's not true. Please catch the killer before he catches you. You're my only link with my daughter."

She was overwrought, of course; that was all. It was that pall of death again, looming like early morning mist that never cleared to let the sun through. Gabriel wondered whether there had ever been a really sunny day for the Gervasonis since their daughter and granddaughter's death and whether there would ever be such a day for Robert Sutton. He hurried down Chesterton Road, aware of how familiar it was beginning to feel. The sight of shops with their colourful awnings and prettily dressed windows made Gabriel think that he really ought to purchase some gift for his in-laws as a way of thanking them for their kindness to him. He could not imagine many other families coping quite so calmly with the sudden appearance of an errant son-in-law after years of absence, bringing with him a whirlwind of drama and death. The inevitable tin of biscuits felt like poor recompense somehow.

When Gabriel arrived on Robert Sutton's staircase, he

was surprised to see Dr Crayford emerging from Robert's rooms. Crayford froze momentarily at the sight of Gabriel before giving an exasperated sigh. "Father Gabriel, you are becoming the veritable bad penny," he said with gratingly forced joviality. "Haven't you a monastery to return to? Or have you been defrocked?"

"The term is laicised," replied Gabriel, as though he seriously imagined Crayford were interested in the technicalities. "I have not pushed my abbot to those lengths yet, *Deo gratias.*"

Crayford's eyes rolled heavenwards as he brushed past Gabriel and made his way down the stairs, leaving Gabriel free to offend Robert Sutton with his unexpected presence. He did not have time to knock at Robert's door, as Robert had overheard the conversation and came to greet him. He stood wraithlike in the doorway, glancing wearily in Gabriel's direction. "He came to discuss my PhD," explained Robert, stepping aside to let Gabriel in. "I feel as though I'm drowning, and all my former supervisor is interested in is how I'm going to finish my doctorate."

"I suppose he's trying to help," Gabriel ventured, shivering involuntarily. There was the faint, sour odour of neglect in the freezing sitting room. It looked as though Robert had refused to let the gyp inside to light the fire and attend to the room for several days, dealing with the problem by wearing his coat and college scarf wrapped tightly about him. Gabriel ignored his own discomfort and sat down. Even the piano stool was cold. "I daresay Dr Crayford is worried that you've worked so hard and might not write up."

"The road to hell is paved with unfinished theses, Father," said Robert tersely, dropping down into the opposite chair as though he were halfway to fainting. "Most people can't blame the loss of their lab head and colleague for the failure. Sorry." He looked glassily into the empty grate, transparently avoiding looking at Gabriel. "What was it you wanted?"

"I wanted to see that you were all right," answered Gabriel truthfully. "I think I know something of what you're going through."

"You know nothing about how this feels," answered Robert, his mottled, rash-covered hands clasped together like the claws of an animal. "Men like you never get close to anyone. It's your job."

"I had a wife and child once," said Gabriel. "I came to the religious life quite late. Our house burnt down, and I was not there. By the time I returned, the place was a raging inferno, and they were trapped. I couldn't get them out."

Robert glanced slowly at Gabriel, horrified. "You're a widower? That's terrible. I'm so sorry; I had no idea. I didn't realise you people could become priests later in life."

"Some of us come late to the vineyard, and we bring our grief with us."

Robert looked searchingly at Gabriel. "Does it ever get any better? When Sarah died, I felt as though I should die too. I can't even describe how it felt—I wanted to run into the middle of a field and scream, it hurt so much. But this time I can't feel anything. That's why it feels like drowning. I feel as though some outside force is killing me, and I just have to sit here and let it happen."

"I promise it does get better," said Gabriel solemnly. "I shan't lie to you and say that life will ever be the same again for you; you will always feel the absence of the people you loved. But eventually, you'll pick yourself up from the floor and stand up again. You will find a reason to live."

"I'm not sure I believe you," said Robert, looking away again. "Plenty of people never recover. Why should I? I'm not a strong man, never have been. I've surrounded myself with strong people who know how to live because I don't. Sarah and Daphne were so alike in that way. They always seemed so excited simply to be alive."

Gabriel noticed the photograph of Sarah that Robert had shown him the other day. "You said that Sarah was Jewish," he said. There was nothing surprising about this, as there were thousands of Jews in London—especially in the East End, where the bombing had been particularly ferocious—but Gabriel was always interested in people's religious backgrounds.

Robert smiled wanly. "She wasn't at all religious, Father. None of her family were. If it hadn't been for Adolf Hitler, I'm not sure she would even have been aware of her heritage. But she stood out in Oxfordshire. She was dark and beautiful. I used to think of her like one of those women from the Old Testament, Ruth or Esther. You would have said she had a Madonna face, I suppose. That was the other thing that Sarah and Daphne had in common. They were both so beautiful, but they didn't even seem to notice. They weren't vain or silly about it."

Gabriel sat in silence letting Robert talk, knowing that the best way to help a grieving man was to sit and listen, but Robert had trailed off and seemed troubled by the silence that descended between them. Gabriel risked the question. "Robert, you did love Daphne, didn't you? The rumours weren't true."

Robert unclasped his hands and touched his head as though he had a sudden, roaring migraine. "I'm not a homosexual, Father," he said dismissively. "I know what people say; I'm not deaf. I suppose I rather wish people would just mind their own business, but they are wrong about that."

"You loved Daphne."

"More than you can imagine, but she could never have been mine. Even if she had wanted to be."

"You have been ill a very long time, haven't you? That's why you were discharged from the army early. I don't suppose you wanted to risk inflicting it on Daphne."

A moan of pain escaped Robert's mouth, and he began rocking to and fro in his chair like a little boy. "You knew all along, didn't you? You're one of these ghastly people who just notices things!"

"All I noticed was that the dates did not quite add up in terms of your studies and that something must have happened to cause you to leave the army in the middle of a major war. And grief and shock certainly take their toll on a man, but your sickness goes beyond grief. If you were avoiding getting involved with a woman you clearly adored, I could only assume one thing about your condition."

Robert stood up and walked over to the wall, pressing his forehead against it, which only made him look even more like a child in disgrace. "Well done, Father. Well done. I've got VD. I'm not an immoral man—I was brought up to be a very nice, clean, respectable boy—but army life can do terrible things. I was only trying to prove that I was one of the chaps. I just happened to pick a whore who'd not looked after herself desperately well. I may have been a bit of an idiot, but I'm not so wicked that I would ever have inflicted this upon a girl I loved. I can never marry; I can't risk passing this curse on to someone else."

Gabriel got up and went over to Robert, but he pushed Gabriel's arm away. "You mustn't despair; there are treatments these days. A doctor might be able to——"

"Not for me, Father. I've been under the care of doctors for years. They've managed to slow down the progress of the disease, but I have not responded to the drugs as well as they had hoped. They've not managed to get me clean, and they're unlikely to now." He sank his fingers into his hair as though he meant to start tearing it out. "It didn't stop me loving her, Father. You must understand, I would have laid down my life to protect Daphne. If I'd been there, I would have pushed her out of that room before she could succumb, even if it had meant suffocating myself. I'm not a chivalrous man—I can't say I'd take a bullet for any woman —but I would have done anything for her."

Then he was weeping. He turned around to face Gabriel, tears streaming down his face, and he slid down the wall, crumpling onto the floor out of sheer exhaustion. Gabriel knelt by his side and placed a hand on Robert's shuddering head, praying silently as the boy cried for Daphne and for Sarah and perhaps even a little bit for the mentor he had battled unsuccessfully to save.

"I should have died!" wailed Robert, slipping effortlessly into another stage of grief Gabriel knew well. "If I had died, nobody would have noticed; it wouldn't have mattered! Daphne's life meant something! She would have changed the world!"

"Your life matters too," said Gabriel, but he doubted Robert could hear him over his own convulsive sobs.

"Everyone loved Daphne! There are so many people hurt by her death; mine would have been different. Even old Crayford's upset, and nobody even believed he had a heart at all!"

Gabriel sat back on his heels. The torrent of grief, guilt and self-pity, Gabriel had expected, but not that. "I understood that Crayford barely knew Daphne."

Robert looked up, wiping his streaming nose on his coat sleeve. Wordlessly, Gabriel handed him his handkerchief. "Didn't you see the state Crayford was in when he left just now?" asked Robert.

"He didn't appear to be in a state to me," ventured Gabriel sheepishly. He wondered whether this was one of the many occasions in which he had misjudged the situation. No, the man had simply looked impatient.

"I suppose he is rather good at putting on a brave face," Robert conceded. "When he hauled me off for tea the other day, he spent the whole time talking about himself and how dreadful it all was. I wished he'd left me with Mr Derrick."

"Dr Crayford seemed to have very little time for Daphne." His mind flashed back to that dinner on the night Daphne had died, to Crayford's patronising dismissal of Arthur's belief in Daphne as little more than a middle-aged man's infatuation. "I rather thought he—"

"You really are one of life's innocents, aren't you?" asked Robert, his face suddenly hard and closed. "I don't imagine Dr Crayford's reputation will have followed him out of this splendid little town, but the man is a lecher. Can't glimpse a skirt without letting his hands wander. Hadn't you noticed?"

Gabriel coughed awkwardly. "Besides Daphne's, there

were no other skirts in the vicinity the evening of the dinner," he said, "and Daphne had you and Dr Kingsley to look after her. He would hardly have tried anything in such a public situation."

Robert made a dramatic show of forcing himself to his feet. "Fair enough, you couldn't have known. Dr Kingsley was besotted with Daphne's mind, and only her mind. He could see the great scientist she would become, and that was what attracted him to her. Old man Crayford could only ever see her as a pretty little doll to be slavered over. He only just avoided a scandal, thanks to the powers-that-be hushing everything up for him. He even tried to get Daphne sent down because he thought she'd squealed to the press."

Gabriel's mind was racing again. "Why did nobody tell me anything about this? A woman and her protector die within days of one another, and—"

"Father, why should anyone have told you anything? What has Daphne's accident and Dr Kingsley's suicide got to do with Crayford trying to get his dirty hands on yet another girl? He didn't get his way, if it helps."

"Did he hurt her?"

Robert chuckled, and Gabriel suspected that he would have given a hearty laugh if he had been in a better state. "No, she hurt him. At least we think she did. He turned up at the buttery for breakfast with a beauty of a black eye. Had us all believe he'd had a nasty fall. Of course, if a woman had said that, we would have been desperately trying to find out the name of the swine who'd thumped her, but everyone was too discreet to pester Crayford. We all knew anyway."

"Did this happen often?" asked Gabriel, appalled. His happy memories of a rarefied university existence were coming tumbling down about his ears.

"The black eyes?" asked Robert, misunderstanding the question. "No. The women didn't usually fight back. Too scared or surprised, I suppose."

Gabriel left Robert's rooms, having promised Robert faithfully not to tell a soul about his condition. Robert had even asked him to pretend that they had been in the confessional, though Gabriel had said that was quite unnecessary. He knew how to keep his mouth shut when he absolutely had to.

The moment his foot stepped down onto the first creaking wooden step, Gabriel was aware of a figure standing behind him. He tried to turn around, but a flabby hand grasped his shoulder, compelling him to continue on his way down the stairs. "Don't let's make a scene here, old chap," came Dr Crayford's clipped tones. "You've heard young Mr Sutton's little fantasies; now I think it's about time I put the record straight."

"It's disgracefully bad form to listen in on a private conversation," muttered Gabriel, reaching the bottom of the stairs with Crayford bearing down on him. "You had absolutely no business eavesdropping."

"It was absolutely my business when I knew I would be the subject of the conversation," Crayford retorted, falling into step next to Gabriel as they crossed the quad. "And since eavesdroppers never hear good of themselves, I have not been disappointed. Contrary to the puerile rumours that floated about this college after the event, I blacked my own eye tripping on the hem of my gown. I'm not in the habit of taking liberties with respectable young ladies."

"You crept up behind me on the stairs to tell me that?" asked Gabriel. "It seems a little melodramatic, if I may say so."

"I know your suspicions, ludicrous as they are," Crayford explained, "and I knew how it might look. I have better things to do with my life than to go chasing after fillies. If I had my way, women would not be allowed anywhere near this university in the first place. It lowers the tone."

If Crayford was attempting to use his own chauvinism as proof of his innocence, it was never going to wash with Gabriel. He knew perfectly well from the undesired male attention Giovanna had attracted that lechers were chauvinists by definition. Crayford might not have wanted female scholars in his precious university, but if he had made a pass at Daphne, it was for precisely the reasons Robert had mentioned. "Is that why you tried to have Daphne sent down then? You didn't believe she had any right to be at your university in the first place?"

Crayford drew in a deep breath. "I think you and I need to take a little stroll," he said. "Then I really would advise you to leave. Outsiders make themselves very unpopular at times like this."

They walked past Westminster College and down towards the Backs, where a long tree-lined road offered them a degree of privacy. What few passers-by they encountered were in a hurry and barely took note of two older men walking at a leisurely pace, deep in conversation. "Are you telling me that you had no argument with Daphne Silverton?"

"That is precisely what I'm telling you," Crayford assured him. "As I have already stated, I never touched the girl. And there was no reason for me to seek to have her sent down. Women may not have the intellectual brilliance of men, they may not have that spark of genius, but I have to hand it to them, they work hard. Daphne worked hard. I could not fault her in that regard."

Gabriel tried a different tack. "Was there anyone else on the fellowship who might have resented Daphne Silverton's presence here?"

"Enough to murder the young wench and make it look like an accident, then convince her lab head that it was all his fault and provoke him into taking his own life, you mean?" Crayford had gone out of his way to make Gabriel's suggestion sound as ludicrous as possible, and it did sound absolutely ludicrous spoken like that. "I think not. Half the members of my department are at daggers drawn with the other half, but there's never been bloodshed—yet."

Gabriel gave himself a moment to gather up his shattered pride. "Would you mind if I ask you another question?"

"I suspect you'll ask it anyway."

"Did Arthur work on the Bomb? He said he didn't, but you see, I'm not a scientist—"

"Evidently," commented Crayford dryly. "No, he most certainly did not work on the Bomb. Different discipline, different field."

"Yes, but Arthur left the university for a number of years, did he not?"

Crayford spun round to face Gabriel. "Now, I think that's enough, Father, if it's all the same to you. As my first-year students might have told you, I do not suffer fools gladly. Arthur spent years away from the university before, not during, the war, a little too early to be working on the development of an atomic bomb. Not that it would have fallen within his field of expertise. Where the devil did you get that notion from in the first place?"

Gabriel took a step back. They had reached the junction with Silver Street, which was a busy thoroughfare, and he found himself looking round to check that no one was listening in. After Crayford's brazen bout of eavesdropping, he was no longer sure that there were any private places left in Cambridge. "Before he died, Arthur showed me an anonymous note that had been pushed under his door, containing the word 'murderer'. He said there had been a few of those over the years. Have you any idea why Arthur might have been targeted like that?"

Crayford gave a contemptuous snort. "If one is a man of science, one gets used to this nonsense. There is a certain kind of ignoramus who believes that all science is wicked, and such people have been encouraged by recent events. The very same people who rage against the Bomb and the development of armaments forget that many of them are alive thanks to medical advances made possible by men like Arthur. Knowledge can always be misused. I suspect that little Daphne's dalliances with the Peace People—or whatever they call themselves—may have attracted a few cranks to Arthur's lab. For all you or I know, Daphne may have sent some of those messages herself."

"But why?" demanded Gabriel, astonished. "If she had found out something about Arthur's work that she believed to be immoral, surely she would have had it out with him face-to-face?"

"You never had to have anything out face-to-face with Arthur, did you?" asked Crayford. But before Gabriel could think up a response, Dr Crayford had stalked off, merging effortlessly with the gaggle of students loitering at the entrance of Queens' College.

It was not the first time Gabriel had investigated a crime involving someone he knew, but this felt very different to the battle he had fought to clear the name of a young doctor he had known only passably well. Investigating the death of a man with whom he held so many cherished memories, whom he had been privileged to call a friend during those heady, formative student days, felt tantamount to grave robbing. It really did feel as though he were trying to dig up his friend's body without any consideration for the horrors that would crawl out of him when he opened the coffin lid. He had never had a major confrontation with Arthur; he had never in the years he had known him, heard him completely lose control of his temper. He had certainly never felt afraid of him. But he was not a young woman or an intellectual rival.

Gabriel knew he could return home now. He could go to the Gervasonis, make his apologies, pack his knapsack and walk to the station. He was not a policeman; no one had asked him to go poking around in the private lives of Daphne Silverton and Arthur Kingsley. It occurred to him that even if he did get to the bottom of what had happened, it was unlikely that the police would take him seriously enough to act on the information he provided. Gabriel made his way onto King's Parade, pausing to listen to a clock chiming noon. Gabriel had not noticed how desperately hungry he was in the tumult of the morning, but he found himself looking round for somewhere to buy something to eat. He walked on an old instinct towards Fitzbillies, where he joined a queue of students waiting to be served.

Gabriel forced himself to remember the distressing details of Arthur's final moments. The struggle, the panic he must have felt. Gabriel recalled his own promise that he would find the person who did this for the sake of Arthur's memory. An inner voice screamed at him that he was doing this only because he could not bear to think that his friend could have committed the mortal sin of taking his own life. But he *knew* Arthur had been murdered.

"A Chelsea bun, please," said Gabriel to the smiling woman behind the counter.

Gabriel watched longingly as the soft, swirling pastry treat was removed from its tray and dropped into a paper bag. "You're lucky, my love," said the woman, giving him an indulgent grin. "It's the last one. Will you be wanting anything to drink with that?"

Gabriel heard murmured groans from the students behind him, at the sight of the last Chelsea bun disappearing from their grasp. "Might I have a bottle of pop? Oh dear, I feel greedy now," said Gabriel ruefully.

"You've bought it fair and square," she trilled, crouching down to examine whatever supply of drinks she still had available. "They know they have to queue up good and early to get one. Here." She plonked two small glass bottles onto the counter. "Lemonade or ginger beer?"

"Ginger beer, please."

The woman—whom Gabriel took to be almost old enough to be his mother—chuckled noisily as she took his money. "You big kid, you! Still, nothing like a taste of childhood on a gloomy day."

It certainly was a taste of childhood. The sticky, spicy sweetness of the ginger beer hitting the back of Gabriel's throat put him in mind of seaside holidays and picnics in the park, on those sultry late August afternoons on which the dreadful spectre of the new school term still felt comfortably distant and the long days merged happily into one another.

The temptation to walk away from Cambridge with questions left deliberately unasked and unanswered was a little like trying to remain in a state of perpetual childhood, Gabriel conceded. He sat on the low wall with the towering monstrosity of King's College's Chapel behind him and thought. Why did anyone ever commit murder? Money—neither Daphne nor Arthur had much in the way of assets; academics never did. Love—if Daphne had been the one victim, it would be the most obvious motive. Will, Robert, even Dr Crayford if Robert Sutton's claims were true—even, heaven forbid, Arthur himself—might have done it. But if Arthur's death was not suicide, it was difficult to see how love could have anything to do with the murder of two such different people.

And there was the next obstacle. If Daphne and Arthur were killed for anything, it was surely for their work—either because of something they were working on or something they had discovered—but Gabriel had no idea how he could find out anything about what they were doing. Even if he could access their lab books or find out where and what Arthur had been up to during his time away from Cambridge, it was unlikely that he would understand any of it. He was a humanities man himself. He was in a university full of the greatest scientific minds in the world, but he could not approach any of them. He had no idea whom he could trust, and if his previous experience of solving crimes had taught him anything, it was that nobody in the circle of the victim could be trusted until the truth came out.

Gabriel looked for somewhere to throw away the empty bottle and crumpled paper bag, feeling a little more energetic, if still as confused as ever. He was going to have to be brave and get Abbot Ambrose involved. Abbot Ambrose was not a scientist, but he knew people, he knew important people who could winkle out information for him. The first thing he needed to find out was where Arthur had been working.

There was a telephone box in the marketplace which Gabriel remembered from his student days. It was still there, red and reliable, the familiar smells of damp and sweat greeting him as he threw open the door. He lifted the receiver and waited for the sound of the operator's voice. "Saint Mary's Abbey, Sutton Westford," he said, fumbling in his pocket for his emergency supply of pennies. He had no idea how long the call would be. To his dismay he realised he had used up much of his change buying food—it would have to be a short call, and he had an awful lot to ask.

"Saint Mary's Abbey," came a ponderous voice at the end of the line. Not Abbot Ambrose.

"Dominic, is that you? It's Gabriel."

"Gabriel, how wonderful to hear your voice!" came a cheery response. "What are you up to?"

"No good, I assure you. Is there any chance you might find Father Abbot? I need to speak to him rather urgently. I don't have very long." Gabriel slipped a penny into the coin slot and hoped it would buy him enough extra time. "I need to speak about a murder."

"He's not here, Gabriel. He's hearing confessions. I don't suppose I can help?"

"I don't suppose you know how many ways scientists have found to kill people in the last fifteen years or so?" asked Gabriel hopefully.

"Are you trying to be funny?" answered Dominic, but Gabriel could hear whispering going on in the background. Dominic had company. "Sorry, I've been told to tell you that there is a present arriving for you at Cambridge station. You need to be there at twelve forty-four."

"What?" demanded Gabriel, looking round for any means to discover the time. There were never clocks or anything useful like that in a telephone box. "But that must be nearly now!"

"No, you have about ten minutes."

"But what's the present?" He could hear the pips warning him that his call was about to end. He searched in his pocket again, but he was officially penniless. "What's the present? I don't have time for this. What's the—"

Gabriel slammed the receiver down and hurled himself out of the telephone box, tumbling headlong into a burly man who had been waiting outside to make a call. The man gave Gabriel a gentle push to help him right himself and began clicking his tongue maddeningly. "You know, if Papists like you were real Christians, you wouldn't feel the need to get angry like that."

"Absolutely," Gabriel retorted, giving the man a smile before moving away. "That Jesus chap was ever so calm as he scourged the moneylenders out of the temple."

He really did not have time to pick a fight. Walking as fast as he could without breaking into a run, Gabriel dashed across the marketplace and hurried through the town, knowing that he would never arrive at the station by 12:44, whatever was arriving for him on that train. If this was Father Dominic's idea of a practical joke, it was in the lousiest possible taste, and Gabriel would be sure to tell them as much when—if—he made his way home to the abbey.

Why *if*? It was a morose thought even by Gabriel's standards. He hurried on towards the station—oh, to have a bicycle! This road had never seemed so long when he was a student, but when he had been a student he had virtually never had to dash to the railway station at a moment's notice. He had ventured to the station only at the end of term and in a cab, his trunk safely ensconced in the boot.

Gabriel slowed his pace as he turned onto Station Road, too hot and exhausted to exert himself further. He knew he was late and only now began to consider that, whatever it was that was waiting for him on that train, it could not have been the original plan for him to pick it up in person. Father Dominic had had no way of knowing that Gabriel was going to call at that precise moment. It occurred to him that Abbot Ambrose might have sent him a telegram earlier and that it might be waiting, accusingly, on Mama's kitchen table, but it was a little late in the day to worry about that.

In the distance, still some five hundred yards away, Gabriel could see the blur of passengers being disgorged by the mighty Victorian station building, all of them passengers from the 12:44 train, no doubt. Gabriel stopped in his tracks and watched as the figures began to disperse into cabs, onto the bus, onto an array of bicycles.

As the pavement emptied, Gabriel was aware of a solitary black figure waiting to be picked up by some late friend. As Gabriel drew closer, he could see that the young man appeared quite lost, looking round about him as though awaiting rescue. He was young enough to be a student, but after a few more steps, Gabriel made out the short, wiry figure of Brother Gerard.

"Jerry!" Gabriel called, picking up speed. "Well, I'm dashed!"

Gerard looked in Gabriel's direction, a mischievous grin spreading across his face. "Gabbers! Thank God you're here!"

"More to the point, what on earth are you doing here?" asked Gabriel, reaching forward to shake Gerard's hand. "I'd no idea you were coming."

"When you sent that daft telegram to Abbot Ambrose saying you were searching for a killer or something, he went a bit bananas," Gerard explained, skipping into step next to Gabriel. They began the walk back up Station Road. "He said, after this, he'll have to lock you up in the abbey and never let you out again, since trouble always find you. Even in this boring place."

"Cambridge is not a boring place!" protested Gabriel, feeling a surge of loyalty to his alma mater.

"Apparently not," Gerard put in. "Mad professors started stabbing each other behind the bookcases, have they?"

Gabriel groaned. "A brilliant young scientist was found dead after an extremely convenient lab accident, and one of my oldest friends was found hanged shortly after, if that's what you mean." This felt like emotional blackmail. Gerard had had no way of knowing that it was Gabriel's friend who had been killed, since Arthur had not been dead when Gabriel had sent the telegram. "Sorry. You weren't to know."

"No, I'm that sorry, Gabbers. It's all right, I'm not here to drag you away. Abbot Ambrose thought you might need some assistance. I shan't be a bother; I'm to go directly to Blackfriars to see if they can put me up."

"You'll do no such thing," declared Gabriel forcefully. "You'll come with me and stay with my in-laws. That's where I'm staying,"

Gerard gaped at Gabriel. "Oh no, mate, I don't think so. I hadn't realised your people were from here. I'm not intruding on that."

"It shan't be an intrusion," Gabriel promised, but he could already see Gerard's problem. Who on earth would want to step into the intense situation of a man spending time with the parents of his dead wife? The thought must have rightly appalled Gerard. "I see what you mean. I do see you might rather—"

"Leave you alone. Quite," confirmed Gerard. "I'll be perfectly comfy at Blackfriars, even if they are Dominicans. Where shall I meet you once I'm settled?"

"I'm going back to Saint Stephen's College to see if I can speak to the master," said Gabriel. "I need to find out where my friend Dr Kingsley went shortly before the war."

"Did your friend never think to tell you?" asked Gerard.

"I never thought to ask, but then I had no idea he was going to die."

"Why don't you just ask to look at his papers?" Gerard volunteered. "There's bound to be something there telling you where he went."

"It feels wrong rooting about in a dead friend's room," Gabriel began, but he was not even convincing himself. "You know, invasion of privacy, I suppose."

Gerard looked sidelong at Gabriel, dragging his feet the way he always did when Gabriel was exasperating him. "You're afraid, aren't you? You want to find out what happened, but you don't really. You're going round and round in circles, wasting time, getting nothing done, so you can say afterwards you tried to get to the bottom of all this and failed."

Gabriel was about to retort, but he knew it was pointless. Like a good surgeon, Gerard knew exactly where to stick the knife, and he had cut him in just the right place. "If he had something to hide, there will be nothing there," Gabriel said, but he was blustering now. "If there were anything incriminating in your past, would you keep it filed away? I'm just trying to be practical."

"You're just trying to be a coward," parried Gerard. "Where's the harm in checking? There now, go and ask for the key to his room and see what you find. If there's nothing there, there's nothing there. Back to square one."

Gabriel staggered towards college, smarting from Gerard's common sense. He suspected that he was about to get a little more of the same from Mr Derrick, but Gabriel arrived in the porter's lodge to find Derrick uncharacteristically subdued, so distracted that he jumped at the sound of the door opening when he would normally have barely noticed it. It was the first time Gabriel noticed that Derrick was wearing a black tie. "Good day to you," said Derrick without enthusiasm. "How you bearing up?"

"It's hard," admitted Gabriel, "but I daresay it's as much a shock to you as it is to me."

"I've never known the like," said Derrick miserably. "There were deaths aplenty during the war of course, fine young men I'd seen go off with a smile on their faces, saying, 'Cheer up, Mr Derrick, I'll be back before you've even noticed I'm gone.' This don't feel quite the same. Folks who lived through war shouldn't be murdered by peace."

Gabriel nodded; he had heard that sentiment expressed many times. Whenever he had investigated a violent death over the past year, someone had always made a remark of that nature. Why should a young woman who survived the concentration camps have come to grief in an English village? Why should a reporter who'd worked in war-torn

Europe have survived the bullets and the bombs to be killed in sleepy Wiltshire woodland? Why? "It's a great injustice," Gabriel agreed, squeezing his hand behind his back to stop himself from flinching. It was the first time anyone else had acknowledged that Daphne and Arthur had both been murdered. Gabriel opened his mouth to ask for an explanation, then thought the better of it and asked instead, "I wonder if I might be permitted to go into Arthur's rooms? It's just that there are some things I was looking for. Nothing important, I suspect, but I shouldn't mind taking a look."

"You'll be wanting to get home, surely?" asked Derrick, and he was not the first person to give Gabriel the distinct impression that he was required to push off. "No point in hanging around here without your friend. His funeral may not happen for weeks."

"I know, I mean to leave," promised Gabriel, and it was not entirely a lie. He would leave eventually. "Might I have the master key? I'll bring it back directly."

Derrick grimaced and stepped into the shadows to retrieve the key. "Not wishing to be rude, Father, but you're not the police. I'm not really supposed to give the key to anyone else."

"You can trust me not to go pinching anything," said Gabriel, knowing perfectly well that this would be the last thing on Mr Derrick's mind. He held out a hand for the key. "I shan't be a minute."

Derrick hesitated. Gabriel suspected that if he had had the presence of mind to do so, he would have thought of a reason not to hand over the key. He might have come up with some college regulation Gabriel would not have been able to contest, but Gabriel's request—like so many of Gabriel's ideas—had come out of the blue and thrown him. Derrick dropped the key into Gabriel's hand.

To Gabriel's surprise, the key he had been given was Arthur's own key, not the master key he had requested. "That didn't take long," commented Gabriel, not sure why it felt so distasteful. "Have Arthur's personal effects already been returned to the college?"

"I don't think so," said Derrick.

"But this is Arthur's key."

Derrick looked bewilderedly at the key, then a glimmer of recognition lit up his face. "Oh yes, one of the students found the key on the stairs and handed it in. Looks like he was so distracted he dropped it on his way out. Of course, he never returned, so he never missed it."

Gabriel nodded and headed across the quad to Arthur's rooms. *He never returned.* It only took a turn of phrase like that to stab Gabriel through the heart. Those little things that reminded a man that a person was dead and would never return. The key unclaimed, the half-empty teapot left to grow cold on a kitchen table, a bed not slept in . . . Gabriel forced himself to unlock the door and walked in, reminding himself that Arthur needed him to be sensible now, even if it meant being detached from the horror of what had happened.

Arthur's rooms already bore the unsettling feel of an abandoned dwelling. Gabriel could not put his finger on exactly what it was. The rooms were always cold if the fire was out, and Arthur had spent precious little time in this place, always dining in hall, with most of his waking hours spent in the lab, but even when Gabriel turned the light on to make a proper search, the room still felt chillingly unwelcoming.

Gabriel was not here to survey the scene this time; he had a much-stronger understanding of what he needed to find, and he set to work immediately. It was a blessing that both the sitting room and the bedroom were small and held little storage space for private items. It did not take him long to discover that he had arrived too late. Arthur's desk looked untouched at a first glance. Nothing had been moved: there was a photograph in a silver frame of a couple on their wedding day, which Gabriel guessed to be Arthur's parents; there were pencils in an open wooden box, a bronze paper knife, a sheet of blotting paper in dire need of changing, a half-empty bottle of ink. The drawers were empty. Every single one. It was inconceivable that Arthur had never used the drawers to store envelopes, writing paper, bills, letters, papers related to his work. Whoever was meddling had not even had the guile to make it look as though the drawers had not been touched—he had taken everything without pausing for a moment to sift out the innocuous items.

Gabriel ran straight back to the porter's lodge. There were a couple of undergraduates checking their pigeonholes for letters and messages when Gabriel burst in; they stared at him in understandable alarm. He immediately stopped and collected himself, glancing across the room at Derrick standing behind the counter. Derrick shuffled from one foot to the other, but for once Gabriel took the hint and walked calmly up to the counter. "I say, I don't suppose you've got this morning's *Times*, have you?" he asked, with what he imagined to be nonchalance. "I've got a wager with the dean that I can complete the crossword in under half an hour, and he's already set the clock ticking."

Derrick rolled his eyes and disappeared from view, making an elaborate rumpus of shuffling papers. Gabriel waited until the two young men had sloped off before joining Derrick at the counter. "What have you done with Dr Kingsley's papers?" he demanded. "His drawers have been cleared out."

"Why should I have had anything to do with it?" demanded Derrick, holding up the counter to let Gabriel in. "If you can't help firing daft questions at me, I'd rather you didn't do it for the world and his wife to hear."

"Who else had access to Arthur's rooms other than you?"

"Anyone else could have got in," Derrick protested, "if the key were lying around all that time. And he might've cleared out his own drawers."

Gabriel groaned. It felt like bad manners, but he could not avoid the observation. "Mr Derrick, there never was a key lying on the floor. Arthur forgot to lock his rooms this morning."

Derrick heaved a sigh of relief. "Well, if the doors were open, anyone could have wandered in."

"And then did you the courtesy of picking up the key on the way out and handing it in so that you'd identify the guilty party when questions were raised?" Gabriel's eyes moved in the direction of the stove that was roaring away nicely, the kindling crackling and curling with the intensity of the heat. "Mr Derrick, what have you done?"

Derrick turned his back on Gabriel. "I had to clear out his things, that's all. He's no family—had no family, I mean. The college wanted the room cleared out."

"Only his papers are missing," Gabriel pointed out. "And if you were going about legitimate college business, why lie in the first place?" Gabriel watched as Derrick slowly turned round to face him, the colour drained from his face. "Mr Derrick, two people are dead, and I think you have known the truth from the start. Now, will you please tell me why you destroyed Arthur's papers?"

Derrick sat heavily in the chair near the stove, hunching forward as though trying to warm himself. "Please don't tell the police. I'm not a killer, and I'm not a common thief. I were trying to help him."

Gabriel sat down beside Derrick, looking back to check that they were not being overheard. "Mr Derrick, have you burnt Dr Kingsley's papers?" Derrick nodded miserably. There was sweat gathering at his temples. "All of them?"

"I had to," he said, sounding alarmingly out of breath. "I knew he were hiding something, and I didn't know what. I didn't know which papers was incriminating, so I burnt everything to be sure."

Gabriel took a deep breath as he considered how best to proceed. Derrick had known before he had crept into Arthur's rooms and made off with the contents of his bureau that he was doing something very wrong; he hardly needed Gabriel to state the obvious after the fact. "Why did you do it? You must realise that this is very serious. Destruction of property is an offence. You could be arrested."

"I had to protect him!" gasped Derrick. "You don't understand; he was the one in trouble. When I found out he were dead, I couldn't bear him to be found out."

"You'd better sit back from that stove before you pass out," said Gabriel, helping Derrick get up and move his chair back a few inches. "There now, breathe." Derrick took several slow, laboured breaths. "That's better. Now, I think you'd better tell me what you were protecting Dr Kingsley from. You know you can trust me."

Derrick stared glumly into the fire. "I overheard him and Dr Silverton having such a row," he said weakly. "It were late, and I'd usually have left by then, so I don't suppose they realised I were listening. I'd never heard any of them angry like that."

"What were they saying?"

"She were saying that he had blood on his hands, that he were a killer."

Gabriel felt the hairs on the back of his neck stand on end, thinking of the anonymous messages Arthur had received before his death. "A killer? How? Did she say anything else?"

Derrick shook his head. "It's all a bit of a blur, she were in such a state. She said the weapon he'd made had caused the deaths of hundreds of thousands of people. He were saying that it weren't his fault, he didn't know. He said that it were meant to do good, he'd not meant to kill anyone."

Gabriel was sweating now, and it had nothing to do with his proximity to a heat source. "Was there anything else? Anything at all that you can remember? Even if it doesn't seem important, it may be."

"Are you going to report me for this, Father?" asked Derrick. "This college is me life. If I lose me position . . ."

"I'm not going to see you lose your livelihood, Mr Derrick," said Gabriel solemnly. "You and your wife were very kind to me when I was a student, and I will not pay back that kindness by doing you any harm, I assure you. I care very much for Dr Kingsley's good name too, but someone killed Dr Silverton, and I need to find out who did it, even if I have to accept that my friend may have been responsible."

Derrick looked up sharply. "He wouldn't have done that!" he protested. "I didn't burn those papers because I thought he'd killed Dr Silverton. I just didn't want people bandying his name about, calling him a murderer after he were dead. Whatever he did in his past, he's dead now. What can it matter? He's a right to rest in peace."

"Mr Derrick, if Dr Kingsley's work really has resulted in the deaths of innocent people, they have a right to rest in peace too. They have a right to justice. Daphne Silverton has a right to justice."

"I can't believe he'd ever hurt her," said Derrick, shaking his head slowly from side to side as though the very idea left him dazed with shock. "She meant the world to him."

"I find it hard to believe him capable of such a crime either, but whoever killed her knew her very well. I have found that fear can drive a man to do all sorts of things of which he would never normally be capable."

"But murder?"

"Mr Derrick, try to remember when you were throwing those papers into the stove. Did you see anything that might explain what Dr Kingsley was doing? A name, an address, perhaps headed paper. Anything at all that looked unusual to you."

Derrick looked desperately at Gabriel. "I wouldn't have known what I were looking for," he said, "and there was so much paper. Letters in different languages, some things handwritten, some things typed, faded ink, bad handwriting. I didn't have time to go looking through all that; I just wanted to get rid of it before anyone found me."

Gabriel rose to his feet. "Different languages? What languages?"

Derrick also rose, perhaps to avoid the sense of a man towering over him. "How should I know? Latin? French? German? It all looks the same to me. I'm . . . I'm sorry."

Gabriel patted Derrick's shoulder and made to leave. "Try not to dwell on it now, Mr Derrick. It's a small consolation to me, but if it helps, I suspect Dr Kingsley—God have mercy on his soul—would have wanted you to burn those papers."

Gabriel stepped outside, relieved by the sudden rush of cold air washing over him. Out on the street, he could hear the normally uplifting sound of young men laughing, and he moved towards the noise, stepping out onto the pavement to find Brother Gerard—surrounded by a group of undergraduates—in full flow. He had obviously just told some hilarious anecdote or other, because four young men in gowns were guffawing noisily with Gerard standing in the middle, grinning like a vaudeville comedian who has just delivered the perfect punchline.

Gerard looked up and saw Gabriel looking quizzically at him. "Gabbers, come and join us!" he called, like the Ghost of Christmas Present, apparently not noticing Gabriel's thunderous face. Gabriel forced himself to smile and joined the merry party. "I've just bumped into a bunch of Preston lads," said Gerard by way of explanation. "Heard them talking. I'd recognise that accent anywhere."

Before Gabriel knew it, he was being introduced to a terribly nice man with a mop of unruly, rusty curls, called Ollie; a short, stocky lad called Percy, who reminded Gabriel a little of Gerard with the addition of three or four stone in weight; and two second-year engineers called Alfie and Jack. After introductions and handshakes had been exchanged, the gigglesome conversation resumed, and Gabriel struggled to distract Gerard long enough to drag him away. "I can't take you anywhere, can I?"

"Aww, you've no idea how nice it was hearing a voice from home. It was like having a laugh with me own brothers."

Yes, thought Gabriel with a faint flash of amusement, *except that I'm pretty sure you were the butt of all the jokes then.* "May I talk about something a little more serious?" said Gabriel as they crossed the bridge. Beneath them, a young man in a boater hat was skilfully guiding a punt along the river. He had two passengers, an elderly couple swathed in tartan blankets, whom Gabriel suspected were the young man's parents, come for a visit they were secretly regretting. "My friend's papers have been destroyed," Gabriel declared. "All of them."

Gerard looked conspiratorially at Gabriel. "Well, that reeks of a guilty conscience. Still, it's not the end of the world. There are plenty of other ways you can find out what he was up to. There will be records of where he travelled, what he did. It might take some time, but—"

"I know where he went," Gabriel cut in. "At least, I know which country he went to. It's a lot worse than I thought it was. I couldn't get the thought out of my head that Arthur was working on the Bomb. It was the way he talked about moral culpability if one helps create a weapon that is used by others to end life. What with Daphne Silverton's involvement with the Peace Pledge Union, it all kept coming back to that. But Arthur wasn't working for the Americans—he was working for the Germans. I don't know what he was doing, but I'm pretty sure I know where he went."

They were standing next to the Round Church, one of those architectural oddities that make Cambridge so charming. Gabriel and Gerard stopped to look at it, as though they were tourists enjoying the view of a building meant to be a miniature Church of the Holy Sepulchre. What could be more natural than two clerics admiring a church? "Are you absolutely sure?" whispered Gerard. "That's one heck of an accusation to make about a dead man."

"I'm sure he was. The person who destroyed Arthur's paperwork said that there were letters in a different language he could not understand. He had no idea what the language was, whether it was Latin or French or German, just that it was a foreign language. Now, let's assume that there are no chemical companies that routinely correspond in Latin. It could have been French, but if Arthur had something to be ashamed of, if Daphne Silverton had confronted him, accusing him of having blood on his hands, it is unlikely that he was working for the French. That rather narrows things down."

"If it were before the war, he weren't working on the atom bomb," said Gerard. "The Germans are good at science; my chemistry teacher was German. They interned him."

"Gerard, what are you trying to tell me?"

"I mean, Brother Tobias always used to go on and on about how the Germans were the best chemists in the world." He put on a comical German accent. " 'Ve lead ze vaaay int science.' Then he'd bore us all to death listing every chemical compound any German scientist had ever invented. If your friend was at the top of his field, it's very likely he would have worked with Germans; he would have travelled to Germany. It wouldn't have seemed so shocking before the war."

"There's one person who might be able to tell me something," said Gabriel. "I don't think he's quite as mad as his lovely wife claims." Gabriel looked Gerard up and down. He looked almost respectable in his clericals, if Gabriel ignored the fact that the laces of Gerard's right shoe were trailing and sodden, and there were at least two buttons missing from his coat. "Look here, don't take this the wrong way, but it might be better if I go to see this family alone. They may be a little intimidated by the sight of two men on their doorstep."

Gerard inclined his head to one side. "You want me to make meself scarce again, don't you?" he demanded. "Are you going to give me some sweetie money, big bruv?"

Gabriel propelled Gerard in the direction of Trinity Street. "No, I want you to make yourself useful. That is why Father Abbot sent you, isn't it?"

"Nah, he sent me to stop you making a pig's ear of everything, as usual," Gerard retorted, laughing as though to compensate for Gabriel's stony silence. "So, what is it you want me to do? Breaking and entering, stumbling upon some hideously battered body . . ."

Gabriel was aware that he had dragged Gerard into some pretty unsavoury situations over the past months, and he did not need an inventory now. "I need you to go to the public library and look at the archives of *Town and Gown*," he explained. "You'll need to look through every issue for the past year until you find anything involving a man called Dr Crayford or any story about a don misbehaving with a female student. Understand?"

"Every issue from the last year?" echoed Gerard. "I thought you wanted me out of the way for the afternoon, not the next month."

"Look, it's a weekly newspaper, so there won't be more than fifty-two editions to look through."

"Glad someone can do maths around here."

Gabriel ignored him. "My guess is that you won't have to go back as far as a year if you start with the most recent editions and work your way back. If there is a story, I believe it will have been quite recent, but I'm putting a limit on a year. I'm fairly sure that if it happened, it did not happen that long ago."

Gerard nodded, looking like a prep school boy who has been given a lengthy detention and is trying desperately to be brave about it. "Where shall I meet you?"

"As soon as you have something, go and wait at Our Lady and the English Martyrs Church. If I finish first and don't find you at the church, I'll come and find you at the library."

"What do we do then? Split up and meet in Prague?"

"Clear off, Jerry!"

Gabriel smiled at the sight of Gerard's retreating figure before going his own way through town towards Daphne's old lodgings. It was only as he was crossing Parker's Piece that Gabriel realised he had omitted to tell Gerard where the public library was, but Gerard was an enterprising fellow, and he guessed that he would find his way there before too long. Gabriel had more pressing matters to attend to. There was no kind way to tell a woman she was a liar, though Gabriel did not trouble to work out what he was going to say before he arrived at the Bellinger residence and knocked on the door.

It almost made matters worse when Mrs Bellinger opened the door and gave Gabriel a gracious smile. "Oh, it's you!" she declared, stepping aside to let him in without further ceremony. "Have you heard anything? Have you found out how Dr Kingsley did it? I was thinking just an hour ago——"

"I came to tell you, Mrs Bellinger, that Arthur Kingsley was found hanged early this morning. He left a note admitting responsibility for Daphne's death."

Mrs Bellinger's hand went up to her mouth, and almost immediately, tears sprang from her eyes. "I knew it was him! I knew it was him; it's just such a terrible shock all the same. My poor Daphne!" Mrs Bellinger all but collapsed into an armchair, putting on such an elaborate show of grief and shock that Gabriel almost believed her. She really was a consummate actress, and she had not lost her touch with the long years of retirement.

"Mrs Bellinger, when your husband became angry at the sight of me, it was because he thought I was Dr Kingsley for a moment, didn't he? It was not a random outburst as you suggested."

Mrs Bellinger nodded her head miserably, pulling out an embroidered handkerchief, which she used to dab her eyes delicately so as not to smudge her mascara. "I didn't want to draw attention to him at the time, Father," she said tremulously. Even the judderings of her grief-stricken voice were carefully choreographed. "It would not have been fair. No one knew exactly what had happened, and it might have prejudiced you against him. But yes, Dr Kingsley did come to the house once. Quite recently. There was a fearful row, and in the end, I had to ask him to leave."

Gabriel waited for Mrs Bellinger to invite him to sit down,

but she was too busy being distraught to ask him, and he sat down opposite her, assuming she would not mind the presumption. "And could you tell me what they were arguing about?" he asked, trying hard to suppress his irritation.

"Daphne had found out about Dr Kingsley's work before he arrived back in Cambridge. He came back to England only as the borders were closing; he would never have left Frankfurt if Britain had not declared war against Germany."

Gabriel's mouth was dry. For a moment, he wished he had brought Brother Gerard with him. He needed someone, some friendly support here, as he enunciated his worst fear. "Daphne had discovered that Dr Kingsley had worked for the Germans, right up until the outbreak of the war," said Gabriel tonelessly. "That was why they were arguing."

"Yes," answered Mrs Bellinger in a whisper. "She was terribly distressed. She called him a traitor, a wicked traitor, a disgrace to science. Words like that. Of course, he was terribly angry and upset."

Of course the man was angry and upset, thought Gabriel bitterly. *The word "traitor" has a nasty-enough ring to it at any time, but in the aftermath of a war, it might have landed him with a rope around his neck.* "Mrs Bellinger, will you please stop lying to me," said Gabriel, and he was sure the words sounded harsher spoken out loud than they had in his head. "I have no doubt now that my old friend was a traitor, however hard it is to believe, but I do not believe that he came here to argue with Daphne. I'm not convinced that Daphne was even in the house when it happened."

Adela shrank back in her chair, appalled. "What on earth makes you say such a thing? Why should I lie to you? Daphne meant everything to me; I want more than anything for her

223

killer to be brought to justice. If the filthy coward is dead, let him at least be exposed as a traitor and a murderer."

"Mrs Bellinger, when I saw Dr Kingsley with Daphne and the others at high table, they did not strike me as two people who had had an irredeemable row. They had argued, certainly. Another witness has told me that they had an aggressive argument, but when Dr Kingsley came to this house, it was not Daphne with whom he was angry. It was your husband."

Mrs Bellinger sprang to her feet. "My husband? But that's absurd; the poor man's away with the fairies. He's not been capable of having an argument or even a conversation in over a year. Most of the time he can't even remember what he had for breakfast."

"No, Mrs Bellinger," answered Gabriel simply. "Your husband may be an invalid, but I'll wager that he is as lucid as you or I. He may not be a professional actor, but he has clearly learnt a thing or two from you."

Mrs Bellinger glared at Gabriel, marching to the door of the sitting room. "You will leave my house immediately," she said with the imperious air of a lady dismissing an errant servant. "If you trouble me again, I shall summon a policeman."

"No, my dear," came a gentle, steady voice from the stairs. Mrs Bellinger started at the sound of her husband's voice and moved towards the doorway, closely followed by Gabriel. Eric stood on the stairs, looking remarkably dignified in his striped pyjamas and worn woollen dressing gown, but they both knew that he had been listening to their conversation all along. "If Kingsley is dead, I think it's best that we all come clean."

224

"Darling . . . ," Mrs Bellinger began, but she stepped back, defeated by the sight of Eric walking unsteadily but determinedly towards them.

"It's no good your trying to protect me, my dear," said Eric as the three of them settled themselves down in the sitting room. Mrs Bellinger, out of force of habit, helped Eric make himself comfortable, plumping pillows and adjusting the white antimacassar behind his head. "I'm not sure this gentleman has much time for theatrical types anyhow." He turned to Gabriel with an unexpectedly sympathetic smile. "You strike me as the sort who'd be bored witless watching grown-ups in fancy dress, pretending to be what they are not."

Eric got the measure of Gabriel so succinctly that Gabriel dodged the remark. "It was you who told Daphne that Dr Kingsley had worked for the Germans, wasn't it?" asked Gabriel. "Your wife mentioned, when we first met, that you had worked in science all over the world. It was your background that caused you to befriend Daphne, not your illness."

"Oh, but that was not entirely a lie," Mrs Bellinger protested. "Eric is very frail, and dear Daphne was so good with him. Wasn't she, darling?"

Eric nodded, a shadow passing across his face. He was the sort of man who could cope with grief only if he were never reminded of the cause. "She was a good girl, a gentle nurse if ever there was one, but I so enjoyed talking with her. It was such a long time since I'd been able to discuss my work with anyone who truly understood." He looked awkwardly at his wife. "Sorry, old girl."

"You know I don't mind."

"Well," he continued, "I told her all about my work in Frankfurt. I'd worked for IG Farben, back in the days when it was a respectable organisation, churning out innovation after innovation. It was a good time to be there."

IG Farben. The name was infamous, so much so that even Gabriel had heard of them. "The devil's chemist," said Gabriel blankly.

"The very same. The top brass are on trial as we speak, and they should all hang for their crimes, though I very much doubt they will." Eric stared down at his hands, which shook constantly. "When I started work with them, they were no friends of the Nazis. Some of the directors were Jewish. But all that changed very quickly. As soon as Farben started donating to the Nazi Party and expelling its Jewish employees, Adela and I came home to Cambridge."

"That was very good of you," said Gabriel, then thought what an understatement it was. A man had given up his adopted homeland and his career on a point of principle when so many had simply bent with the wind.

Eric sat up as straight as he could. "I'm not a religious man, Father," he said, "but one thing my Jesuit education taught me was the importance of a well-formed conscience. I could not in good conscience work for a company that was intent upon feeding the Nazi war machine. I firmly believe that with knowledge comes great responsibility. So many scientists forgot all about that principle when war came; they were prepared to sell their souls for the sake of a little more funding. I'm not such a man. I could never have held up my head again if I had done any different."

Gabriel found it impossible not to admire Eric, and he wondered whether, under different circumstances, they might have forged a friendship, but Gabriel was reeling at the sensation that all his beliefs about Arthur Kingsley were falling away. He had learnt very soon after Daphne's death that Arthur had a dark past, but Eric's principled stand threw Arthur's mercenary choice into brutal relief—if it had been an entirely mercenary choice, and Gabriel prayed it had. "So, Dr Kingsley did not leave. That was where you knew him, at IG Farben."

Eric gave a contemptuous shake of the head. "He was far too comfortable to inconvenience himself by leaving. Said he'd only just got himself settled. It's amazing how far a man will compromise himself for a comfortable life."

Gabriel shuddered at the understatement of the decade. If there had been more men like Eric and fewer men like Arthur, the war might never have happened in the first place. "I have to ask you this, I have to know, or I will never stop thinking about it. Was Arthur Kingsley a Nazi? Did he really stay with the devil's chemist for a comfortable life, or did he believe in what they were doing?"

Eric sighed, and Gabriel noticed that contempt had given way to sadness in a matter of seconds. "Arthur Kingsley didn't have a political bone in his body. That was the trouble—he didn't care for whom he worked or what they did with his work. As long as he had a lab and a team and the freedom to pursue his own interests, he did not care who was funding him. Until Daphne confronted him, I don't think he'd ever stopped to think about the hundreds of thousands of men, women and children who died thanks to his work. Perhaps more people than that, perhaps millions. The Nazis tried so hard to cover their tracks."

Gabriel felt himself trembling. He recalled the conversation he and Arthur had had in which Arthur had asked whether the man who designed the first gun was responsible for every single person who had ever died at the end of a bullet. He had been trying to confess, but he had not had the moral courage to admit even to his friend what he had done. "I cannot believe he could have wanted to do so much harm."

Eric leaned forward towards Gabriel and attempted a smile. "When Daphne mentioned his name, I told her everything I knew about his work. I regretted it almost immediately. She was distraught. I wondered whether I had had any right to broach such a subject with her; she was having such a hard time as it was. It's no easy business being a woman in science, fighting off unwanted advances, being belittled by men with half your intelligence. I should have let it go. But I was so furious with him, I thought somehow that she ought to know."

"Dr Bellinger, you did the right thing!" Gabriel exclaimed. "Daphne surely had a right to know. She was a mature adult; she did not need protecting from the truth." *But Arthur needed protecting from himself,* thought Gabriel grimly, *and two people died because you told the truth.* "He must have confronted you after he had argued with Daphne," Gabriel put in.

"Hardly confronted me, old boy," Eric retorted. "Pleaded, more like. The man was a gibbering wreck when he came to the house, raging at me that I was dragging his name through the mud, that I was poisoning his dear little protégé's mind against him. Then all the excuses started—oh so many excuses, Father! He'd never meant those little pellets to be used to kill people; it was an insecticide. It was supposed to be used to fumigate prisoners' clothing. Never mind that it still made him a collaborator with the Nazis; never mind that he was contributing to that diabolical concentration camp system! He swore and swore that he had not known about the gas chambers, that he'd never intended to create a weapon against the innocent. They didn't start gassing people until some years after Kingsley had left Germany." Eric halted in full flow. "I say, old man, are you all right?"

Gabriel's mind was wandering again, to those monochrome newsreels and the piles and piles of emaciated bodies, too many to count—mothers, fathers, sons, daughters . . . and the stunned, disbelieving voices of friends: *But how could this happen? How so many and so quickly?* "I'm sorry," Gabriel murmured listlessly, but he felt numb. His mind drifted from those hellish images to Arthur—avuncular, courteous, so very ordinary—sitting smoking a pipe with friends after a jolly meal. If he thought about it any longer, his brain would fall to pieces. "It's a little too much to take in."

"I wouldn't try if I were you, old man," said Eric with the kindly manner of a physician. "I'm not sure anyone will ever make sense of all this. I'm not sure anyone would dare."

"Daphne dared," said Gabriel, almost without thinking. He squeezed his hands together until he could almost hear his knuckles cracking with the effort. He had to pull himself together. "I have to ask you: Is it your belief that Arthur Kingsley murdered Daphne? Regardless of what happened to him afterwards, do you believe he killed Daphne because he could not trust her to keep her mouth shut?"

Eric grimaced. "He was clever enough to do it," Eric conceded, "but I don't believe he would have killed her in that way. Let's face it, Daphne was gassed. It was a painless, rather quicker death than those poor wretches must have suffered in the camps, but she was gassed. She died by asphyxiation. A man struggling with guilt about his part in the development of poison gas is unlikely to have killed his protégé that way. Too close to the bone.''

Gabriel stumbled in the direction of Parker's Piece. He had not gone far before he felt a tightening in his stomach so painful that he lent against a tree for support, stooping forward as his guts knotted up. He vomited once, then again, his body rebelling against a revelation more terrible than he could ever have imagined. His friend had been a war criminal. For all his pretences about insecticides, Gabriel could not swallow the truth that Arthur had worked for and taken money from men he had known to be evil to the core.

Gabriel stood up slowly, running a hand over his clammy forehead. He noticed two old women walking past him and thought for a moment that they were going to stop and offer him help, which would have been most embarrassing. Instead, they picked up their pace at the sight of him standing unsteadily by a tree next to a pool of vomit, one of them muttering to the other: "Typical! Blind drunk at this hour of the day. They've no shame whatsoever!''

Gabriel allowed himself a hollow laugh before continuing on his way, forcing himself to walk with his back straight and his head up, apparently in good spirits. Inwardly, his mind was still a blur. Gabriel knew there was no possibility that Eric could have killed Daphne—he had neither the motive nor the physical capability. True, he would have been perfectly capable of rigging a booby trap involving liquid nitrogen, but it was rather less likely that he would have had the strength to carry her dead body into the lab afterwards, slightly built though Daphne was.

Killing Arthur was another matter. If Eric were bluffing and believed that Arthur really had killed Daphne, then Eric would have an excellent motive for killing him in revenge, and Gabriel was not at all convinced by Eric's line of reasoning about Arthur's innocence. Certainly, there was a cruel irony in the manner in which Daphne had been killed, but it was also a relatively humane way of ending a life: Arthur would not have had to overpower her or feel her struggle; he would not have had to witness the execution itself. There would have been no blood or mess, and most of all, it would have been so easy to make it look like an accident.

Gabriel shook his head impatiently. Even if Eric had wanted to kill Arthur, he certainly could not have done it alone. The man might be in possession of his marbles, but his hands trembled continuously with the symptoms of neurological disease, and Gabriel doubted that Eric would even have had the strength and coordination to hold a knife to a man's throat, let alone to force a struggling man into a noose.

Gabriel made his way to Our Lady and the English Martyrs Church, but he never needed to enter. Sitting in the narthex, chatting away as though to an old friend, was Brother Gerard—in the company of none other than Will Valentine.

11

There was no reason to ask Gerard what the devil he thought he was doing; Gerard was more than happy to do the talking. "I found your story," he said delightedly, reminding Gabriel of a Labrador who has just presented his master with a dead rat. "Daphne Silverton and a number of other women accused a certain Dr Crayford of molesting them."

Gabriel looked quizzically at Will Valentine. "I don't suppose the two of you met at the library, by an extraordinary coincidence?"

Will was about to make some sort of an explanation of his presence, but Gerard burst in. "I hope you don't mind, but I was trying to find me way to the library, and I just thought, well, it were a bit daft going through hundreds of pages of print when I could just go to the newspaper itself and ask them. So I did."

"You did," answered Gabriel sardonically. "And Mr Valentine here has obligingly given you the information you require."

"It's quite all right, Father," Will put in, in the tone of a man trying to defuse a tense situation, though Gabriel was more exasperated than angry. "I was perfectly happy to help him, and since I wrote that story, I could give him plenty of information that wasn't even written down."

"Did Daphne know that you planned to write a story

about this unfortunate situation before she spoke to you?" asked Gabriel in as neutral a tone as he could muster, which was not neutral in the slightest. "Or was this a repeat of your feature about science and morality?"

Will blushed, his pale face blotching like a man in a fever. "I did try to apologise to Daphne. You know, it's awfully difficult churning out good copy, day after day, with an editor always expecting everything done yesterday. You've no idea how hard it is."

"You really should find a new excuse, Mr Valentine; you've already used that one up," said Gabriel tersely. "And I'll spare my sympathy for Daphne Silverton, if it's all the same to you. I'd imagine that story got her into even more trouble than the previous one. Reporters are dangerous men to know."

"No, no, it's not what you think," answered Will; he was almost wheedling. "She came to me for help. Crayford was all over her; she was scared."

"Wouldn't she have gone to Dr Kingsley with a problem like that?"

"No, she said Dr Kingsley was very kind to her, but he didn't really understand women. And she couldn't go to the police, because they'd never believe her anyway. Next thing I know, that swine Crayford's banging on my door. He said if there were any truth in the story, he would have been arrested, but we both knew that wasn't the case."

Gabriel allowed his attention to be drawn to a large spider attempting to spin a web in the corner of the narthex closest to the outside world. Gabriel was not a fan of eight-legged creatures as a rule, but he had to admire its persistence in the

234

face of a hostile draught. "What did the story actually say?" asked Gabriel finally. "That's all I need to know, though I doubt now that it has much to do with anything."

Gerard put his hand up like the impatient boy at the back of the class. "I'm sure it's got everything to do with it!" he protested, determined that his work would not go unrecognised. "This lassie Daphne says in the story that Dr Crayford was making the lives of women impossible in the department. Two secretaries had already left because they couldn't bear his advances anymore. She said he'd threatened to have her sent down if she told anyone, but Dr Kingsley had defended her."

Gabriel turned to Will. "To your knowledge, did Dr Crayford make any attempt to have Daphne removed from the university, or was it merely a threat?"

Will was relaxing now, aware that he was of some use to the two men. "Yes, I believe he made some halfhearted attempt, but Dr Kingsley squashed it pretty quickly. Dr Kingsley was better regarded than Dr Crayford, and his opinion carried more weight."

"Thank you. You have been most helpful."

"I can't see why you got your knickers in a twist over this," Gerard protested as he struggled to follow Gabriel's irate march back in the direction of town. "I got you what you needed to know, didn't I? You don't have to thank me or anything."

Gabriel slowed his pace just enough to allow Gerard's little legs to catch up with him. "If I had wanted you to go in search of Will Valentine, I would have told you as much," snapped Gabriel. "I didn't want him to know I was looking into his news stories. I certainly did not need him to filter what we learnt."

"Gabriel, I saw the stories meself; he didn't add to or take anything from the story. What's the harm in asking a man a few questions?"

Gabriel lowered his voice, though he doubted the conversation could be heard over the hubbub of cars and the chattering clusters of people going about their business. "It may do a lot of harm if Will Valentine is our killer. I overheard him arguing with Daphne the night she died, and until I know for certain who killed Daphne and Arthur, I have to treat everyone as a suspect. Particularly people who don't bother to volunteer information until I find it out."

Gerard spotted a pub sign and dragged Gabriel by the arm in its welcome direction. "Come on, Gabbers, let me get you a pint. You must be running a bit short of funds by now."

Gabriel found himself seated in the snug of a public house he would not have been seen dead in when he was a student. If it hadn't been for Gerard manhandling him into the establishment, he was not sure he ought to be seen dead in here now, but he sat compliantly, peering through the fog of cheap cigarette smoke at the grimy, nicotine-stained walls and the reassuring sight of Gerard walking towards him with two pints of warm beer.

"Get outside of that," ordered Gerard, plonking one glass tankard before Gabriel, but neither man had the chance to take a swig before a voice roared at them from the nether regions of the bar. "Oi! Friar Tuck! Gimme my beers back!"

Gerard looked from the two tankards back to the dark figure approaching them through the smoke. "I bought two pints," said Gerard. "Ask the landlord."

Gabriel groaned, wondering whether Gerard was going to add beer snatching to his list of blunders that day. He stood up to greet the owner of the voice, a man with the vast, flabby figure of a former soldier who has let himself go. Before Gabriel could say anything, the man barked at Gerard, "You bought two different pints, you scouse git. Yours are at the bar; these are mine."

"I hail from Preston, not Liverpool," said Gerard to the man's retreating back, after he had scooped up the two beers and stormed off. "Sorry, Gabbers, I could have sworn the landlord were pulling those pints for me. Two ticks and I'll be back with ours."

Gabriel sank back in his chair, relaxing at the happy avoidance of a confrontation. It was an easy-enough mistake to make with multiple people standing at the bar, ordering more or less the same thing. An easy mistake . . . "Jerry?" called Gabriel into the gloomy void, but Gerard was well out of earshot, chattering with the landlord.

Gabriel closed his eyes. He was being assailed by a deluge of emotions from guilty relief to shame at his own stupidity. He watched, as though from the other side of a murky window, as Gerard tottered back with the correct pints and sat down opposite him.

"You all right, Gabbers?" enquired Gerard when Gabriel failed to pick up his drink and continued to stare into space. "Is there anybody there?"

Gabriel looked at Gerard with the vague expression that warned Gerard his friend was about to come out with something random. "You may put me down for a blithering idiot. I'm a blithering idiot."

"It were only a couple of pints," Gerard reassured him, "and I'm the idiot."

"Arthur didn't kill Daphne. My instinct was right: he would never—could never—have killed her. Even if he hadn't quite obviously adored her, she was his ticket to the fame and fortune he had himself been denied. She was brilliant; she might have won a Nobel Prize one day. And he would have basked in the reflected glory. That was always my feeling. Whatever she had found out about him, he would have found some other way to work things out with her. He was a clever man; he had huge influence over her. He never needed to kill her."

"If he didn't kill her, I take it you know who did?" asked Gerard, taking a long swig of his beer. He wrinkled his nose. "They definitely watered this down."

"That was always the problem. Nobody wanted to kill Daphne, however much she talked to the press—well, Will Valentine, to be precise—or however much she got involved in campaigns that horrified other scholars. I just could not find a compelling reason why anybody would have gone to the trouble of killing her." Gabriel lowered his voice, aware that he was talking too loudly in his excitement and might attract attention. "Don't you see, Gerard? She was never meant to die. I should have noticed that right at the start. I was told she never worked late, that she was always up with the lark. It was Arthur Kingsley who burnt the midnight oil. Whoever set that trap knew the comings and goings of the different members of the lab and meant Arthur to walk into that trap."

238

"Did your friend realise?" asked Gerard. "You told me earlier that he was full of guilt and said that he was a murderer. Was that what he meant? That he'd cost this girl her life because he knew he was the intended victim?"

"It puts everything he said in a rather different light," admitted Gabriel. "And if he knew he had been the intended target, he almost certainly knew who was responsible. And of course he knew why." Gabriel sat back in the chair and closed his eyes. "If only he'd felt able to confide in me," lamented Gabriel. "If he'd only trusted me enough to tell me what he'd done and why he was being hunted, he need never have died."

"Perhaps part of him wanted to die," ventured Gerard. "If he knew he'd been responsible for the deaths of innocent people, part of him must have thought he deserved to hang. Plenty of other war criminals have. Or will."

Gabriel rose to his feet. "I need to speak to Will Valentine," he said, pushing his untouched pint glass in Gerard's direction. "Stay here until I return."

"You don't really think . . ."

"It really would be better if you were not there. This is not going to be an easy conversation."

With that, Gabriel picked up his coat and hat, and left.

It was over an hour later that Gabriel found himself walking steadily through the gloaming back to Saint Stephen's College. It seemed a very long time since he had walked through this very entrance, soaking wet, ready for a few days' journey down memory lane. He stepped into the porter's lodge and found Mr Derrick like a faithful sentry, standing at the counter. "I've come to say good-bye," he said, extending a hand to the porter. "I shall be leaving in the morning. I'm all finished here."

"All finished?" asked Derrick, hesitating to take Gabriel's hand.

"Yes. I've done everything I can. I think it's time I returned to my monastery. Somehow, I'm not sure I'll return again."

Derrick shook Gabriel's hand warmly. "I hope you do return," he said, and Gabriel knew he meant it. "In happier times. Come in the summer months when the days are long. I'll take you punting down to Grantchester. How would you like that?"

Gabriel smiled, remembering long summer afternoons after the Tripos exams, when they had punted down to Grantchester Meadows with a hamper full of food and at least one of the party dripping wet from having fallen in. Yes, he should like to make that trip again very much indeed, but he doubted that he ever would.

He crossed the quad, ignoring the bustle of students coming and going, getting ready for a relaxed and probably drunken evening out. He noticed the lights were on in Robert Sutton's room, and he picked up his pace, fumbling inside his coat before knocking on the door. Gabriel was surprised to see Robert dressed for dinner when he appeared in the doorway, but not at all surprised that Robert looked displeased to see him. "Oh, Father Gabriel," he began awkwardly. "It's good of you to drop by, but I'll be going in to dinner in half an hour. I'd invite you to join me, but it's a little late——"

"This won't take long," promised Gabriel, brushing past Robert into the room when his host failed to invite him to enter. Gabriel felt irrationally annoyed at the sight of the young man dressed for a smart dinner when he had been a wreck just a few hours before. The young were fickle like that. "I'm leaving Cambridge in the morning and thought you'd like to know what I've discovered. I know how much Daphne meant to you, and seeing as you had the misfortune to discover Dr Kingsley's body, I thought you had a right to know first."

Robert raised an eyebrow, a supercilious pose which did him no favours. "Well, thank you. It's awfully decent of you to think of me." He looked at his unwelcome guest, but Gabriel did not move. "You'd . . . I suppose you'd better sit down."

Gabriel headed towards the piano stool near the roaring fire whilst Robert opened a cabinet and brought out a decanter of sherry. "It's good to see you looking a little better," said Gabriel, ignoring Robert's small, agitated movements that betrayed the continuing emotional turmoil going on beneath the surface.

"I hope you shan't think it heartless of me going to hall," said Robert, pouring a glass of sherry for Gabriel. He did not pour one for himself. "But Dr Crayford was rather insistent that I join him. He said I'd never recover, hiding in this room all day."

"He's right, of course," said Gabriel, accepting the glass with a polite nod. "I'm sure Daphne—God rest her soul —would want you to come to terms with what you have done."

Robert looked sharply at Gabriel. "Not sure I understand what you mean."

"We all make mistakes, Mr Sutton, and you were telling

241

me the truth when you said you would have done anything to protect Daphne. That was exactly what you did on the night she died, wasn't it?'' Robert continued to shake his head in bewilderment, but Gabriel could see him twisting the tassels of his silk scarf, fingers fidgeting as he tried to work out what Gabriel was going to say next. ''It seemed a little odd to me that Daphne became unwell with a headache, having been in such good form all evening. It was not as though she had overindulged. What did you put in her drink?''

Robert said nothing.

''Mr Sutton, you are a chemist. It can't have been difficult to put together some compound or other to make her feel a little headachy and out of sorts, to make absolutely sure that she would go straight home to bed rather than go back to the lab. That was always the risk, wasn't it? You knew her habits—you knew she worked early, not late—but you could not be absolutely sure that she would not go back to the department on some errand or other. You had to be certain that she would not step into that study, because you knew what would be waiting if she did.''

''I didn't put anything in her drink!'' blustered Robert, but he had given up any pretence of not understanding Gabriel, as Gabriel had suspected he would. ''She never worked after dinner. Never, and she was creature of habit.''

''But you had to make sure that it was Arthur Kingsley, not Daphne, who walked into that room. Only the three of you ever used that room, and you were obviously not going to be foolish enough to step inside, knowing that the booby trap you had set would knock over a canister of liquid nitrogen and kill you within seconds. But there was always a risk that Daphne might. And you had been planning Arthur's death from the moment you discovered what he had done."

Robert sank into the sofa, staring fixedly at the floor. "Father, I loved her so much! I don't know what went wrong; she should have felt too unwell to go anywhere near the department that evening. I can't understand how she ended up there. It doesn't make any sense to me at all!"

"When did Daphne tell you that Dr Kingsley had worked for IG Farben?" asked Gabriel.

"Not long after she'd found out herself, I suspect," answered Robert quietly. "And I think she regretted telling me at all, but she was desperately worried and didn't know whom to trust. But you have to understand, Father, Dr Kingsley's crimes were none of my business. I was shocked, of course; I'd already decided that I would never work with him again after completing my doctorate. I was in discussions with Dr Crayford about getting a postdoc in his lab, but I didn't have any reason to kill anyone. It was none of my business!"

Gabriel studied his glass thoughtfully. Outside the room, he could hear the cheerful shouts and chatter of students coming out of chapel to smoke and gossip before going into hall, but the two of them seemed to be stranded in an isolated place where no one could reach them. "When the whole world has been through such a crucible, it is hard to pretend any longer that one man's war crimes really are none of one's business. For you, it was very personal indeed."

Robert watched warily as Gabriel stood up and picked up the photograph of Sarah from its place of honour. "Leave that alone!" he demanded, but he did not have the energy to get up and take it from him. "Don't touch my things!"

"I made the classic mistake when you told me that Sarah had been an evacuee, of assuming that she had been evacuated from London like thousands of other children. I should have realised my mistake when you told me that other children had mocked her accent. The cockney accent might have sounded a little odd in rarefied Oxfordshire, but there were thousands of Londoners billeted about the English countryside. But if she'd had a German accent, that would have caused her serious difficulties."

"Father—"

"Then, of course, there was the extreme way she had responded to those film reels of the liberation of the concentration camps. I assumed that she had been so distraught because she was Jewish, and when she saw the bodies of all those dead Jews, she saw the terrible fate she might easily have suffered herself if the Germans had occupied England. It was a natural-enough reaction, but what you did not tell me was that she might well have been looking at her own dead family. That was what took away her will to live."

"I didn't hide anything from you, Father," Robert put in, finally summoning up the energy to get up and snatch the photograph from Gabriel's hands. "Sarah is dead. Keep her out of this."

"You hid nothing, but you did not volunteer the information that Sarah had come to England on the Kindertransport. She was one of the many girls and boys who were put on trains in Germany, in Czechoslovakia, and brought to the safety of England, leaving their parents and relatives behind forever.''

"They were supposed to join her,'' said Robert, looking fixedly at the photograph of Sarah to avoid Gabriel's glance. "That was always the plan, but they couldn't get out in time. I did tell you that she died of a broken heart, and that much is true. We searched and searched for her family through the Red Cross, but we found out that her entire family—her parents, her older brother and sister, her uncles, aunts, grandparents—had died in the gas chambers at Auschwitz-Birkenau.'' Robert blinked away tears, but more came to take their place. He swiped at his face impatiently, as though imagining that Gabriel would think the less of him for breaking down once again. "She was so broken, Father; she was so broken. All the years she was with us, she chose to come to church every Sunday. She said it didn't matter where she prayed for her family's protection. She was like Ruth in the Old Testament: 'Wherever you go, I will go. Wherever you live, I will live. Your people shall be my people, and your God my God.' When she found out that they were all gone, she couldn't go on anymore. When the illness was squeezing the life out of her, she'd cry to me, 'Not one! God could not spare me *one!*' ''

Gabriel watched the young man huddled up in his sofa— ailing, pale, exhausted and heartbroken. Gabriel knew that Sarah was one of the many indirect casualties of the war who would never be remembered on any cenotaph or memorial but who, nonetheless, had lost their lives as a result of a conflict that had cast its long shadow across the world, leaving no safe havens anywhere. "I'm so sorry, Robert. I am

245

truly sorry." He handed Robert his glass of sherry. "I think you'd better drink something before you answer my next question. Did you come up with the plan to kill Dr Kingsley on your own?"

"Yes," said Robert, a little too quickly and emphatically. "I knew there was no point in reporting him to the police. Who on earth cares about some fuddy-duddy old chemist safely ensconced in his Cambridge college? I knew he had powerful friends. I knew he'd find some way of worming his way out of the whole thing. He'd say he didn't mean it; he'd say he didn't know what it was being used for. He'd no doubt have said he was only a scientist and only doing his research. It wasn't his fault how it was misused. I couldn't bear even to hear it. And yes, I did choose liquid nitrogen to make a point but mostly because it was an easy way to kill a man and make it look like an accident. It happens; it happened here not so very long ago."

"Then another innocent person died instead."

Robert gulped down the rest of the sherry, almost choking as it slid down his throat. "If they ever find out it was me, I know I'll hang, but it will be Daphne I remember when I go to the gallows. When I found her dead on the floor early that morning, it was the worst single moment of my entire life. It was worse even than watching Sarah die. She was still warm when I picked her up and carried her into the lab. She was still *warm*, Father! It was as though I could have just woken her up like the princess in the fairy tale."

"When you went on to kill Arthur, are you sure you had no assistance then either?" asked Gabriel. "Even holding a man at knifepoint, it would have taken considerable time to force him to write a long letter, to tie a noose to that beam and then to make him climb up onto a desk. From the state Dr Kingsley's fingers were in, he put up quite a struggle at the end."

"He was a broken man, Father," said Robert, and Gabriel found himself looking away as Robert's face broke into a sneer of contempt towards the man he had killed with his bare hands. "He had hardly eaten or slept since Daphne's death; he made it easy for me. I only had to wait until I saw him cross the quad, follow him to the department and do what I had to do. There was no one around at that hour of the morning. By the time I started to hear footsteps outside the room, he was already hanging like a dead fish. He struggled to loosen the noose around his neck only when he was already half-choked, and it was far too late then. His fat old carcass was pulling that rope tighter and tighter."

Gabriel pressed his knuckles against each other. It was grotesque, practically patricide on Robert Sutton's part. Arthur had been a murderer; there was no other way of putting it. No one with an ounce of compassion for his fellow man could have assisted in the creation of a toxic gas and placed it in the hands of the Nazis in the belief that it would not be used to hurt anybody. It was childish reasoning, and Gabriel knew it. If his friend had been hanged following a fair trial, Gabriel would have wept for him and prayed for his salvation, but he was sure he would not have felt the intense revulsion he felt now.

"I am truly sorry about what happened to Sarah and her family," said Gabriel, his voice trembling with the effort of remaining calm. "But you had no right to make yourself Dr Kingsley's judge or his executioner; his life was never yours to take. By taking the law into your own hands, you killed a brilliant young woman whose only mistake was to confide in you."

A sound came out of Robert's mouth like the whimper of a wounded animal. "I know, and I shall have to live with Daphne's death, somehow or other, for as long as I have left."

"You must give yourself up to the police," said Gabriel. "You must go straight to the police and confess what you have done."

Robert looked at Gabriel in blank astonishment. "I shall do no such thing! Daphne's death was an accident, not murder. I never intended to kill her."

"It may be manslaughter—you would have to take advice from a lawyer—but it is still a crime. And you cannot wash your hands of Dr Kingsley's death."

"I shan't sacrifice my life for ridding the world of a monster like Kingsley. There's no evidence I did anything wrong. If you hadn't been such a Nosy Parker, even you would never have guessed."

Gabriel reached inside his coat and pulled out a large metal cuboid with a trailing wire, painted in the khaki of the armed forces, which looked not unlike a radio receiver. "Wars have a tendency to unleash innovations onto the world," Gabriel explained, "most of them wicked, but not all. A reporter I know lent me this newfangled recording device. If anyone had such a thing in his possession, I guessed it would be him."

Robert made to snatch the device from Gabriel's hands, but he quickly slipped it back inside his coat. "I'm giving you forty-eight hours to turn yourself in," said Gabriel, "or

I will go to the police myself. Daphne's family has a right to know the truth."

For a moment, Robert looked as though he might strike Gabriel, but a pounding on the door broke the spell between them, and Robert threw himself at the door, yanking it open. Dr Crayford stood in the doorway, impeccably dressed and ready to take his place at high table. "There you are, young man," he said impatiently. "Hurry along now; we'll be late."

Robert looked back at Gabriel and then again at Dr Crayford. "I'm . . . I'm coming," he said uncertainly.

"I say, are you all right?" asked Crayford solicitously. "You look as though you've seen a ghost."

"I'm quite all right," snapped Robert, pushing past him. "Let's go."

Crayford faltered in the doorway, as though trying to decide whether it would be rude to leave Gabriel on his own in the room, or a little ruder to leave his guest to go to dinner by himself. "Why don't I walk with you as far as hall?" suggested Gabriel, putting Crayford out of his misery. Crayford waited whilst Gabriel switched off the lights and closed the door before joining him on the stairs.

"What on earth is wrong with young Robert?" demanded Crayford as they struggled to catch up with him and eventually gave up on chasing his retreating figure. "I've been desperately trying to help the lad to buck himself up, but I'm not at all sure this dinner was such a good idea. He has to eat, of course, but he'll be unbearable all evening."

"You can always slip a little something into his drink to help him relax," said Gabriel with a helpful smile. "If you were quick enough, he might not even notice."

Crayford gave Gabriel a sidelong glance, not slowing his pace for an instant. "I'm sure it would be desperately un-ethical to drug a man without his knowledge."

"But not a woman, perhaps," Gabriel persisted. "One hears such terrible stories of innocent young girls being drugged and coming to harm in their confusion. I gather that there are drugs so clever these days, it is impossible to taste or smell them. One cannot even trace them in the body after death. It's a frightening prospect."

Crayford was silent a moment too long before answer-ing. "A frightening prospect indeed. I'm glad I never had daughters—far too much to worry about. But thank you for the warning, Father. I daresay I had better keep an eye on my own glass this evening."

They reached the Senior Combination Room, where Robert was skulking in a corner, keeping himself apart from everyone else. Gabriel suspected that in the absence of Arthur and Daphne, Robert would have been condemned to stand on the outside of every conversation, whatever his state of mind. He looked up warily at Gabriel and Crayford as they neared him. "I was just joking to Dr Crayford here," Gabriel told Robert, all smiles, "that he ought to put a little something in your drink tonight to help you relax. I'm sure it's been done before."

"What a marvellous sense of humour these clerics have," answered Crayford, exchanging glances with Robert. It al-ways amazed Gabriel that no one ever seemed to work out that it was possible to see a person even when not looking at them directly, but Gabriel said nothing.

"Dr Crayford, Father knows," said Robert irritably. "He knows you drugged Daphne to try to keep her away from the murder scene. I don't imagine he is the brightest button in the box, but he must therefore know that you knew of my plans."

Crayford looked icily at Robert but betrayed no anger or anxiety whatsoever. "He may surmise what he likes, but unlike his ilk, I rely upon evidence before drawing a conclusion."

"Alas, it is impossible to prove that you tampered with Daphne Silverton's drink that evening," Gabriel admitted regretfully, "and one man's word against yours is unlikely to be very harmful to you. Nor can I prove that you gave her a rather lower dose than you promised Robert you would give her, just enough to make her a little confused, a little unfocused. Likewise, I cannot prove definitively that, once she was in that state, you insisted to her that she must go to Arthur's study on her way home. I cannot prove that you provided her with some urgent reason why it could not wait until the morning, knowing perfectly well that she would step into a lethal trap, and in her numbed state would find it virtually impossible to find her way out of that room once she'd knocked over the canister of liquid nitrogen. I cannot prove—though it would make logical sense—that you held the door shut to prevent her escaping."

Gabriel watched as a look of utter horror spread itself across Robert's face until he resembled one of the death masks a morbid tourist might find in Madame Tussaud's. "But . . . but . . . ," he began, turning from one man to the other. "But why?"

"Because that newspaper report was true," said Gabriel simply. "Daphne was right. Good night, gentlemen."

12

Gabriel walked out of college and stood on the bridge, looking down at the dark waters. There was no traffic on the river now, and he counted off the chimes of seven o'clock from the college tower, knowing that in the Great Hall, hundreds of students and their professors were settling down for the evening meal, the master chanting the words of the grace as the master of college had done thousands and thousands of times over the centuries. He tried to imagine Dr Crayford and Robert Sutton sitting side by side at high table, wondering how on earth they would be able to get on with the mundanities of eating and drinking and putting a calm face on things in front of the others. Not that it was really his business now.

It was as he was pondering the situation that he suddenly remembered Gerard. Where on earth was Gerard? His pulse raced, and he began to march down the road through the town, feeling not unlike an adolescent boy who has accidentally lost his little brother at the park. He remembered that he had left Gerard in a pub with two beers to drink and a pocket full of coins—far too much time to drink far too much beer.

He was still some fifty yards away from the entrance to the pub when he heard a chorus of rowdy voices singing uproariously, so tunelessly that Gabriel could only just make out the song.

> Tha's been a-courting Mary Jane
> On Ilkley Moor bar tat
> Tha's been a-courting Mary Jane
> Tha's been a-courting Mary Jane . . .

Gabriel hurled himself through the door and found himself in the midst of a half-drunk chorus of "On Ilkley Moor" being led by a little chap in clericals with a fine baritone voice. Gerard spotted Gabriel immediately and gave him a cheeky wave, but Gabriel grabbed Gerard by the arm and yanked him in the direction of the door. "Party's over," pronounced Gabriel over the din.

There was much waving and cheering as Gerard waved good-bye like a minor celebrity taking his leave of an ecstatic audience; Gabriel all but threw Gerard out onto the street. "Who's rattled your bars?" demanded Gerard as Gabriel frog-marched him along the pavement.

"What on earth did you think you were doing?" barked Gabriel. "I can't leave you alone for five minutes!"

"You were a heck of a lot more than five minutes, mate," answered Gerard reasonably. "What was I supposed to do, left alone in a pub for hours?"

"A little over an hour," Gabriel corrected him. "How much have you had to drink?"

"It's all right, I never bought a single pint after them two," Gerard promised, which did not reassure Gabriel in the least. "Folks are very generous round these parts. Did you nab your killer?"

Gerard groaned with the impatience of a man desperate

to be taken seriously by the family clown. "I'm not a policeman, Jerry. I could only confront the killer and pretend I had a recording of his confession. I could hardly arrest him."

"But that's good, int'it?" asked Gerard seriously. "If he thinks you've got a record of his confession, he'll have to go to the police."

"Or he may realise that a secret recording would not be accepted as evidence," Gabriel explained. "He may even have twigged that I couldn't possibly have recorded his words without the presence of bulky and expensive equipment. The one silver lining is that guilty men have a tendency to panic and act irrationally, which may work in my favour."

"Why did he do it?"

"The reason so many of them commit murder," answered Gabriel. "Love, of a sort—just love for a different person to the one I'd imagined. Unfortunately, the man who discovered Mr Sutton's plan to kill Arthur used it to lure Daphne to her death. Unless he confesses, it is highly unlikely that he will ever be brought to justice."

Gerard suddenly looked a good deal more sober. "The first death wasn't a mistake then? I thought you believed that the girl wasn't the intended victim."

"She wasn't," confirmed Gabriel. "Not Robert Sutton's intended victim, anyway, but Dr Crayford knew what Sutton was planning. He found some way to persuade Daphne to go to the place where the trap was set. To be honest, I'm not sure what the police would charge him with, even if he did confess. He had nothing to do with propping up the canister of liquid nitrogen in such a way that it would overturn when a person crossed the room; he simply urged a young woman to walk into a study she entered every day. He may have held the door shut to stop her escaping, but he may have left her to it, knowing that she would be too groggy to get out in time anyway."

"It's horrible," said Gerard simply. "Two killers, and one or both of them may go scot free."

"I suspect Robert Sutton will give himself up to the police at some point, whether or not my bluff worked with him. I doubt he'll be able to live with himself," said Gabriel. "Dr Crayford, I'm not so sure. That's always the risk with playing God, you see. One might make a mistake; or worse, provide another person with the means to do harm."

They stood on the corner of Chesterton Road, but Gabriel felt a sudden reluctance to let Gerard go. He knew that his spirits would sink as soon as Gerard had gone on alone to the friary, and he found himself delaying the point of departure. "I have to go, Brother," said Gerard, noting Gabriel's morose expression. "Come along, Gabbers; go home to your family. They're waiting to welcome you."

"Shall I come and meet you tomorrow morning?" suggested Gabriel.

"No, I'll come to you," said Gerard firmly. "Go home, have your dinner, stay up late and talk. Sleep as late as you need. I shan't come anywhere near the house until late morning. When you're ready, and only when you're ready, we'll make our way to the station."

"Thanks, Jerry."

Gerard grinned and went on his way, leaving Gabriel standing alone for a moment before walking slowly along Chesterton Road, with its smart Victorian terraced houses and its long riverbank and brightly painted houseboats. And at one particular house on this street, there was good company and food and wine and a warm bed awaiting him. *Deo Gratias*, he whispered.

Mama made no comment when a haggard Gabriel turned up at the door. She behaved almost like the mother of a schoolboy might, when she suspects her son has been up to no good but would rather not enquire too deeply into his activities. He helped her lay the table for dinner, finding the strength to tell them what had happened only when they were sitting down to eat.

"What a mess," was the only comment Papa felt able to make when Gabriel had finished. "But surely those two men will not get away with it? Two people dead, one of them only a young girl."

"The trouble is that in the eyes of the law, there were no crimes committed," Gabriel explained, but he had already been over the unfortunate circumstances with Gerard and could hardly bear to have to describe the hopelessness of the situation again. He distracted himself by helping himself to more of the chicken risotto on his plate. Gabriel could not remember the last time he had enjoyed such a rich blend of flavours all on one plate, and he tried hard not to consider that there was probably one fewer chicken clucking about in the back garden tonight.

"But there were two crimes!" protested Papa. He was not about to let the subject pass.

"The police believe that Daphne died as the result of an accident and that Arthur hanged himself. Of course, there will be inquests, but it is unlikely that a coroner will come to a different conclusion, unless Robert Sutton can be persuaded to confess. If he does, it is possible that Dr Crayford will also be implicated, but I'm not the police. I can only work out what happened; I have no authority to arrest anyone or press charges."

"I suppose the one consolation is that you at least know the truth," said Mama, "but truth without justice is not much consolation. As we all know."

They descended into silence. It was a sad fact that Giovanna and Nicoletta had never been granted justice either. The fire had been ruled to have been arson, due to a quantity of petrol having been poured through the letterbox, but no one was arrested and the trail had gone cold within weeks. The police had had better things to do than to pursue the killers of a couple of foreigners who could be quickly forgotten about by anyone who mattered.

"I'll keep an eye on the local newspaper, in case your man does do the decent thing," said Papa. "If there is any news, I will send it to you."

"Yes," said Mama more brightly, "we will send you any newspaper cuttings in our next letter to you. We will be writing a lot more from now on, won't we?"

Gabriel reacted to the pointed question with an embarrassed smile. "I promise I'll write every week," he said, "not that there is always much news with the life I lead."

"I do not believe that for a single second!" laughed Mama. "Giovanna always said that you were a walking disaster. Wearing a habit hasn't changed that."

Then they were laughing, and Papa was filling up Gabriel's glass for the second time that evening. "Thank you for welcoming me so kindly," said Gabriel, forcing himself to look his mother-in-law in the eye. "I've done precious little to deserve it."

"We were always here, my son," she said, taking his hand. "And we knew you'd come home one day. Like the prodigal son."

"I promise I haven't spent your money on a life of debauchery," said Gabriel.

"More's the pity, my love," answered Mama, and Gabriel saw it again, that twinkle in the eye, that naughty smile that brought back Giovanna's impish face. He knew he would not want to leave in the morning because it meant walking away from a place where he felt close to the two females who had once been his whole world. But he needed to leave. He needed to return to a life he had made himself, or he would never stop looking back.

When it came to it, the parting was made a good deal more painless by Gerard's presence in the kitchen when Gabriel came downstairs after a long sleep and a hot, honey-scented bath. "Kicked you out, have they?" asked Gabriel, glancing up at the kitchen clock to ensure that he had not slept in until midday or something awful like that. It was nine o'clock, and Gerard was tucking into a plate of scrambled eggs, washed down by a large cup of coffee.

"I got a bit fidgety," explained Gerard between mouthfuls. "Let's face it, the Dominicans gave the world the Inquisition; we Benedictines gave the world hospitality. No offence or anything; they're a nice-enough bunch."

Gabriel was presented with a stack of buttered toast to munch on whilst the eggs cooked. "You make sure you have plenty to eat," said Mama, sipping her own morning coffee as she attacked a frying pan full of eggs and milk. "You have a long journey. Will you need a taxi to the station? It's a long way."

Gabriel had the urge to walk. He could see brave slivers of sunshine outside and patches of blue where the cloud cover was breaking up. He and Gerard were in no great hurry, and he wanted to take a last tour of the city before they got on that train. As they parted company on the doorstep, amid many hugs and kisses and promises to write frequent long letters, Gabriel found himself saying, "Come and visit me at the monastery. We have a guest lodge for family. I should so like to welcome you there."

"God willing," said Mama, folding him in a last embrace. Gabriel savoured the sense of being loved and wanted, appreciating a little too much the realisation that she was reluctant to let him go. *Arrivederci.*

Arrivederci. Not *addio.* If Providence allowed it, they would meet again.

Epilogue

Two weeks later, with the adventures of Cambridge comfortably in the distance, Gabriel sat in the monastery garden, looking over the two letters he had received that morning. One was a long letter in Italian from his father-in-law, accompanied by a newspaper cutting bearing the headline "Scholar Confesses to Murder". The other was a letter from Will Valentine, which was rather terse and to the point:

Dear Father Gabriel,

You have presumably heard the news that Robert Sutton went to the police last week and told them everything. He is now in custody pending trial. Dr Crayford is also facing questions, but he will probably get off without charge.

I wondered whether you might see your way to giving me an exclusive interview about how you solved the puzzle? Readers are frightfully interested in crime, and I have no doubt that they would be interested in hearing from a real-life Sherlock Holmes.

If you are not allowed to leave your monastery, I could come and visit you for the day if that is acceptable to you. Please let me know by return of post.

I remain,
yours sincerely,
Will Valentine

Gabriel smiled and placed the letters in his pocket. He would have to write three letters during his time of recreation. One would be a matter of business, politely turning down Will Valentine's request, in the knowledge that the young man would probably make up the interview anyway; the second would be a matter of pleasure, writing to thank his father-in-law for sending the article and to give him his news. He was not sure how to categorise the third. A letter to Dr Crayford, which would be simple and to the point. A reminder from one mortal man to another that there is often no justice in this world, but there is in the next.